VINEYARD CHILL

A Martha's Vineyard Mystery

PHILIP R. CRAIG

SCRIBNER

New York   London   Toronto   Sydney

SCRIBNER
A Division of Simon & Schuster, Inc.
1230 Avenue of the Americas
New York, NY 10020

First Scribner hardcover edition June 2008

SCRIBNER and design are trademarks of Macmillan Library Reference USA, Inc.,
used under license by Simon & Schuster, the publisher of this work.

For information about special discounts for bulk purchases,
please contact Simon & Schuster Special Sales at
1-800-456-6798 or business@simonandschuster.com.

Text set in Baskerville

Manufactured in the United States of America

1   3   5   7   9   10   8   6   4   2

Library of Congress Control Number: 2007045855

ISBN-13: 978-1-4165-3558-4
ISBN-10: 1-4165-3558-6

For all of the family, friends, and readers
who encouraged and supported
Phil's lifelong passion for writing.
You added more than you know
to that great ride.

For the living know that they shall die: but the
Dead know not anything, neither have they any
More a reward; for the memory of them is forgotten.
Also their love, and their hatred, and their envy,
Is now perished; neither have they any more a
Portion for ever in any thing that is done under the sun.

—ECCLESIASTES 9:5–6

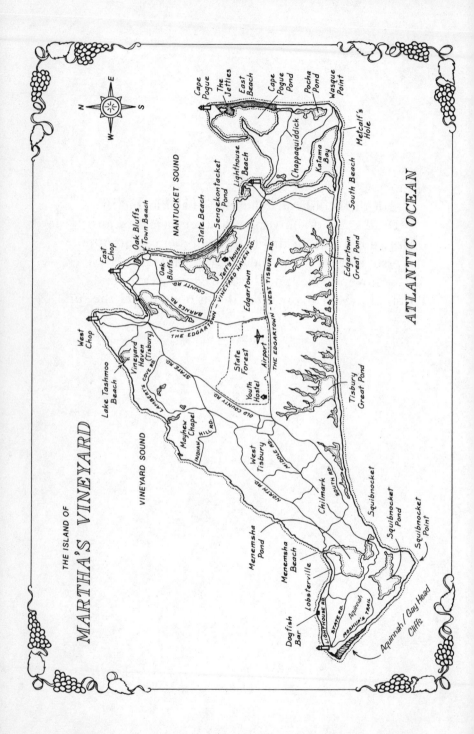

VINEYARD CHILL

— 1 —

We were getting ready to head to East Beach to get a load of seaweed for the garden when the phone rang. Clay Stockton's voice was the last one I expected to hear on the other end of the line. I'd not had a better friend than Clay in the army, or later, when I was on the Boston PD, but aside from a rare letter or Christmas card, I hadn't heard much from him since before I'd met Zee, so a lot of water had passed under the bridge. And unless Clay had changed, there was a fair chance some of it was hot water.

"Where are you?" I asked.

"I'm up here in Boston, but I thought I might drop down to the Vineyard for a visit. You still have a spare bunk?"

"You bet. The guest room will be waiting. How are you?"

"Fine. I'll give you the details when I get there. It'll be good to see you again, buddy! I'll catch the bus and call you when I get to Woods Hole."

I hung up, a smile on my face.

"Who was that?" asked Zee. "Whoever it was made you happy. Not an old girlfriend, I hope."

I put my arms around her. "You're girlfriend enough for me, wifey. No, that was Clay Stockton. He's coming down from Boston."

She looked up at me. "The Clay Stockton who writes you a note about every other year? He's the adventurer, isn't he? The one who actually lives a life that sounds like a novel?"

"That's Clay. I'm almost surprised he's still alive, but he's a really wonderful guy. You'll like him. All the ladies do. Men, too. He has charm." I gave her a kiss. "Like me."

She kissed me back. "You have charm, Jefferson, but not too much. We can always use a little more around the house. If we're going to the beach, we'd better get started. The kids are already in the truck."

I glanced at my watch. The bus from Boston wouldn't get to Woods Hole for at least a couple of hours, so we had time for a seaweed run.

It was a bright, snowless mid-January day, chilly but not cold. Just right for a drive on the Chappy beaches. We could enjoy the ride and bring back several big, industrial-strength trash bags full of seaweed for the garden. Two good reasons to go. So we went.

January and February are the only months in the Martha's Vineyard year when mainlanders are rare. They start trickling down in March, and in April the trickle becomes a small stream. By May, parking places downtown are harder to find and by June, the summer season has begun in earnest. During July and August the streets are mobbed, the roads are filled with cars, and the beaches are bright with umbrellas and towels. Even after Labor Day, by which time most families with school-age children have gone home, there are still a lot of out-of-state cars parked where you want to park and lined up at stop signs. People pour over from America for the Columbus Day weekend, for Thanksgiving and Christmas, and for Last Night festivities. It's only after the turning of the year that silence falls over the island and we year-rounders have the place to ourselves for a few weeks before the cycle starts again. It's during those weeks that you have a fighting chance of actually knowing the people you meet.

But few of those people would be out on Chappy in mid-winter.

We got into the old Land Cruiser and drove up our long sandy driveway. We were well bundled because I'd never managed to get the truck's heater working properly. At the Edgartown–Vineyard Haven road, I turned left and drove through Edgartown to Katama, passing the P.O., the Stop and

Shop, and Al's Package Store without even slowing down—an almost impossible feat during the summer, when taking that route means dealing with the village's worst traffic jam.

When we crossed the herring creek, I shifted into four-wheel drive and we headed east on Norton Point Beach, open now to traffic but often closed during the summer because of laws in defense of piping plovers. To our north was the cold, shallow water of Katama Bay and to our south was the colder water of the Atlantic Ocean, stretching dark blue to the southern horizon, where it met the ice blue sky.

A couple of years earlier, a seventy-foot fishing boat had gone ashore on Norton's Point, causing consternation among plover protectors, who feared that curious sightseers might step on an egg or fledgling while eyeballing the grounded boat. Concern for the boat and its owners was considerably less than concern for the birds, and everyone breathed a sigh of relief when a tug finally managed to drag the fishing boat off the sand and back out to sea.

The boat was now only a memory and the plovers had all departed for those warmer places plovers visit in the winter, so we were able to fetch Chappaquiddick without delay.

When I was a boy, we could drive from Norton Point Beach over the sand directly to Wasque Point on the southeast corner of Chappy, but times had changed, so we took the road to Dyke Bridge—still, almost forty years after the accident that had made it famous, the most popular tourist site on the Vineyard and, according to those who yearned for the old days when only they and a few others knew of Chappy, the spark that had ignited the Vineyard's unfortunate flame of popularity.

Other calamities had occurred and were still occurring on the island: planes crashed, boats sank, people drowned, people shot or stabbed other people or hit them with bricks, teens killed themselves and their friends by driving into trees, people overdosed on drugs or went missing and were never seen again. The most recent of the latter was Nadine

Gibson, the girl with the strawberry hair, so called because of her long, brightly dyed tresses, who had left work at the Fireside bar in Oak Bluffs the previous March and had disappeared. Had she gone back to the mainland? Had she shaved her head and moved into a nunnery? Had her apparently frantic boyfriend killed and buried her after some lovers' quarrel? No one knew. But though such disasters as these continued to occur on the island, no tourists sought out most of the fatal sites.

On the east side of the bridge, we turned and drove to Cape Pogue Pond and points north, seeing not another soul en route. We rounded the cape on the outside, following the narrow track between the water and the cliff, and spotted a seal heading toward Wasque, its sleek head disappearing underwater only to reappear farther to the south.

On the rocky north shore of the elbow, we could clearly see the Oak Bluffs bluffs, the far shore of Cape Cod, and the white houses of Edgartown. There were gulls on the water, and the waves slapped on the shingle beach.

I crossed over the neck to the pond side of the elbow, hooked a left, and there we were, on a flat beach windrowed with seaweed blown ashore by the southwest winds of recent days.

"Pa, can we fish?" Joshua asked.

"Sure, but I don't think there's much out there right now."

"You don't know if you don't throw."

Like father, like son. I got the small rods off the roof rack and gave them to Joshua and Diana, who went down to the water and began to make short but straight casts. They were both better at it than I had been at their ages.

"When did Joshua learn that cliché?" asked Zee, pulling plastic bags out of the back of the truck.

"That's not just a cliché," I said. "That's ancient fishing wisdom." I was watching Diana. She was very intent and was making nice casts for an eight-year-old. She looked like a miniature Zee: blue-black hair, dark eyes; a young panther. I

VINEYARD CHILL

allowed myself an early worry about the boys we could expect at our door in not too many years.

"Come along, dear." Zee handed me a bag and we started filling them with seaweed. Our garden loved seaweed and we used a lot of it. As we worked, Zee said, "Tell me about Clay Stockton."

How could I describe Clay Stockton? "I imagine I've told you most of what I know," I said. "We met in boot camp and hit it off right away. I ended up in Nam. He didn't. We bent a few rules together and he got me out of a couple of jams. He was the only guy I knew besides me who read for fun. He introduced me to Nietzsche."

"Smart."

"And he has magic hands. He can build anything and fix almost anything. He's built wooden boats and he can do finish carpentry. And did I tell you he's a hypnotist?"

Zee finished stuffing one big bag. "You told me about the boats, but I don't think I've heard about him being a hypnotist. Here." She gave the bag to me. "You're a manly man. Put this in the truck."

"What would you do without me?" I asked, coming back from the truck and joining her in filling the next bag.

"I'd do without you." She gave me a sweet smile. "Is he a Svengali?"

"I don't think he's ever transformed a Trilby into an opera singer, and as far as I know he's never hypnotized a fair maiden into doing anything she might not otherwise do."

Zee's smile became a grin. "A lot of fair maidens would be glad to be hypnotized into doing things they might otherwise not do."

"Sexist. No, Clay used to hypnotize guys in our barracks just for fun, but only if they wanted him to, and never in a way to make them look foolish. The most interesting thing I saw him do was get a guy's permission, then hypnotize him and stick a needle through the guy's hand without causing any pain or bleeding. I never have figured that one out."

"Did he ever hypnotize you?"

"I volunteered but it didn't work. I was too busy analyzing what was happening to take the suggestions he was giving. I'm a bad subject."

"I can vouch for that. I've had a hard time teaching you anything."

"He was interested in psychosomatic relationships, and hypnotism was a way for him to experiment. I think what he really wanted to do was learn to hypnotize himself."

"Did he manage to do that?"

"Not while I was around."

"What's he look like?"

"A good-looking guy. The last time I saw him was when we were both in Boston. I was a cop, going to Northeastern part-time, and he was at BU, studying philosophy and building a Tahiti Ketch down in Quincy. We were both married by then." I carried the second bag to the truck and brought back another one. "He's about six feet tall, on the lean side of average weight, blue eyes, brown hair. I think he might be what you call a hunk, but I'm not sure because I've never understood just what qualifies as hunkiness."

"Leave that decision up to me, hunk. Well, he sounds pretty good so far. What's he do for a living?"

I thought about some of the things I'd read in his rare letters and said, "Maybe you could call him a pilot, because he's done some flying jobs here and there, but he's done other things, too, so I don't think you could say he has a profession. He's like me since I left the Boston PD. No steady job."

"You keep busy."

"So does Clay."

"What else can you tell me?"

"I trust him."

"Does he have children?"

A potential sore spot. "He's mentioned more than one child by more than one woman. He's been married two or three times, as near as I can figure."

Zee and I had both been married before but had survived to try again, successful examples of the triumph of hope over experience.

"Why so many wives?" asked Zee, not being judgmental.

"You can ask him. I'd say it was because he's not a nine-to-five kind of guy and he has a lot of friends who live on the edge. Most women want a little more security than he offers. He writes about plans to settle down, but then something happens."

"Like what?"

"Something that makes it better for him to move along."

"Like what, Jefferson?"

"Well, once it was the woman's first husband. She hadn't gotten around to divorcing him before she married Clay. I think that was the same so-called marriage that involved some jewelry of dubious ownership. Clay thought it was his but the woman and her brother and some of the brother's friends thought it was theirs, so Clay had to slide out of town at night and couldn't go back. That sort of thing."

"That sort of thing."

"Another time, I remember, the wife got saved and wanted them to join a commune of fundamentalist Christians, but he didn't care for it when they got there, so he left but she stayed."

"And he remained unsaved, I presume."

"As far as I know."

"How long does he plan to stay with us?"

"I didn't ask him."

Joshua had gotten tired of fishing where there were no fish and had put his rod on the sand so he could skip stones for a while. I left the seaweed bag and walked down to him.

"You never put your rod on the sand," I said. "You can get sand in your reel. If you're through fishing, put your rod in a spike on the front of the truck."

Joshua's lower lip went out.

"And if that was my reel, I'd rinse it off," I added, and walked back to the seaweed bags.

Being a boy isn't easy, and neither is being a father. I pretended to be concentrating on filling the next bag, and after a bit, Joshua and Diana both came up from the water and put their rods in the rod spikes in front of the radiator.

Diana came closer and smiled a good-girl smile. "I didn't put my rod on the sand, Pa."

"Good girl."

"I rinsed my reel," said Joshua.

"Good boy. I almost ruined a reel once by getting sand in it, and I don't want it to happen to you."

"Can we go exploring, Pa?"

"Where?"

"Back there at the cliffs." He and his sister both pointed east.

"That's a bit of a walk."

"We'll go along the beach."

I glanced at Zee, but she was staying out of this one. "All right," I said. "But don't climb the cliffs and make sure you're out of the way if a car comes along. We'll be done here soon, and when we are we'll drive back that way and pick you up. Be careful."

"We will, Pa."

They walked up and over the rocky elbow and dropped out of sight on the other side.

Zee bit her lip. "Are you sure they'll be all right?"

"Not much can happen to them. The water's shallow and the waves are small."

She took a deep breath, then let it out and stuffed more seaweed into her bag. "I don't think I ever heard that story before about you ruining your reel." She lifted her eyes and stared at my legs. "I think your pants are on fire."

"Fables and out-and-out lies are different things," I said. "It's a well-known fact. Fables are told for the good of the listener; lies are told for the good of the liar."

"And of course you'd never tell your child a lie?"

"Never," I lied.

As I carried the latest bag of seaweed to the truck and studied the remaining space, trying to figure whether another one
would fit, I heard the sound of an engine on the other side of
the elbow, and I turned to see an almost-new Jeep pickup
coming over to our side and turning toward us. The Jeep was
driven by Eleanor Araujo, who stopped and stuck her head
out the window.

"Great minds. You leave any seaweed for me?"

"Plenty," said Zee. "You see two kids on the beach this side
of the cliffs?"

"They were about halfway there and were comparing
horseshoe crab shells when I came by. Well, I'd better get to
work."

"I'll give you a hand," I said.

"You won't make any money, but I can pay you with a
pleasant smile."

"A pleasant smile is better than the wisecracks I've been
getting," I said. "Let's get started."

"I don't think we can get any more in the Land Cruiser,"
said Zee. "So I'll join your crew, too. With three of us working, we'll be done in short order."

And we were, because there was plenty of seaweed. While
we filled the back of the pickup, Zee and Eleanor chatted
about this and that but never touched on the midlife crisis
that had led Mike, Eleanor's ex, to divorce her and marry the
woman known to Eleanor's angry friends simply as "the
Bimbo." When the truck was full, Eleanor drove away via
the road over the big sand dunes, and we put the rods on the
roof rack, then climbed into the truck, turned around, and
retraced our route to the Cape Pogue cliffs.

"She seems to be doing okay," said Zee.

"How come you didn't talk about the divorce?" I asked.

"We didn't want to talk about the Bimbo."

Ahead of us I saw the children nearing the cliffs.

"The Bimbo must have a name," I said. "What is it?"

"I wouldn't know."

I glanced at her pants but saw no flames. So much for moral poetry.

We caught up with the kids at the cliffs and loaded them aboard. It was a tight squeeze because of the bags of seaweed.

When we got home, I emptied the bags out by the garden. We had a good pile of seaweed but would need more by planting time.

I was putting some wood in the living-room stove when the phone rang. It was Clay Stockton.

"I'm catching the next boat. It's about to pull out of Woods Hole."

"I'll meet you in Vineyard Haven. I'm glad you're coming."

"No gladder than I am, buddy."

The sound of his voice rolled time backward. I was almost thirty years younger and Clay and I were sitting in a bar in West Palm Beach. I had been telling him about my plans to join the Boston PD and start college when a man came in and sat down beside us.

— 2 —

The man looked about forty and was trim. His hair was short and blond.

After he had picked up his glass, he looked at Clay and said, "Tom Gilbert tells me you're the guy who brought the *Miramar II* down from Boston."

"That's right," said Clay.

He put out his hand. "I'm Fred Marcusa. Tom speaks highly of you. Glad to meet you." He looked at me and arched a brow.

I gave him my name and he nodded and turned back to Clay. "That had to be a pretty rough trip, especially for somebody short-handing a boat that size through that gale off Hatteras."

"I didn't do it alone," said Clay. "Tom told me he had a crew for me but the guys didn't show up the morning I was leaving, so I talked J.W. here into coming along."

Marcusa nodded. "Booze or women probably."

"Probably."

"So you left anyway."

"We didn't see any reason to wait."

"I've seen the *Miramar.* Tom's glad to have her here, but she took a bit of a beating coming down."

"She'd have taken the same beating if I'd had a bigger crew."

"It must have been pretty hairy out there."

"It could have been worse."

Marcusa sipped his drink, smiled at me, then sipped

again and said, "You boys have any plans for the next few days?"

I shrugged. "Go back to Boston, I guess."

"I don't have any plans," said Clay, taking another drink.

We sat in silence for a while, then Marcusa said, "If you're interested, I can give you some work. A guy wants me to take a forty-four-foot yawl out to Freeport and then bring it back here. I can probably do it by myself but I'd rather have a crew that can handle things if something happens to me. It'll only be a two- or three-day job, but the pay is good."

He mentioned the pay and it really was good. Too good. "You boys interested?" he asked.

"What could happen to you?" I asked.

He smiled. "Oh, it's not going to be dangerous or any-thing like that, but you're both sailors, you know that things can happen out there. You can get sick, you can make a mis-take and break something. I'd feel better with people aboard who could take over if they had to."

I thought about the pay. If Fred was offering me that much, he must be making a lot more himself.

"You just need a crew going and coming. No more than that?" asked Clay.

"No more than that. We'll sail to Freeport, tie up for a few hours, then come back. You ever been to Freeport?"

"No."

"Great town. Free trade zone. Lots of cruise ships. Lots of action. You'll get half your pay when you go aboard and half when we get home again. What do you say?"

Two or three days. Half the money up front. Clay and I looked at each other.

"Sounds okay to me," I said, and Clay nodded.

The *Lisa* was fast-looking and had a pretty sheer. When I went aboard, Fred handed each of us an envelope. Mine was full of fifties. I put it in my duffle bag, and we headed out.

We took turns at the helm and lines, the three of us work-ing smoothly together just as Clay and I had done on the

Miramar II, and were well offshore by sunset. Fred cooked up a good supper, and during the night we took four-hour shifts at the helm. Fred struck me as one of those rare people, like Clay, with whom I could companionably sail long distances. We had a smooth trip and the next day we tied up against a pier in Freeport.

"There's a bar right down there," said Fred, pointing. "Owner knows me. You boys go have some lunch. I'll go find the guys with our cargo. We'll load up and be out of here before you can say Jack Robinson."

He stepped ashore and walked out of sight. He hadn't mentioned cargo before, but it was what I'd been expecting. Clay smiled and said, "Cargo. Why not?"

We walked down to the bar and sat down. The bartender came over and nodded toward the door. "Fred just stuck his head in and told me you'd be coming along. Said to put what you want on his tab. What'll you have?" We enjoyed beer and sandwiches before heading back to the boat.

The cargo arrived not too much later in the form of several closed boxes marked with the name and logo of a well-known television manufacturer. The crew of Bahamians, directed by Fred, stowed the boxes in the center cabin. When the Bahamians left, Fred grinned. "I bet you never knew these things were manufactured out here in the islands."

He was right.

"I have to see a guy," he said. "Have another beer on me, and when I get back we'll cast off."

He went ashore and we went back to the bar, where we had another drink and talked with the bartender, who seemed to like Fred.

By and by, Fred came in. "Okay," he said, "time to make sail."

"Maybe not," I said, looking through a window and seeing a half dozen armed uniformed men coming along the pier.

"Damn," said Fred, looking out the window. "I'd better see what this is all about. If I can't get rid of these guys, deliver those televisions by yourself. Somebody will meet you when you get to West Palm."

He stepped outside and went to meet the uniformed men. They surrounded him and when they took him away with them, they left one man behind guarding the boat.

Clay and I exchanged looks and bent over our glasses.

"Guard's got a rifle," said Clay.

The bartender had taken everything in. He was busy for a few minutes, then came over with a bottle of beer in his hand. "Fred always treated me right," he said. "I don't know how long they're going to keep him, but I think you boys and the boat better be gone before too long."

"There's a guy with a gun out there," I said.

"I know that lad with the rifle," said the bartender. "He likes his beer. Go chat with him and give him this bottle."

He moved to the far end of the bar.

Clay and I took our glasses and stepped outside, glanced around and saw that no one was watching, then went to the guard and looked in the direction his companions had gone with Fred.

He shrugged and followed our gaze.

"Hot day," I said. I handed him the bottle of beer. "Here. It's on me. I was in the army once, and I know what guard duty's like."

He grinned, checked to make sure no one was watching, and pulled on the bottle.

"Good," he said. We touched our glasses to his and we all had another drink.

By the time he finished his bottle, the guard seemed about half asleep. I led him into an alley and sat him against a wall behind a barrel while Clay threw the rifle into the harbor.

"I wonder what the barman put in that beer," said Clay. "Pretty fast-acting."

"Let's not wait to find out," I said.

We went aboard and cast off the bow and stern lines and

motored out of the harbor. Clay and I didn't say much. Nobody followed us, so about an hour out of the harbor, we put up the sails and turned off the engine. The creak of the rigging and the hiss and slap of the water were the only sounds. Clay and I looked astern and still saw no other boats, then we looked at each other and shook our heads, grinning.

The next day we tied up at the dock in West Palm where we'd boarded the *Lisa* a couple of days earlier. We were ashore with our duffle bags when a man came down the dock.

"Where's Fred?"

"The last time we saw him he was walking off with the Freeport police," said Clay.

He frowned. "You two brought the boat over?"

"Yes," I said. "But so far we've only gotten half our pay."

He gave me a look, then turned back to Clay. "You take a peek at the cargo?"

"No," he said. "We're not interested in TVs. Why don't you go aboard and check for yourself. None of the boxes have been opened."

"I'll do that." He went down into the cabin and came back. "Everything looks fine."

"Is Fred going to be all right?" I asked. "He seemed like a nice guy. I wouldn't want anything to happen to him."

"He'll be okay," said the man. "They don't have any evidence against him, thanks to you guys. How much does he owe you?"

We told him and he grinned and said, "Cheap bastard. I'll have to get it for you from the bank. Come on."

We followed him to two banks where he cashed two checks and gave us the money. As I put mine away with the other fifties, he studied us and said, "You fellas interested in more work?"

"No thanks," I said. "I'm going back to Boston."

"Not right now," said Clay.

"Well, if you change your minds . . ."

"I'll look you up if I do," I said.

*　　*　　*

But I didn't look him up because back in New England I passed my examinations and joined the Boston PD, and then started taking classes at Northeastern, using my Palm Beach money to pay my way.

As far as I knew, Clay never saw him again either, because he used his money to take flying lessons, then went out west to find work. He'd heard there were a lot of jobs for pilots out there along the border and apparently there were, because a couple of years later, he came to Boston with a new wife and enough money to rent himself a nice apartment and get his BA from Boston University.

By that time I was married, too, and the four of us saw a lot of each other before he and his then wife sailed his now completed ketch south so he could take a job he'd been offered.

And now he was coming again.

"What are you thinking about?" asked Zee, bringing me back to reality. She had a quizzical smile on her face. "You haven't moved since you hung up the phone."

"That was Clay," I said. "He's on the next boat. Hearing his voice, I got to thinking about a couple of sails we took together. I think I've mentioned them. One down to Florida from Boston and another out to the Bahamas and back."

"I remember you telling me about the one to Florida, but I don't remember the other one. Wasn't the Florida sail the one where you ran into a bad storm?"

"Yes. You know what they say about sailing: hours of boredom interspersed with moments of stark terror. But it was a good boat so we lived to tell the tale."

"Tell me about the Bahamas trip."

"Not much to tell. No storms. No problems. We sailed the boat out to Freeport, then sailed it back to West Palm. Fair winds both ways."

"What's Freeport like?"

"All I saw of it was a dock and the inside of a bar."

"I should have guessed! Well, you'd better get started if you're going to meet that boat. I'm looking forward to getting to know the mythical Mr. Stockton."

"You'll like him."

I drove to Vineyard Haven and had no problems finding a parking place in the Steamship Authority parking lot. The wind had shifted to the northeast and was coming off the water, so it was chilly. I stood inside the ticket office and watched the brand-new ferry, the *Island Home,* come into sight around West Chop. The *Island Home* was the pride of the Great White Fleet, and rightly so. It was only unpopular with those people who thought there were already enough people on Martha's Vineyard and didn't want to encourage more to come.

There weren't too many passengers aboard, and as they streamed down the gangplank, I immediately saw Clay, backpack slung over his shoulder, traveling light as always. He looked good.

I went out to meet him as he walked toward the ticket office and we wrapped ourselves in each other's arms, then stepped back and looked at each other, grinning.

"Haven't changed a bit!" Clay said.

"A thing of beauty is a joy forever."

"How long's it been?"

"We'll figure that out over martinis at home. Come on."

As we walked to the Land Cruiser, he glanced once back toward the boat. Then, walking on, he slapped my shoulder. "We have a lot of catching up to do."

"You don't get to leave until I know everything."

"Suits me. You sure your wife doesn't mind me visiting?"

"She thinks you're a myth. You get to prove you're not. It may take some work because I've been telling lies about you for years."

"Probably better than telling the truth!"

"Probably!"

We drove out of Vineyard Haven and headed for Edgartown. The bare trees let us see deep into the woods on either side of the road, revealing houses that were out of sight during the summer. There weren't many cars on the road.

"Never been here in the winter before," said Clay. "Last time I came here, we were both in college."

"That was a while back. Our place has changed a bit. New rooms for the kids, another bathroom, a woodstove in the living room. The bunk room is the guest room now, and my dad's bedroom is the master bedroom."

"Any work available this time of year?"

"If you build houses or wooden boats," I said. "Not much else. Most people think of rich people when they think of the Vineyard, but the island is one of the poorest counties in the state. When the tourists aren't here, there's a lot of unemployment and all of the problems that go along with poverty. A lot of it's generational: fathers beat up their wives, and their sons beat up their girlfriends. Brainless parents produce brainless children. The same kid steals from his mother, gets his girlfriend pregnant, drives his car into a tree. That sort of thing. Five percent of the people cause ninety-five percent of the cops' problems."

"Sounds like every small town."

"Or city. The percentages don't change much. You looking for work?"

"Maybe. But don't worry. If I decide to do that and if I can find a job, I won't be mooching off you. I'll get a place of my own." He laughed that good, infectious laugh of his, and I heard my own laughter in response.

"You can stay as long as you want," I said. "Hell, it'll take a month just to catch up on what you've been doing since the last time you wrote."

We passed the Felix Neck Wildlife Sanctuary and a bit later, turned down our long sandy driveway. I parked in front of the house beside Zee's little Jeep, and we both got out and went through the screened porch into the living room.

Zee and the children came to meet us.

"You must be Zee," said Clay. "I'm Clay." He put out his hand and took hers, holding it just long enough. "It's very nice of you to allow me into your home."

Her eyes danced. "It's a pleasure."

"And you must be Joshua and Diana. Your father has told me of you in his letters." He shook their hands and said, "He's very proud of both of you."

They beamed.

I pointed to the guest room. "You can put your gear in there, Clay, and I'll fix us some drinks."

He excused himself and disappeared into the guest room, and I went to the kitchen and got the Luksusowa out of the freezer. I poured three glasses, added two olives to each, put the glasses on a tray with crackers, cheese, and smoked bluefish, and came back into the living room just in time to find Clay introducing himself to Oliver Underfoot and Velcro and distributing small gifts: perfume to Zee (her favorite; how did he know? I must have mentioned it in a letter), a pocketknife to Joshua (his first; I'd only recently decided he was old enough for one, but hadn't told him so yet), and a tiny blue sapphire ring for Diana (just the right size, too).

"How about me?" I asked, putting the tray on the coffee table next to my delighted family members.

He gestured at them. "You already have everything here a man could want."

I looked at Zee, who was smiling at everyone in the room. It had taken me years to capture her heart. Clay had done it in five minutes. Even the cats were rubbing against his legs.

I felt good. I picked up my glass and raised it. "Here's to us all," I said. "God bless us, every one."

The next morning, Zee was back at work in the hospital ER, and the kids were in school by the time Clay came yawning into the kitchen, where I was reading the paper and having another cup of coffee.

"If I had more character, I'd be embarrassed," he said, finding himself a cup, filling it from the pot, and sitting down across from me.

"It's the Vineyard Sleepies," I said. "You remember them. It happens to everybody. You come down to the island and the first thing you feel like doing is taking a nap, and the next morning you oversleep. Maybe it's the salt in the air. It even happens to me if I've been off-island for a while. What'll you have for breakfast?"

"I see some toast here and a couple of slices of bacon. I'll fry myself a couple of eggs to go with it." He started to rise, but I put out a hand.

"You sit. I'll fry. You're a guest." I fixed his eggs and sat down again.

While he ate, his eyes roamed around the room. He looked happy, and I was happy to have him there. Friends are scarce and rare.

"Place looks mighty fine. Not to criticize your housekeeping, J.W., but I think having Zee around has improved things quite a bit."

"No doubt about it."

"I imagine there've been a lot of changes since I was here last."

"More than you know. After you finish eating, I'll take you

on the two-wheel-drive tour and you can check things out for yourself. What you won't see is the hundred thousand tourists we get in the summer."

"Mostly locals here now, I guess." He finished his meal and rose before I could. "No, I remember the rule, and it's a good one: the cook doesn't do the dishes; the eater does. Makes for peace in the valley."

He carried his dishes and my now empty cup to the sink, washed everything, and stacked it in the drainer. Like everything else he did, he worked smoothly and without wasted effort, as though every movement had been choreographed. When he was done, he came outside to where I was refilling the bird feeders. The two cardinals that sat in the catbrier between visits to the feeders were waiting for me to leave.

"Pretty birds," said Clay.

"They're even prettier when it's snowed," I said. "Bright red against all that white. Christmas card stuff. If you're ready for the ten-cent tour, make sure you wear that coat. My heater has never worked right."

Overhead the sky was gray-blue, with high, thin clouds moving down from the northwest, dimming the midwinter sun. The wind was chilly and the trees around the house were bare ruin'd choirs.

We drove up our long sandy driveway, where I turned left and headed into Edgartown.

"A lot of these buildings weren't here when I was last here," said Clay, as we passed through the Y and went on. His eyes never stopped moving.

"True." When I'd first come to the island, Edgartown's Main Street had been lined with useful stores and shops: drugstores, grocery stores, a paper store, hardware stores, and clothing stores. Now it was all T-shirt shops, pricey resort-clothing shops, and souvenir stores, most of which were closed during the off-season. If you needed anything useful, you often had to go to Vineyard Haven or Oak Bluffs to get it.

"Cannonball Park's still here, I see."

"True again. And the cannons and cannonballs still don't match."

"I remember when some drunk college kid tried to steal one of those cannonballs. The cops let him try to carry it for a couple of blocks before they arrested him."

"It's challenging to purloin a ten-inch ball of iron."

We drove down Main and to the docks, where we saw scallop boats going out toward the ponds, manned by fishermen thick with clothing.

"These guys earn their money," I said. "I do some winter scalloping, myself."

Clay nodded. "Fishing is a wicked way to make a buck. I fished out of Alaska one season, and a couple of times I didn't think we were going to make it back to land. Some of those guys go out in tubs that will hardly float."

"They're probably a lot like the fishermen around here. They have to choose between fixing up their boats, buying insurance, or buying fuel. Most opt for the fuel because that's the only way they can get out to the grounds and maybe make a profit for a change. When were you in Alaska?"

"Oh, I thought you knew. A few years back. My second ex sicced the police on me and I had to get out of state, so I went north. I'd never been there, so I figured I'd be fine until the dust settled. And I was. Never missed a meal, although I'll admit I had to delay some." He grinned. "Worked up above the Arctic Circle for a while. Wicked flies and mosquitoes up there. If you're out in the woods and you have to take a crap, you wait as long as you can because when you drop your pants, your ass is covered with mosquitoes faster than you can shit!" He laughed.

I drove up to North Water Street and out toward Starbuck Neck. To our right we could see the little three-car On Time ferry heading across the entrance to Edgartown Harbor over to Chappaquiddick.

"A floating gold mine," I said. "If you ever decide to go

back to sea, I recommend you buy that ferry. You've got a monopoly on traffic, and prices go up whenever you want them to. A lot of very happily retired people once owned that business."

"And it's always on time because it doesn't have a schedule. My kind of boat."

We passed the great captains' houses and the big Harbor View Hotel at the end of the street. "They have a Sunday brunch here with an open raw bar," I said. "Even you could finally get your fill of littlenecks and oysters."

"It hasn't happened often."

"Why was your second ex mad at you?"

"Child support. I thought we had a deal. I signed over all of our money and property except for my tools. She even got the plane I owned then. It amounted to quite a bit and we agreed that it was enough to see our boy through high school. Then, a few months later, she changed her mind and wanted more that I didn't have. I'd almost finished building a nice little twenty-seven-foot cutter, but I had to abandon it and get out of state. I heard later that she got the boat, and then sold it."

"You still a wanted man?"

He shrugged. "There are forty-nine other states. I'd like to see the boy, though."

"Well, you can hunker down here as long as you need to."

He gave me a swift look. "I may stay a few days, at least, if that's okay."

"You can stay as long as you want."

We drove back to Main, then out on South Water Street, passing under the giant Pagoda Tree, which had originally been brought to the island in a flower pot by a sailing captain and recently had dropped one of its huge, ancient limbs on top of an unfortunate automobile that, happily for its owner, was unoccupied at the time.

To our left the harbor was empty save for work boats, one of which was moored to the stake where we tie our eighteen-foot catboat, the *Shirley J.*, in the summer. At the end of the street we turned left toward Katama, where Clay had opportunity to comment that huge houses were growing like weeds in Eden.

"There's a lot of money floating around these days," he said. "I see this happening in every pretty place in the country. Big money from out of state. Mansions built beside lakes, up on mountains, out in the desert. Most of them only used a few weeks out of the year. It's like the guys who buy the really big yachts. The bigger the boat, the less the owner uses it." He shrugged. "I've helped build these kinds of houses and I've lived in them, and I've helped build those kinds of boats and I've sailed on them. It's wonderful to have a budget that lets you build with the very best materials and take the time to do the best possible work, and the products are magnificent. When you live in those houses or sail in those boats, it's like being in a movie."

"Sounds good."

"It is good, and it's a lot of fun." He paused. "But it's make-believe. It might not seem so to the people who live that way all the time, but I've lived with those people, and most of them have no idea about any other kind of life. Their money protects them from ever having to know. I always have to leave. The time comes when I go down to some bar and have a beer, then look for a job where I can use my hands."

We drove out along Meetinghouse Way, the roughest corduroy street in Edgartown—guaranteed to shake your car to pieces if you go over fifteen miles an hour—until we came to the Edgartown–West Tisbury road, where I took a left and headed up-island.

I showed him the driveway down which then-president Joe Callahan and his family had lived while enjoying their summer island holidays.

"I think you wrote that you'd met the daughter," said Clay.

"Cricket Callahan. Yes. Nice kid. I think she's in college or grad school now."

"According to the magazines, this place is crawling with celebrities."

"More every year, they say, but most of them stick to themselves. Every now and then you get one who wants to be seen, but that's pretty rare. I don't know much about the celebrity scene, I'm afraid. My friends are mostly neighbors, fishermen and people who sing in the community chorus. Not a celeb among them."

A car came up behind us and Clay turned and studied it. Beyond the mill pond, the car went right, and I turned left and drove past the field of dancing statues. Even in January happy-looking people were out there imitating the poses of the statues and having their pictures taken beside them. I've been told that thousands of such photos have been mailed from all over the world to the gallery beside the field.

"I may come up here and pose, myself." Clay grinned. "My kids might get a kick out of seeing me being a goof."

"You pose and I'll take the picture."

"It's a deal. Not today, though. Too cold. Later."

"How many children do you have these days?"

"Three. Two girls and the boy. Different mothers. None of the marriages lasted. What about you and Carla? I know you split but you never said why. I liked her."

"And she liked you and me, but she was a schoolteacher and finally couldn't take being a cop's wife because she never knew when I might end up in a box. When I got shot, it was the last straw for her. She waited until she knew I'd be all right, then divorced me and married another schoolteacher so she'd have a husband with a safe job. They have two kids now and live out west somewhere."

He stared ahead as I turned up Music Street and headed for Middle Road. "It's rough when things fall apart, but what starts out good doesn't always end that way. You have no idea how I envy you. A wife and kids and all the house you need. I've known a thousand guys like me, and every one of them would trade all their travels and capers for what you've got."

"They write books about those people but not about people like me."

"Believe me," he said, "you don't want people writing about you." He slapped my knee and grinned. "You know: police blotters, IOU's, wanted posters, angry e-mails, and all like that!"

"Fame can be demanding," I agreed, laughing. It was good to be with someone I didn't have to explain things to, and I thought he felt the same.

We passed the field where the long-horned oxen grazed. I was driving slowly so I could look at the land on both sides of the road and see new things, and it wasn't long before a faster car appeared behind me. I pulled over into the entrance to a driveway and let the car go by. Clay looked at it with interest until it was out of sight in front of us.

"Not much traffic this time of year," I said, "but most of it is still faster than I am."

"You've got the right idea. Slow and steady is best."

Middle Road is the prettiest road on the island, with farms and fields and fine stone walls on either side. As we got toward its western end, we could see the Atlantic rolling south toward the horizon, cold and wintry under the darkening January sky.

We came to Beetlebung Corner and drove to Menemsha, a fishing village so cute it looks like Walt Disney designed it. Clay ordered me to stop so he could buy us two lobster rolls for a snack.

As he climbed back into the Land Cruiser, he said, "After we admire the Gay Head cliffs—or are they the Aquinnah cliffs these days?—a liquor store is the next stop. We need a bottle of Rémy Martin for after dinner."

"For a homeless man, you've got expensive taste."

"I've slept under the stars more than once, but right now

I'm in the chips and staying in a nice little place in Edgartown. Other people's houses are the best, you know, just like other people's boats. You get all the benefits and none of the responsibilities or expenses, so you can blow your money on lobster and Rémy Martin."

"It sounds like a plan."

His eyes had surveyed the parking area and then the road ahead as I drove around Menemsha Pond and followed the highway to the top of the famous cliffs, at the westernmost point of the Vineyard. We were all alone at the observation area, and the wind was cold in our faces as we looked out across the whitecapped sound toward the huddled Elizabeth Islands.

"Snow coming," he said.

I nodded. "I like snow when I'm inside and it's outside. I'm a few years past loving cold weather. At home we can sit in front of the fire and look through the windows at the flakes coming down."

As we walked back down to the truck, another couple, shoulders hunched against the wind, came up the path. They smiled and said hello and that, yes, it looked like snow, and passed on up the hill. Clay glanced at them over his shoulder as we went on.

Back down-island, we stopped in Oak Bluffs, where we lunched on Sam Adams and burgers at the Fireside.

Bonzo was there, bringing beer up from the basement. When he saw me, he came right over to our table. Long before I'd met him, he'd gotten into some bad acid and had doomed himself to a life of gentle preadolescence.

"Hey, J.W., how you doing?" He smiled his childish smile.

"I'm good, Bonzo." I introduced him and Clay to each other as old friends, and they shook hands.

"J.W. is my old friend, too," said Bonzo to Clay, "and if you're his friend, that means that you're my friend, too."

"I'm glad to have a new friend," said Clay.

Bonzo beamed. "Hey," he said to me, "you know what? I

got a new recorder and a new mike and as soon as spring comes, I'm gonna go out and get the best bird songs I ever got! You want to come?"

"Sounds like fun, Bonzo. You can go on my land, if you want to. I've got a meadow back in my woods where you might pick up some good songs."

"That's a good idea, J.W. I never been there. I might hear a bird I never heard before!"

"I guess it could happen. When you're ready, you give me a call and we'll do it."

Bonzo was suddenly serious. "You know who would like to go, too? Nadine. I wish she'd come back. She liked birds. She went with me to listen to them once."

"Maybe she'll come back in the spring, Bonzo."

"You think so? I hope you're right. That would be very good."

Bonzo went back to work and Clay smiled. "Nice guy."

"Very."

"Who's Nadine?"

"Nadine Gibson, a girl who worked here last winter. Long red hair. One night last March, after work, she headed for her house and hasn't been seen since. Bonzo liked her."

"Skullduggery?"

I shrugged. "Who knows? No body's been found, so that's good. Most people who go missing do it on purpose or don't even know that people think they're missing. They just go off and don't bother telling anybody because it never crosses their minds that they should. When they find out that their friends have been frantic, they're shocked."

Clay drank some beer. "Well, let's hope that's what happened to Nadine."

We finished our meal and then walked up the street so Clay could buy some Rémy Martin.

"Pretty steep price for cognac," he said, climbing back into the truck.

"Freight," I said. "You ask the liquor store guys why it costs

fifteen dollars to buy a bottle you can get for ten on the mainland and they'll tell you: freight. The same goes for everything else on the island. The only thing that's cheap on the
Vineyard is taxes. And that's because all these McMansions
pay big real estate taxes but don't use a lot of services."

"Maybe I can go into the freight business," said Clay.
"There seems to be money in it."

"You need money? I have some stashed away."

He shook his head. "No. I can always find a way to get
money if I need to. It's not hard to make money if money is
what you want. Besides, I have a little stash of my own. You
need any?"

"No. We don't use much and we have what we need."

"That's what I call being rich."

We drove home just as the first fine flakes of snow began
to spiral down.

I stirred up the fire in the stove and Clay made coffee. We
poured some cognac into the coffee cups and sat down in
front of the fire.

The children would be coming home from school in an
hour or so, and Zee wouldn't be far behind.

"Who's after you?" I asked.

— 4 —

"Nobody that I know of," Clay said, giving me a thoughtful look. "Don't worry. I didn't come here to bring you trouble."

"You haven't," I said, "but ever since you arrived, you've been looking over your shoulder and studying everybody who gets close."

"I think that's mostly habit." He smiled. "You know me. I'm peaceful as a lamb, but from time to time there have been people more interested in talking to me than I was in talking to them, so I've been obliged to keep my eyes open and to move on a few times when I really didn't want to."

"Like the move to Alaska."

"Like that. I have nobody to blame but myself, of course. I've had plenty of chances to walk the straight and narrow, but every time I've started down that road, I've managed to wander off into the jungle. About half the time it was some woman sort of beckoning to me, and other times it was some job that looked interesting. I'd meet a lady and we'd hit it off, or I'd be talking to a guy and he'd ask me if I'd be interested in some work that sounded better than what I was doing, so I'd throw away the good life and go off with the girl or off to the job." He paused. "I'll tell you, though. I'm getting too damned old to be gallivanting around, following my pecker wherever it leads me. That straight-and-narrow path is looking better and better to me."

"What do you want to do?"

"I have to work, of course. Not right now, because I've got enough for the moment, but eventually. What I'd really like to do is get another plane or boat. I like flying and I'm good at it. Stupidest thing I ever did—well, maybe not the stupidest but stupid enough—was giving Samantha my airplane when we split. I should have kept it. If I'd have done that, I could have made enough money to keep her happy and piled up some retirement cash of my own. I'd be sitting pretty by now. But I was trying to do the right thing in a hurry, so the plane went to her and I've never gotten another one."

"I didn't know there was that much money in flying."

"You'd be surprised. I've flown planes in several countries, and I could still be doing it if I wasn't getting so old and conservative." He grinned. "You've got these castles all over this island. There's a lot of money in this world, and a fair part of it travels by small plane. Remember Fred, all those years ago down in West Palm?"

"Sure. I was just thinking about him yesterday, in fact."

"Remember the cargo we brought home for him?"

"I do."

"You know what was in those cartons?"

"I know they weren't TV sets."

"And that's all you know, and all I know, but we both know those boxes contained something that was pretty valuable. Well, there's a lot of freight being moved around these days, and if you don't look in the boxes, you can do all right for yourself."

"Sounds like it could be dangerous."

He made a small dismissive gesture. "Not really. The secret is to play straight with the people you're working for and to keep the authorities from getting interested in you. You do that by always having some legit reason to be flying where you're flying or by having a boss who knows who to buy off." He sipped his coffee. "You have to be careful, of course. You always have to be careful."

"Is that the kind of work you want to do now?"

He looked into the fire. "I think I'm too old for some things I used to do," he said, "but I still have some contacts and I can still fly."

I said, "Well, we have two working airports during the summer and another one that small planes use from time to time on an informal basis. There's a lot of air traffic to and from the island during the tourist season, but things slow down this time of year, so the Katama airport is closed until Memorial Day."

He finished his coffee and looked at his watch. "I think I'll stay on the ground for a while, until I work out a long-range plan. When I was a lad, we used to get out of school about this time. When do your kids get home?"

"Any time," I said, looking out at the falling snow. "The bus drops them off at the head of the driveway. Zee should be coming home not too much later."

"You the cook?"

"I am. Tonight is leftover night. We're having yesterday's black-bean chili again tonight."

"It was good last night and it'll be good again, but we used up the corn bread, so I'll whip up some more. You have the makings?"

"I do."

"Since you and I were young, I've become a world-renowned corn-bread baker, and I'm anxious to show off my skills." He stood up. "Point me at the ingredients."

Because chili and corn bread go together like Damon and Pythias, I got right out of my chair. "I never argue with someone who wants to do my work," I said. "Follow me to the kitchen."

He did, and when he discovered canned chili peppers in our cupboard, he announced that his corn bread would be the Mexican variety, which was even better than the normal kind. By the time Joshua and Diana came stomping into the living room from the screened porch, their jackets and boots wet with snow, Clay's batter was mixed and he was ready to bake.

I helped the kids out of their storm gear and sent them to their rooms so they could get into their loafing clothes and slippers. I put the wet coats and boots behind the woodstove to drip and dry and got to work making warm cocoa for the youngsters and, in expectation of Zee's arrival, heating cider for the big people to mix with rum, cinnamon, and cloves.

When Zee got home, the snow was falling in earnest and changing the landscape into a black-and-white world as the short winter day darkened toward night. She added her coat and boots to those already behind the stove, gave kisses to me and the kids and a smile to Clay, then sniffed the scents from the kitchen.

"Smells good."

She disappeared into our bedroom and returned in sweats and slippers, walking like a panther out of her den. We sat in front of the fire and the children told us how things had gone in school that day. Diana's day had been uneventful, but Joshua's had included an altercation with another boy.

At this news a silence fell and stayed until I said, "Tell me what happened."

"Oh, not much," said Joshua, seeming surprised that the event merited further discussion. "Jim Duarte pushed me and I pushed him back, and then he pushed me again and I hit him in the nose just like you showed me, Ma, and he cried and I had to go to Patagonia."

Patagonia, I knew, was a chair in the corner of the classroom where students served their terms as class disrupters. What I didn't know was that Joshua knew how to punch someone in the nose. I looked at Zee, who lifted her chin slightly.

"Are you giving boxing lessons now?" I asked.

"I don't want my children to be bullied," said Zee coolly. "I just taught them a couple of things so they can protect themselves."

"Diana, too?"

"Girls need to know self-defense."

True. I turned to my children. "I just want to be sure that you don't start fights. When you know how to hurt people, you have to be especially careful not to do it."

"I didn't hurt him," said Joshua in a serious voice. "We're still friends."

"That's good."

"Pa?"

"What?"

"Did you ever hurt anybody?"

"Yes. But I almost always wished it hadn't happened."

"Did anybody ever hurt you?"

"Yes. But I never wanted that to happen, either."

"Sometimes," said Clay, leaning forward from his seat and speaking to the children, "people think they have to hurt other people. It's usually because they're afraid of them. If you're not afraid, you're usually better off."

"Pa says being afraid sometimes is good," said Diana, looking at Clay. "Like being afraid of a lion or a Tyrannosaurus rex."

"Well, of course," said Clay. "You should always be afraid if you meet a lion or a Tyrannosaurus rex. And you should be afraid of other things, too, like jumping out of an airplane without a parachute or putting your hand in a fire. But if you get afraid of too many things or of other people, you risk becoming somebody who hurts other people and thinks it's the right thing to do." He paused and gave me a rueful, amused look. "I think I'm drowning here."

"You're not drowning," said Diana. "You're just waxing philosophical."

"Waxing philosophical?" He laughed. "Is that what I'm doing?"

She and Joshua both nodded. "Pa says we're waxing philosophical whenever we talk about something we don't understand. You know, like God or gravity."

Clay glanced at me, then back at the children. "Do you talk about God and gravity a lot?"

"No," said Diana, "but we do sometimes and we have books about that stuff."

"And a computer, too," added Joshua. "We can look things up if we don't have a book about it."

"Ah," said Clay. "An intellectual household." He sipped his cider.

"Actually," said Zee, "we talk more about food and fishing than about philosophy."

"Smart," said Clay. "I have a degree in philosophy, and food and fishing are a lot more interesting than most philosophizing. Speaking of food, I think my corn bread must be ready to come out of the oven." He got up and went to the kitchen and I followed to tend to the chili.

After we'd eaten and had washed and stacked the dishes, we went back to the fire. I poured cognac for the big people. Outside it was now too dark to see the falling snow, but I knew it was still coming down because it was so quiet. Silent snow, secret snow.

"So you had to go to Patagonia today, eh?" asked Clay, looking at Joshua.

"Only for five minutes," said Joshua.

"That wasn't too long," said Clay. "I'll bet you could serve that sentence standing on your head. I was in the real Patagonia once."

"The real Patagonia is way down at the tip of South America," said Diana, perking up. "They have penguins there. Did you see some? How did you get so far away?"

"It's a long story," said Clay.

"Tell us!"

And he did, for among his other talents, he had that of a teller of tales, who could weave words into a web that captured his listeners and held them until his story ended.

"Well," he began, "I didn't see any penguins, but it was a good adventure anyway. It started when I met a girl from Argentina who wanted to see America. I was driving from Florida out to Oregon, so I offered her a ride. . . ."

And she had accepted and they'd had a splendid trip, at the end of which she offered to show him Argentina. He'd accepted the offer and had ended up in Buenos Aires, some coastal towns west of there, and finally in a nameless little village in the Andes. The girl, it turned out, was rich, so for his first few weeks in Argentina, he had lived in mansions and on yachts, but then he'd grown tired of luxury and of people who, though charming and well-educated, never worked, and he had thanked them for their hospitality and traveled on toward the Andes until, at last, his money was gone and he had no way of getting home. With his last coin, he'd gone into a bar and bought a beer to sip while he figured out what to do.

"It's what I do whenever I'm at the end of my rope," he explained to my wide-eyed children, "I take my last dollar and buy a beer while I decide what to do next and hope for a miracle."

"Does it always work?" asked Joshua.

"So far," said Clay, and he went on to tell how the Patagonia miracle had happened in the form of a man who sat down beside him and who, they discovered as they talked, needed a pilot to fly a cargo to Peru.

"So you see," said Clay, "miracles do happen, even in these days." He grinned that infectious grin.

"Gosh," said Joshua.

"If you hadn't met the man, you could have gone to church," said Diana, who had friends who did that. "God lives there."

"I guess I could have," said Clay.

"God must live in bars, too," said her brother.

"No more waxing philosophical," said Zee. "It's bedtime for you two. Off you go."

Following the usual *gee*'s and *gosh*'s and *do we have to*'s, they left after getting the promise of another story from Clay the next night.

"Quite a tale," said Zee when the kids were gone.

"And all true, too," said Clay, "but that reminds me." He went to his room and came out with a tiny leather bag. "I left out a few things that I didn't think the kids needed to hear." He sat back down beside Zee, loosened the drawstrings of the bag, and emptied its contents into his open palm. Jewels and gemstones glittered in the firelight.

"Take your choice," he said to Zee. "And take one for Diana, too."

"I can't do that," she said, catching her breath.

"You'll give me great pleasure if you do, and make me sad if you don't. The red ones are rubies and the green ones are emeralds. The yellow and white ones are diamonds. They're very pretty, but I have no use for them, so help me out by taking two off my hands."

She touched them. "Where did you get them?"

He smiled. "Well, without going into too much detail, let's say I got them for flying into Peru. I brought them home in the heels of my boots. That was in the days before the shoe bomber, fortunately."

Zee's fingers roamed over the stones.

"Take what you want," said Clay. "I personally favor the rubies and emeralds. Diamonds have never interested me very much."

"I already have a diamond," said Zee, wiggling her ring finger. "All right, I'll take this emerald for me and this ruby for Diana. She'll lose it if I give it to her now, so I'll put it away until she's older."

"Good!" He cupped his hand and poured the remaining stones back into the bag.

"What did you take into Peru?" asked Zee, holding the stones in a clenched hand.

"I'm not quite sure. We'd sewed small packages into the lining of my suitcase. After I landed in Lima, I left the airport in a taxi and went to a hotel where we'd agreed I'd go. A man was waiting for me in the lobby. I about wet my pants because I was sure he was a cop, but he wasn't. He took me and my suitcase to a mansion outside the city. The next morning, when I got up, I had a new suitcase and my old one was gone."

"Who was the guy you met in Patagonia?"

"He said his name was Bill. He was a Frenchman, if I got his accent right."

He yawned and finished his cognac. "I'm getting to be an old man. I can't stay up the way I used to." He rose and said good night and went into the guest room.

Zee opened her fist, and two eyes, one green, one red, gleamed up at us.

"You have interesting friends," she said to me. Then suddenly she put her arms around me and pulled me to her. "I'm glad you're not an adventurer," she said, putting her lips to mine.

— 5 —

The next morning the snow was six inches deep and still coming down. It was the wet, heavy kind that's so good for making snowballs, snowmen, and snow forts. When I looked through the falling flakes, the woods around our house were black and gray and my sense of distance was vague and uncertain. My ancestors, when they lived in caves, probably worried about what gray-black things were out there looking back at them. The sound of the falling snow was the sound of silence, and the sounds of the woods were muffled and hard to locate. There was no wind.

I liked it.

We were all standing in the screened porch, where I'd come after shoveling the steps and the walkway and cleaning the snow off of Zee's Jeep. She was going to drive Diana and Joshua up to the bus stop on her way to the ER. The kids were bundled up for school and Zee was wearing her big furry hat and her other winter garb.

"This reminds me of the time I got lost in Alaska," said Clay.

"Tell us, tell us!" cried the children.

"Not now," said Zee. "You're going to school."

"Tonight," said Clay. "After you do your homework."

Zee and the children waded out to Zee's little red Jeep and drove away, leaving clean tire marks in the snow. Fortunately for us, both the Jeep and my Land Cruiser did well in the white stuff.

"Well," I said, "I imagine I have to go to work, too."

"What's the job?"

"I drive a snowplow for a guy who cleans driveways. He's got two trucks with plows, and he drives one and I drive the other. He prays for snow every winter, but lots of years we don't get enough to plow, so when a storm like this comes, he's anxious to be out there raking in the dollars before the snow melts."

"I drove a plow one winter," said Clay. "Up in Montana. I was working on a ranch and one of my jobs was to keep the snow off a runway and five miles of private road that led to the state highway. I didn't think that winter was ever going to end, but I liked the work while it lasted."

"Come on in while I call Ted to see if he needs me."

We went inside, but before I could call Ted, the phone rang. It was Ted calling me. He was frustrated. Wouldn't you know, he'd broken an arm and couldn't drive his plow? Worst time of the year to break something. Dad blast it! I'd have to do the plowing by myself, so I should come on over right away and get started.

I told him he was in luck. I had a visiting friend who was a Montana plowman. All he needed was somebody to show him where to go to work. Ted said that was good news, and that he'd ride shotgun and show the Montana plowman where to plow.

"I just got you a job," I said to Clay. "You can say no if you don't want it."

"I've never minded working," he said. "Let me get my coat."

When we got to the Edgartown–Vineyard Haven road, we found it plowed. The Highway Department at work. The town guys didn't mind the work because it meant a lot of overtime. They did the school parking lots and all the other official lots, but they didn't do private driveways, at least, not very often. Every now and then such a driveway got plowed but just who did it was an official mystery. Mostly, private driveways were plowed by people like Ted Overhill.

"When he isn't plowing snow, Ted uses his trucks in his

landscaping business," I said as we drove to his place. "His sister works part-time for the Steamship Authority and keeps him informed about cars and passengers. He sees himself as the island's eye on tourism. Too little is bad for businesses; too much is bad for everybody else; just right has never been defined."

"Wasn't it Davy Crockett who said, 'Make sure you're right, then go ahead'?"

"Something like that."

"The problem is knowing when you're right."

"You might want to take a peek into Ted's barn. For as long as I can remember he's been building a boat in there. Right up your alley." I turned on to Ted's side street—not yet plowed—and saw the earlier tracks of a couple of vehicles whose owners had to get somewhere, snow or not.

At the end of Ted's drive, I parked the Land Cruiser in front of the barn, beside two big pickups armed with plows, then we took our coffee thermoses and stomped and kicked our way to the house. I performed introductions on the farmer's porch as Ted came out to meet us.

"What happened to your wing?"

"Ice skating with my grandson down on the pond there." He waved his good arm at a flat white space beyond the barn. "Not as limber as I used to be. Nowadays I break easier than I bend. You figure you can drive that rig, Clay?"

Clay followed his gaze and nodded, smiling. "I figure you'll let me know if I'm doing it wrong."

"You figure right. Well, let's go, so I can get rich before things melt. You know where to go, J.W. Do my sister's drive first, then when you've got the other places plowed out, come back here."

"Okay. Who put the plows on? Job takes more than one arm."

"My son Dan. Came over last night. Figured he owed me because I'd wrecked my arm skating with his boy, Little Dan."

"Guilt is a powerful tool."

I brushed the snow from the older of the two trucks, then let the cab warm for a few minutes while the steam cleared from the windows and I refamiliarized myself with the workings of the plow. By that time Clay and Ted were clearing the area between the house and the barn and, from what I could see, Clay knew what he was doing. Leaving them to that work, I plowed the driveway as I went out to the street. There, even though it was a public way, I plowed my way up to the highway to make things easier for the neighbors until the big town plows came by.

It wasn't an easy matter to move the heavy snow where I wanted it to go, but by being patient and not asking too much from my equipment, I could clear it away.

I drove a mile toward Vineyard Haven, then turned off and started cleaning Eleanor Araujo's driveway, pushing the snow off, first to this side, then to that, until I got to her yard, where I cleaned the parking area in front of her house and two-car garage. There was an apartment over the garage that she rented out during the summer, but its windows were dark with emptiness.

As I was finishing the job, Eleanor came out with a half dozen fresh-baked bran muffins still steaming in the winter air. I knew they were delish before I even tasted them, because I'd given her the recipe.

"Here you go," she said, handing me the paper plate. "Something to keep you alive until noon."

"Thanks. How are things with the Great White Fleet?"

"Slow, just like you'd think. This time of year you know most of the people on the boats, and more of them are leaving than arriving. Headed south to Naples or out to Scottsdale, looking for warm weather. They'll be back in the spring."

Naples and Scottsdale are known by some as Vineyard South and Vineyard West, because of the number of islanders who winter there to escape the rock. I personally liked our

Vineyard winters at least as much as our summers because of the quieter pace, the sense of greater empty space, and the feeling of small-town comfort that comes when you recognize the people you meet at the grocery store or post office.

Off-islanders are often surprised by anyone's affection for the island in the wintertime and wonder what people do out there when they can't go to the beach. I tell them that though I am inclined to stay at home with my family, I could, if I wished, be out every winter night listening to music of every sort or performing it, attending lectures or plays or otherwise partaking of island culture, for there may be no other place so small that produces more good art in all its forms than does the Vineyard. Writers, actors, painters, sculptors, wood carvers, musicians, and other artists hunker down in their houses and work during the short days and long nights of winter, showing up to exhibit their excellent wares onstage, in galleries, or in bookstores.

"No exciting news to report?" I now asked, not expecting any.

"None," said Eleanor, "unless you consider higher ticket prices exciting." She looked up into the falling snow. "The weather lady says this should be pretty much stopped by noon, but the Montreal Express is coming down, so it'll be a while before it melts."

"Good news for the kids who want to go sledding," I said. "But I'd better get moving before this stuff freezes solid."

I drove away and went first to my own driveway and yard, which, as a perk, I cleared before moving on and cleaning the driveways of Ted's customers. I worked steadily all morning, plowing and pulling a couple of stuck cars out of ditches and snowdrifts. By noon I was hungry in spite of having downed my coffee and muffins, but I kept on working as the snowflakes slowed and then stopped. About one in the afternoon, a bit of blue sky showed and an hour or two later, the gray clouds had moved off completely, leaving the snow cover glittering in the light of the southern winter sun, and the trees, each branch white with snow, looking like a fairyland. Is anything prettier than such a winter landscape? It made me feel happy and about six years old.

By four o'clock I was through with my jobs. I drove the truck to the gas station and filled its tank with the country's most expensive gasoline, put the fuel on Ted's tab, and went on to his place as the long night began to come down. I'd parked the truck and gotten the heater, such as it was, going in my Land Cruiser when Clay and Ted came in with the other truck.

"You didn't tell me that Clay was a boatbuilder," said Ted when I met them. "Come on, Clay, you might be interested in this." He led us into the barn and showed us his boat. The hull filled the center of the building and seemed complete. The barn was warmer than I'd anticipated and I saw why: it was weather-tight and insulated and it had heat, though the thermostat was set low.

"Been working on her off and on for fifteen years," said Ted. "Thought I might get her into the water this coming summer but because of this bum arm, it may take longer."

Clay went to the boat and touched the stem, then, while Ted watched proudly, he circled the hull, climbed a ladder, and looked at the cockpit.

"Go on aboard," called Ted. "Look inside. You'll see what still needs to be done."

Clay nodded, stepped aboard, and disappeared.

"Nice fella," said Ted. "Said he could plow and he can. Said he's built a couple of wooden boats." He gave me a quizzical look.

"I saw the first one," I said. "A Tahiti Ketch. Saw pictures of a schooner he worked on later in Florida and a little sloop he was building in Oregon. All of them beautiful. He's got magic hands."

Clay came back down the ladder and nodded. "Nice boat. Chapelle design?"

Ted smiled. "You recognize it?"

"Forty-two-foot schooner. I almost built one years ago but I got sidetracked. You do this yourself?"

"A lot of it. I had some friends help out now and then when I needed to be two places at once."

Clay nodded. "It helps to have several hands sometimes. You've done a good job. She's strong and solid and she'll be beautiful on the water."

"I want to take her a ways before I get too old and rickety. Not too many years left before that happens."

Clay was looking at the boat. "Not too much left to do. Mostly inside-finish work and rigging. You have your masts yonder, I see. You might get in the water this summer."

"Not with this wing."

"No."

Ted had apparently been thinking, for now he made a decision. "You interested in the job? Pay you a living wage."

Clay looked at him, then looked back at the boat, then nodded. "I can use a job, and I can do this one. What's a living wage on Martha's Vineyard?"

Ted named a fair-sized figure. Clearly he wanted to see the schooner afloat. Clay nodded again and put out his hand, which Ted shook.

Clay looked at the boat with a new expression: that of a builder. "Unless there's some problem I don't know about, we should have this vessel ready for a summer launching." He rubbed his chin. "Of course, there are always problems you can't anticipate, but we'll take care of them as they come."

"You take a look at my inventory," said Ted. "I think I have almost everything we'll need. I've been collecting it for years. Anything we don't have, we'll buy."

"I'll have my hand tools shipped to me," said Clay. "A friend is storing them for me out in Sausalito." He looked at me. "I'll have them sent to your place, if that's okay with you."

"Fine," I said.

"You may not have to do that," said Ted. "I've got all the tools you'll need."

"A man likes his own tools," said Clay, "but I'll use yours until mine get here."

"Fair enough."

Clay seemed as pleased as Ted. "Only two more things, then," he said. "I'm going to need a place to stay and a truck of some kind to get around."

"You can stay with us as long as you want," I said.

"No, I can probably leech off you for a few more days, but then I'd start to feel bad. My folks were churchgoers but the only part of religion that stuck with me was guilt. I'm sort of like Byron; he said that his religious upbringing never prevented him from sinning but always prevented him from enjoying it as much as he wanted."

Ted frowned, then brightened. "We may be able to kill two birds with one stone. My sister Eleanor has an apartment over her garage that you can probably rent cheap during the winter. And she's still got that old Bronco she planned to sell when she got her new pickup. She might give you a good deal on it. Nothing wrong with it, really. Just old."

"The same is fairly true of me." Clay laughed.

"I'll call her and sound her out," said Ted, sounding pleased.

"And we'll head for home," I said. "If Eleanor's interested in this deal, have her give Clay a call at our place."

Ted pulled out a roll of bills and awkwardly peeled off wages for both of us. Then, as he walked toward his house, we drove away toward mine.

The promised cold wave was already crisping the snow when we pulled into the darkening yard, and we were barely in the house when the children came smiling up to Clay.

"We've done our homework and now we want the story about being lost in Alaska!"

"Give me five minutes to shed my coat and boots."

"And another five for me to do the same and get us some drinks," I said.

"I want to hear this, too," said Zee, helping me out of my coat.

The fire in the stove was dancing and the room was warm. Oliver Underfoot and Velcro were stretched out, enjoying the heat. We sat in the living room and Clay sipped his hot cider and looked at Joshua and Diana.

"Well," he said, "it happened like this."

— 6 —

His tale was of being a last-minute copilot on a routine winter flight from Bettles Field north to the oil fields along the Alaskan coast, of leaving in sunshine and flying into a sudden and unexpected snowstorm where all landmarks were blotted out, of having a compass that didn't work because of the magnetic pole, of gradually running out of gas, and then, suddenly, unexpectedly, through a miraculous opening in the clouds below, seeing a tiny airstrip punched out of the tundra by a bulldozer driver for some reason, of landing the plane in howling winds, of stepping out into the storm and having hands that shook so badly he could barely light a cigarette, of shivering in the plane through the night and then, the next morning in bright sun, flying back to Bettles on the fumes from their gas tanks, and greeting friends who were sure they were dead.

His voice cast a glamour over his listeners, entrancing us. He could have been a skald of old, a scop, an Egil Skallagrimsson weaving such a tale of words that Eric Bloodax, his captor, allowed him to live. When he finished his story, there was a silence, then Diana spoke.

"Clay, don't you know that smoking's dangerous?"

The big people laughed and Joshua smiled uncertainly, not sure what was funny.

Clay brushed his hand across Diana's dark hair. "You're right. It is dangerous. I smoked then, but I don't do it anymore."

"Do you still fly airplanes?" asked Joshua.

"I can," said Clay. "But right now I don't have one to fly."

"I want to be a pilot," said Joshua.

"You'd like it."

"I'd like it, too," said Diana. "Can you teach us how?"

"Well," said Clay. "I can teach you some things, but to really learn we'd need an airplane."

"Is it like driving a car? We drive our car on the beach sometimes, sitting in Pa's lap."

"It's something like that. If you can drive a car, you can probably learn how to fly an airplane." Clay smiled at me. "So you're letting them learn on the beach, eh? When I was a kid out in Wichita we all learned by driving around in the fields."

"We'll switch to fields when they get a little bigger."

I went with Zee into the kitchen and helped get supper while Clay and the children discussed cars and airplanes.

"I see how he managed to get married so often," said Zee. "He's got a voice that casts spells."

"Put cotton in your ears," I said. "You're already married to me."

"Maybe you can take locution lessons."

"I'm the strong, silent type."

"Pardon my repressed laughter."

"Speech is silver; silence is gold."

"Silver apples of the moon." She kissed me.

"Golden apples of the sun." I kissed her back.

We called everyone to the table and afterward, when the dishes were cleaned and stacked and the kids were in their rooms reading and the adults sat over coffee and cognac in front of the fire, the phone in the kitchen rang. It was Eleanor Araujo calling for Clay. While he talked to Eleanor, I told Zee of Ted Overhill's job, housing, and transportation proposals.

She arched an eyebrow. "Really? Clay must have made a pretty favorable impression on Ted. One day working together and he offers him a full-time job and finds him a car and an apartment, too."

"Clay inspires confidence."

She nodded and glanced toward the kitchen. "He does that, for sure."

Clay came back and sat down. "Well, it looks like you won't have to put up with me much longer. Tomorrow I'll go over to Eleanor's place and take a look at her old truck and her apartment. The prices she mentioned seem right, and if things work out I'll be out of your hair."

"We don't want you out of our hair," said Zee. "You just got here and you haven't told us half of your adventures."

He gave her that smile of his. "Adventures are always more fun afterwards. While they're happening, you often wish they weren't."

"This is afterwards," she said. "And Jeff hasn't seen you for a long time. You two talk, and I'll listen and keep the drinking horns filled."

"You know what they say about fish and guests," he said, grinning. "And tomorrow will be my third day. I'd stay longer if I thought I wasn't going to see you again for another ten years, but it looks like I'll be your neighbor, so we'll have plenty of time to bring each other up to date. Besides," he put a hand over his cognac snifter, "I don't imbibe as much as I used to, so I don't need my drinking horn filled again tonight."

"Tell me what happened to that Tahiti Ketch you built when you were at BU," I said. "I never did get that story straight. The last time I saw it was when you and Margaret sailed south for Florida."

"Ah," he said, sitting back and making a wry face. "Where to begin? The problem was Margaret's inner ear." She was seasick all the time they sailed, and when they got to Fort Lauderdale, where his job waited for him, he knew she would never step aboard again, so he sold the boat and bought a share in a plane. But it turned out that Margaret got sick in planes, too, so he sold his share of the plane and bought a van, and . . .

By the end of his tale, Margaret had, as the result of a

complex series of events, ended up with a wealthy Mexican ranchero driving a white Rolls-Royce toward Texas, and Clay had ended up with a used van full of his worldly possessions, most of which were tools, and all of us, Clay included, were laughing so hard, tears were streaming down our faces.

"That's enough for tonight," said Clay when he'd caught his breath. "I'm going to bed." And he did.

Alone in the living room, Zee looked at me and laughed again. "My God," she said. "What a life. He lost his boat, his airplane, and his wife. It must have been a terrible time, but he made the whole thing sound incredibly funny!"

"Byron thought we laugh so we won't cry."

"I know that quote: 'And if I laugh at any mortal thing, 'tis that I may not weep.' Maybe that's what we have to do."

I didn't know whether life was comic or tragic. Perhaps it was both, though I suspected it was neither. But Zee was real and good, so I put my arms around her and said, "Let's go to bed."

Dawn brought blue skies and a landscape that was a fantasy of snow: white, shimmering trees; white, sparkling earth; slanting light dancing off silver drifts and the icy pond beyond our garden; glinting snow on the far barrier beach and beyond it the cold blue waters of Nantucket Sound. Winter! The owl for all his feathers was a-cold.

We bundled the children in their warmest clothes and sent them up the driveway to wait for the school bus, because it's good for kids to know they're tough enough to go to school even though it's colder than an oyster on ice. They were not long on their way when Zee pulled the electric dipstick out of her Jeep's engine, kicked over the motor, and headed to the hospital. She left a few minutes early, in fact, because although her motive was never officially announced, she wanted to make sure that Joshua and Diana actually got on the bus.

That left Clay and me to have a last cup of coffee, clean up the breakfast dishes, and drive to Eleanor Araujo's house.

The trees glittered at us as we passed them and the brilliant sky looked like blue ice.

Clay turned up the collar of his coat. "The older I get, the less I like cold weather," he said. "But this is beautiful."

"We've had some winters that got cold and snowy early and stayed that way until spring, but usually our snows melt before too long."

"The gulf stream?"

"So they say. It usually keeps us warmer than the mainland in the winter and cooler in the summer."

"Paradise enow."

The purity of the snow made it easy to think so, covering, as it did, all signs of sin and woe.

There weren't many cars on the highway, but the road was clean thanks to the Highway Department guys who'd made good overtime money with their plows.

We turned down Eleanor's driveway and stopped in front of her garage. She came out of her house, pulling on her coat, and crossed to us. I introduced Clay and the two of them shook hands.

She looked up at him, then down, then up again. "So you're a friend of J.W.'s."

He smiled that smile. "For many a year."

"What brings you to our fair island?"

"I came for a visit and I'm staying to work."

"My brother says he's going to give you a job on that schooner of his. You a boatbuilder?"

"I've built two or three. I like to work with wood."

She nodded. "Well, he'll want things done right. He's been building that boat for years, and he's very picky."

"So am I."

"Are you, now? Good. Come on. I'll show you the apartment. I turned on the heat and water last night. After that, you can take a look at my old Bronco, if you want."

She led us to a stairway to the second floor of the garage.

"I even shoveled the snow off the stairs just to create a good impression."

"Works for me," said Clay, following her up to the landing, where we kicked the snow off our boots before going inside. I'd never been there before. It was a comfortable place with all the amenities plus a porch on the back that looked out to the east. Between two barren trees, I could just see a slice of the dark waters of Nantucket Sound.

"What the Realtors call an ocean view." Eleanor grinned. "In the dead of winter, when all the leaves are gone, you can see a teeny bit of water. Jacks up the price."

"Location, location." Clay nodded, looking around as he walked through the small rooms. "Well, this is just fine. The price you mentioned is right, too. You want me to sign a lease?"

She waved a hand. "No. You're a friend of J.W.'s and that's good enough for me. Besides, if you do me wrong I'll sue his ass for bringing you here."

He beamed. "An excellent idea. And if you do me wrong, I'll sue his ass for the same reason. Consider yourself a land-lady. Let's take a look at that Bronco."

We went down and she threw open one of the garage doors. Inside was the elderly blue Ford four-door, showing wear around the edges but nothing serious.

She waved at it and handed him the keys. "Take it for a spin. I'll be in the house. When you get back, come inside and tell me what you've decided. The apartment's yours whether or not you want the truck."

She walked away.

"I'll go with you," I said to Clay.

He checked the oil, then warmed up the truck while he familiarized himself with the dashboard. Then we backed out and drove up the driveway to the highway. We took a right and drove past the high school and turned left toward the airport. At the site of the Frisbee golf course, we turned and drove off the pavement, the four-wheel-drive traction moving us easily through the six inches of hardening snow on the parking area. Back on the highway, we drove to the Edgartown–West Tisbury road, took another left to Edgartown, where we wound through the narrow, snow-piled streets, then went back along Vineyard Haven Road to Eleanor's house. The old Bronco chugged along smoothly.

"I've driven worse cars than this clear across the country," said Clay.

We put the Bronco back in the garage and went to the house, where Eleanor waved us inside and our noses led us to the kitchen, floating on the scent of fresh-baked gingerbread. There we sat and had coffee and gingerbread while Clay's eyes took in the kitchen, and Eleanor's, more subtly, surveyed him.

"Well, what do you think of Old Blue?" she asked after we'd done some chewing and swallowing.

He nodded his head. "Seems just fine. Anything I should know that I don't know?"

"Uses a little oil. Nothing serious, but you should keep an eye on it."

He raised his coffee cup. "In that case, name your price."

She did and he nodded and the deal was made. He pulled out a checkbook and scribbled a check. "You'll want to be sure this clears," he said. "It's for the truck and the first month's rent. Should take a couple or three days. I'll be back then."

"Move in any time you want," she said. "This bounces, I'll take it out of J.W.'s hide."

"The risks I have to run for my friends," I said.

"I'll tell you what," said Eleanor, ignoring me. "I don't have to be at work until noon, so why don't you and I take the Bronco up to the registry right now and do the paperwork that transfers ownership. That way you'll have wheels and I'll have the truck off my back."

Clay nodded. "Good. Let's do it."

"And you get a bonus," said Eleanor. "A free garage for

your Bronco. My ex took our other car when he left, so that garage stall is empty."

"Is this a wonderful country or what?" said Clay.

We finished our coffee and gingerbread and left the house. I got into the Land Cruiser and headed for home. As I pulled out onto the highway, I glanced in my rearview mirror and saw the blue Bronco coming out behind me. I envied its excellent heater and was happy for Clay, and then for some reason I thought of Nadine Gibson, the girl with the strawberry hair, and hoped that she was in some place warmer than this.

The January thaw arrived a week after Clay moved to his new quarters. The winter sun seemed warmer, the snow sank into itself, and little streams flowed down the shallow ditches beside our driveway. Within three days the only snow left was a bit here and there under the boughs of evergreen trees, and some of us were in our shirtsleeves.

That week and afterward, Clay came by most evenings after supper, so we could tell yarns and exchange tales of the lives we'd led since he and I had last spent time together. The house seemed warmed by his presence, so when his visits began to slow, we felt his absence before we lapsed back into our traditional, comfortable, all–Jackson family evenings. We wondered for a while what was keeping him away, but at the hospital, one of the island's major gossip centers, the explanation was soon being bruited: Clay and Eleanor Araujo had been seen together in public places.

Zee brought home the news. She, like many women I know when word of a romance reaches their ears, was fascinated and enthusiastic about the prospects for a serious relationship. I was more cautious.

"She's on the rebound and he's been married at least three times," I said. "I don't think you should get your hopes up."

"Piff!" she said. "You and I were both married before and look how great things have worked out for us!"

I looked at my fingernails. "Yeah, but most women aren't as lucky as you were."

She reached up and grabbed my ears and gave them a

small yank while she stood on her tiptoes and stuck her nose up toward mine. "You're the lucky one, meat!"

I quieted her with a kiss. "The point is," I said, "that she's just divorced and he's never been able to resist a woman."

"She's good-looking and she's smart, and so is he. Her ex, Mike, is such a bore that I never understood what she saw in him. Clay must seem like a ray of sunshine. Someone who can actually hold an adult conversation. No wonder they like being together."

"Having talks in restaurants isn't the same as being married."

"They're not just having talks, they're dancing and going to the movies."

"You and I go to the movies. You and I dance, as long as I don't have to move my feet."

"You're making my point," said Zee. "They're going places together and they're happy. And Ted Overhill approves. He thinks Clay is terrific."

True enough. Ted had kept an eagle eye on Clay's work on the schooner and had soon realized that Clay was a master craftsman. He had been flawless using Ted's tools, but seemed to get even better after his own had arrived from the West Coast. When Ted heard that his sister and Clay had started socializing, he'd been very pleased.

"She needs a good man in her life for a change," Ted said to me a couple of weeks after the hospital gossip had reached my ears. "Mike is a nice enough guy, but a little too short of gray cells to keep her interested. I understand that the girl he's going with now is so dumb she thinks he's smart, so they're both happy. More power to them, but Clay can give Eleanor a better life than Mike could even imagine."

Who was I to roil the waters of romance? "Sounds good," I said.

We'd had a streak of harder-than-average winters, so I was pleased when this one seemed to be a fairly normal one. We got some small snows in February, but they melted fast so that we had a mostly open winter, which was nice for the grown-ups but not so nice for the kids, who didn't get to do much sledding or skating.

I kept to my usual winter jobs, tending to houses I'd been hired to open in the spring and close in the fall, doing some scalloping while there were still some around and the price made it worthwhile, and occasionally driving Ted Overhill's second snowplow.

March arrived, bringing the promise of spring but not the reality. It was Zee's least favorite month because of the false hopes it raised, and she often said that if we ever got enough money to travel somewhere, we weren't going to do it in February because then we'd come back in March; instead, we'd do it in March so we could come back in April, when winter was actually gone even though it might still pretend to reassert itself.

On a bitterly cold day, after checking several houses, I stopped to warm up in the Dock Street Coffee Shop in Edgartown and was surprised to find Eleanor sipping coffee with her brother. I sat down beside them at the counter, accepted a cup of coffee from the waitress, and said, "What are you two doing here? I thought you were both gainfully employed, making America great by earning honest dollars so you can pay your taxes."

"Even normal people get some time off," said Eleanor.

"What's new with the Steamship Authority?"

"Well, we brought over a yellow Mercedes convertible from California," she said. "That's pretty unusual for this time of year."

"Top up or down?"

"Definitely up."

"Some movie star looking to escape his or her fans?"

"No. Two guys wearing summer clothes."

"California clothes?"

"Not New England clothes, for sure. If they plan to stick

around, they'll have to get themselves some heavier duds or they're going to freeze their bippies."

"There are worse things than frozen Californians." I looked at Ted. "How's the wing and how's the boatbuilding?"

He waved his bad arm at me. "Cast is off. Almost as good as new. I can do some of the work myself now, so between me and Clay, things'll go even faster. Boat'll be ready to launch in June."

"Then what?"

"Then we'll do some shakedown cruises, and in the fall we'll head for the Caribbean."

"Who are *we*?"

"Why, me and Clay and Eleanor. We've been talking about it. I want to get some blue water under me while I'm still young enough to enjoy it, and Clay and Eleanor here are ready to go with me. We'll winter down south and then decide what to do next."

Many a friendship has broken up after the friends spend time on a sailboat, but I didn't say that. What I said was, "You'll have the tall ship. All you'll need is a star to steer her by."

"I don't need a star. I'll have global positioning."

"A GPS isn't as romantic as a sextant."

"We won't need a sextant for romance," said Ted. He glanced at Eleanor, who actually blushed.

"Well, it sounds like a plan," I said. My own blue-water sailing days were long since over, but I still remembered the voyages with Clay down the coast and out to the Bahamas. Nowadays, though, I was quite satisfied to sail our eighteen-foot Herreshoff America catboat in local waters.

Someone left the café, and before the door closed behind him, a wave of chilly air wafted past us. "Not a good time to be driving a convertible," I said.

"Spring is coming," said Eleanor optimistically. "You'll wish you had a convertible when it gets here." Maybe love was affecting her brain.

"Could be," I said. "Be nice for the ospreys if they had some good weather when they come back."

March was usually when we saw the first of the ospreys nesting after their long flights north from their winter quarters in Central America and points farther south. They had once almost been extinct on the island but with the help of conservationists, who erected many tall poles with crossbeams to entice the few remaining birds to nest and reproduce, they were now abundant once more and generally loved, except by the rare old-timer who blamed them for catching all the fish he often no longer could catch but remembered as being abundant in earlier, osprey-less days.

"Danged birds! They should shoot them all!"

It was a minority sentiment. Personally, I loved ospreys and blamed whatever party was in power in Washington for my failures to land fish.

Only days after I'd chatted with Ted and Eleanor, the weather took a New England twist and suddenly summer seemed to arrive. The wind sank to nearly nothing, the sun was bright, temperatures soared; people appeared in T-shirts and even shorts; gardeners cleaned vegetable and flower beds and planted their peas; fishermen, still in waders but no longer wearing jackets, contentedly threw their lines into the empty waters even though they knew the blues wouldn't be arriving for two more months.

It was a most unusual experience for us all, and when I stopped by the Fireside for an early afternoon beer, I found Bonzo with mikes and recorder in his backpack, preparing to go forth to capture birdsong along the edges of a meadow deep within a favorite forest.

"Say, J.W.," he said, his face aglow in anticipation, his innocent eyes wide, "you want to come with me? I know a good place where there's lots of birds. They won't be nesting till May or June, but there's some out there right now."

I was tempted, but had promises to keep. "Another time,

Bonzo. I've got to go home and get the garden ready. If you get some good sounds, though, I'd like to hear them. You can tell me which birds are making which sounds. I'm not very good at that."

"Okay, J.W. I been working all morning, but now I got a whole afternoon off and I got to get going so I don't waste my chance. We don't get much weather like this in March, you know."

"I know."

He went out, all elbows and knees and happiness, and I wondered, not for the first time, if he was really worse off for having taken the bad acid that changed him from a promising young man into an eternal child. His life was simple, his emotions fresh and innocent, and his innate goodness was never altered by the random evils of life. He remembered the good things and, for the most part, forgot the bad. He was like the blinded angel who, when asked why he'd saved the man who'd put out his eyes, replied, "Angels have no memories."

Good old Bonzo.

The next morning, just after the kids had left for school, I got a call from his mother, a schoolteacher who had only minutes before she had to go to work. Bonzo was her heart's all.

"My son found something. I want you to see it and tell us what to do with it. I have to leave for work, but can you come by the house? He'll be here waiting, and he'll show you what he found."

There was a strained quality in her voice, the sort produced by worry.

"Of course," I said. "I'll come right up. Are you both all right?"

"Yes, yes. We're both fine. But do come and look at this nest. It disturbs me and it's made Bonzo unhappy. Let me know what you think we should do."

Nest?

"I'll be right there," I said.

Zee paused on her way out the door. "Who was that?"
I told her what I'd heard.

"Nest?" asked Zee. "Are you sure you heard right?"

"I'll soon know," I said, finishing my coffee.

I got into a light jacket and followed her in the Land
Cruiser as she drove up our long driveway and headed for
the hospital. At the intersection of County Road and Wing
Road we parted ways, as she drove on toward the hospital
and I turned to the right and drove to Bonzo's small, neatly
kept house.

Bonzo met me at the door. "Gee, J.W., I'm glad to see you.
My mom and me aren't sure what to do, but you're my
friend and you'll know."

The house was as neat within as without. The furniture
was old and comfortable and there were doilies on the end
tables. Knickknacks—souvenirs of travels and memorable
events—were the principal decorations. On the small piano
in the corner of the sitting room was a photo of proud parents and their little boy: Bonzo's family in the happiness of
youth, before the smiling wife became first a widow and
then the mother of an eternal child.

"What is it that you found, Bonzo?"

"A robin's nest. You know how I was going out yesterday
to see if I could get some songs? Well, I went up there in the
woods where I like to go. There's a meadow there and an old
foundation. I think it must have been a farm once. You
know the place I mean?"

"I'm not sure."

He seemed a bit uneasy. "I don't remember if I ever took
you there, but I go there sometimes because the birds sing
there and I can get their music on my tape." He looked at
me with his huge, half-empty eyes. "Yesterday there wasn't
any singing, but I found this nest on the ground. I think it
must have been blowed down by the wind. I got it in my
room. Come on."

I followed him into his bedroom. The bed was made and

there was no clutter. His mother had taught him how to be neat and he had learned well. Along one wall was a bookshelf mostly holding tapes, bird books, and recording devices. He went to a bureau and brought me a round plastic container that had once held something from a local deli.

I took off the lid and looked inside.

There I saw a medium-sized cup nest. It was battered but mostly intact. At first I didn't see anything unusual about it, but then I saw the hairs that had been incorporated into the nest by the bird that had built it. They were long, strawberry-colored hairs, too fine to be from a horse's tail or mane, too long to have been from any animal but a human being. My mind leaped back to the previous March.

"Nadine has hair like that," said Bonzo in an unhappy voice. "I never seen anybody else with hair like that. How did that bird get Nadine's hair?"

— 8 —

When Nadine Gibson had disappeared, people—her boyfriend in particular—had been questioned and communications had been exchanged between the island police and her people on the mainland, but no clue had ever been discovered as to what had become of her. In early March, Nadine had walked out of the Fireside after her shift and had never been seen again, but like most people, I'd guessed that she'd just left the island and hadn't bothered telling anyone where she'd gone or why.

Until now.

I stared down at the nest.

"Where did you find this, Bonzo?"

He fidgeted. "Up there where I told you I go. It was there on the ground at the edge of the meadow."

"I think you'd better show this to the police."

He looked very nervous. "I don't know, J.W., I don't know."

"They'll want to see where you found it."

He twisted his hands together. "Gee, that's what my mom said, but I didn't like that idea, so then she said that I should talk to you and now you're saying the same thing she did. Gee . . ."

"What's the problem, Bonzo? What's bothering you?"

"You aren't going to be mad, are you?"

"No. Your mother wasn't mad, was she?"

"No. But the police might be. I don't like people to be mad at me."

"Tell me why you're worried."

It came in a rush. "It's because I was up there on that land that belongs to the Marshall Lea people! You know how they don't like people being on their land and they put up all them No Trespassing signs? Well, I go there anyway and I never see anybody watching so I hide my bike and go past the sign and I go to see birds and get their songs! That's where I found the nest, up there on Marshall Lea land, and the police won't like it when they find out and they won't let me go up there anymore!"

I nodded. The Marshall Lea Foundation was my least favorite island conservation group. They had so many restrictions on the use of their land that I called them the No Foundation. No fishing, no hunting, no picnics, no horseback riding, no walking, no this, no that. No trespassing at all. Except for their own members, of course.

"I don't think the police will be mad at you," I said. "I think they'll be proud of you for finding this nest. I think it may be important. So don't be afraid. I'll go with you to the station."

He looked doubtful but relieved. He'd been under quite a strain.

"You're important," I said. "You're the only one who can tell them where you found the nest."

He thought about that, then nodded. "You're right, J.W. I'm the only one."

"I think the state police are the ones to talk to," I said. In Massachusetts the state police handle all homicides and unattended deaths outside of Boston, which has its own homicide people. I put the lid back on the plastic container. "Come on. We'll go in my truck."

The state police office is on Temahigan Avenue, in Oak Bluffs, about a city block from the hospital where Zee worked and a long mile from Bonzo's house. Sergeant Dom Agganis and Officer Olive Otero were stationed there year-round, and additional cops came down during the tourist season. It wasn't considered hardship duty to summer on the Vineyard.

I parked in the lot behind the office, and Bonzo and I went in. Dom was doing something on his computer, whacking the keys with his sausage-sized fingers. He looked relieved when we arrived and gave him an excuse to stop what he was doing.

"Are you working on your blog?" I asked.

"I don't even know what a blog is," he said, pushing his chair away from his desk. "What brings you two here?" He nodded pleasantly at Bonzo. "How are things at the Fireside?"

"They're good," said Bonzo, who had served Dom enough beer and burgers to recognize him as a friendly customer. "Gosh, I didn't know you were a policeman, Dom. I never seen you in a uniform before."

"Well, now you know," said Dom. "I wear my civvies when I'm off duty." He looked at the plastic container that I had placed on his desk. "What's this?"

"It's a robin's nest that Bonzo found yesterday while he was out birding. We thought you should take a look at it."

"I'm no birder," he said. But he took the lid off the container and looked at the nest.

"It may not be anything at all," I said, "but those red hairs look the same color as Nadine Gibson's. The girl who went missing just a year ago."

Dom was instantly all business. His friendly look went away and he tipped the container toward the light. "I never knew the woman," he said, "but I take it that you did." He put the cover back on the container.

"She worked at the Fireside," I said. "I saw her there. Pretty girl with amazing red hair. This is the color I remember."

"You agree?" asked Dom, looking at Bonzo. "You should know. You worked with her."

Bonzo nodded. "Nadine was nice and she was pretty and she had this really good, pretty hair that was the color of fresh strawberries. You know what I mean? I never seen anybody else with hair like that." He frowned. "I don't know how that robin got her hair. I don't like to think about it."

"Can you show me where you found this nest?"

Bonzo looked at the floor.

"He can show you," I said. "But he found it on Marshall Lea land and he had to go by a No Trespassing sign to get to the place. He's worried that he might get in trouble for that."

"You won't get in trouble," said Dom. He put the plastic container in a desk drawer and reached for his phone. "Tell me where you went and I'll have a couple Marshall Lea people meet us there, just so their noses don't get out of joint."

The property was off Barnes Road and was, as Bonzo had said, adorned with a No Trespassing sign.

"See," he said as we waited there for the Marshall Lea representatives to show up. "There's that sign, just like I said. I put my bike across the road behind that bush so nobody will know when I sneak in."

"Lemme show you something," said Dom. "Look at the back of this sign. What does it say?"

"It don't say anything," said Bonzo, studying the blank wood.

"That's right," said Dom. "Keep that in mind."

"I didn't know you were a Woody Guthrie fan," I said.

"There's a lot you don't know," said Dom.

A Range Rover stopped behind Dom's cruiser and my truck. A lean man and a leaner woman emerged, both gray-haired and both wearing the informal but expensive clothes favored by people known to their critics as limousine liberals. I recognized Justin Wyner and Genevieve Geller, dedicated conservationists.

Genevieve eyed me with disapproval. We'd met several times before at meetings where we'd disagreed about how much access normal human beings should have to conservation lands. I was for more; she was for less and took the disagreement personally.

"Well, Officer, tell us again what this is about, if you will." Her husband shook Dom's hand and looked attentive.

Dom told him and added, "I told Bonzo, here, that you'd be as pleased with him as I am. I'm sending the nest to the lab, but meanwhile I know we'll all want to see where he found it. This could be a break in that case."

"Of course, of course," said Wyner. "Lead the way, Mr. Bonzo."

So we all walked by the No Trespassing sign and went into the woods.

The ground was spongy and covered with last year's leaves. The new leaves weren't out yet, so we could see quite a ways on an overgrown dirt road through the trees. Scrub oak and other undergrowth clutched at us as we passed. After a bit we came to a small meadow that was slowly being infringed upon by trees. On one side, with a tree growing up through brown weeds and collapsed floors from what had once been a cellar, were the remains of a small house. Not much more than a stone foundation and some ancient, rotting timbers were recognizable.

"Old farmhouse," said Wyner. "Used to belong to the Ormsteads. The foundation's owned the place for the past ten years or so. We're letting it revert back to its natural state."

Its natural state was woodlands. Already there were more woodlands on the Vineyard than there had been for over a hundred years. A century earlier the island had been mostly open farm and grazing land, but that had been before the tourists had found it and transformed its economy. Among conservation groups on the Vineyard was some debate now about just how far back in time land should be allowed to revert. Some favored letting nature take its course but others preferred to select the landscapes they thought best. I knew of at least one woodland that had been cleared of trees to form a sand plain.

My thoughts on the subject mostly had to do with the constant and increasing loss of access to fishing spots and hunt-ing areas. I had pretty much stopped hunting, myself, but I didn't like having conservation groups and new landowners shutting their properties to gunners whose fathers had used them for generations during deer and bird seasons.

"Show me where you found the nest, Bonzo," said Dom, and Bonzo dutifully pointed to the far end of the meadow.

"This used to be a hay field," said Wyner as we walked. "When I was a kid, my pals and I used to come up here in the summer to hunt rabbits. It was a good deal bigger then. The trees are closing it in pretty fast."

And the grass, too, covering all, doing its work. Hearing Justin Wyner tell about hunting here long ago made me like him better for some reason. I wondered if his wife was equally human. I hoped so.

"Right here," said Bonzo, stopping and pointing first to the ground and then to a large oak whose barren limbs thrust out over the meadow. "I know because I remember looking up in this here tree and wondering if maybe that's where it fell down from."

We all looked at the tree and then swept the ground and the woods with our eyes, as if hoping we'd see something important.

"It's a robin's nest," said Bonzo. "They build them in the spring when they're mating. In May and June, lots of times. So this one is old. Last year, at least." He paused and frowned and became silent, pressing his lips together.

"How far will a robin go to find material for its nest?" asked Dom.

"Not too far," said Genevieve Geller. "Robins like a shel-tered, secure place to build, like up in the crotch of this tree, for instance. And they build where they can find materials. The female does most of the building but the male helps out. It takes less than a week for them to make a nest."

Bonzo gave her a pleased look. "That's right, lady. I like robins because they stay here all year and they sing in the wintertime, not just in the summer. They're very nice birds. They like worms, you know."

"I do know that," said Genevieve Geller in a kinder voice than I expected. "They like fruit, too, and berries."

"So it's safe to say that the birds that built this nest got their materials from close by," said Dom. "Is that right?"

"Correct," said Genevieve.

"There are five of us here," said Dom. "If you're all willing, let's get about twenty feet apart and walk in a big circle with this tree at the center. When we finish the circle we'll go out to its edge and make another, bigger one. If we have to go farther, we'll need to get more people. I don't know what to tell you to look for, other than for anything that looks unusual: a mound of dirt, a piece of cloth, a sunken spot in the ground, anything like that. If you see anything, sing out and stay where you are." He didn't mention a skull or bones.

I was the last person in the line and had the farthest to walk. I'm not Daniel Boone, but I used to hunt and know how to move through the woods. I made the big circle, walking slowly and letting my eyes roam ahead and on either side of my path. I saw nothing, which wasn't surprising considering the depth of the brown leaves that layered the ground. When I finished my circle, the others were waiting for me in the meadow.

No one had found anything so we all walked out farther from the oak tree and made another circle. When we gathered again in the meadow, again no one had seen anything of interest. Dom seemed neither surprised nor disappointed. Patience is a requisite if you're to be a career police officer.

He looked at Justin and Genevieve. "If the lab tells me that it's real human hair in the nest Bonzo found, I'm going to want to come up here with a bigger search party and go over these grounds with a fine-toothed comb. Do I have your permission to do that? If I have it, I won't have to go to a judge."

"You have it," said Genevieve. "We'll cooperate in any way we can."

"Thank you. You can start by keeping this whole thing to yourselves. The fewer curiosity seekers we have up here, the better."

Justin Wyner smiled a small smile and glanced at Bonzo. "Maybe we can put up a bigger sign."

But Bonzo was thinking about something else and kept on thinking about it as we walked back to our cars. When we got there, Justin and Genevieve drove off first and Dom was about to leave when Bonzo made up his mind about what he should do and said, "I think you should know something, Dom. Once Nadine and me came up here together. She liked birds and we had a good time. It was last year, just before she went away."

Dom frowned. "You brought her here?"

Bonzo nodded and looked up at Dom with his wide eyes. "Yeah, I did. Just that one time. She liked the old house and the meadow and the birds. She said she didn't know you could be so alone on a crowded island like Martha's Vineyard. I told her there was lots of places you can be alone and that I'd show them to her if she wanted to see them, and she said that would be good, but then she went away and I never did show her them places."

Dom studied him. "Are you sure you never came here with her again?"

Bonzo seemed to shrivel before his gaze. "I never did. I was only here with her that once. You believe me, don't you, J.W.?"

"Yes," I said. "I believe you."

But Dom was a cop and cops are careful about what they believe. They have to be, because they live in a land of liars.

Two days later I got a call from Dom as Clay and I were having morning coffee in my kitchen. "Just thought I'd call and see if you're interested in being a member of a search party," he said. "The lab confirms that those red hairs are human, so we're going out this morning to see if we can find where they came from."

"Can I bring a friend?"

"As long as he's got good eyes. Be there in an hour."

"Yes."

I told Clay what was happening.

"I need a break from the boat," he said. "I'll be glad to join you."

— 9 —

The skies were still clear, but there was a north wind bringing chilly air down from the mainland. When we got to the No Trespassing sign, we found the sides of Barnes Road lined with cars and had to park quite a ways from where we entered the woods.

There were forty or fifty people gathered in the meadow, including officers from many of the island's police departments. Because of ancient traditions and rivalries among the six island towns, Martha's Vineyard has ten different police agencies, and it's not unusual for them to view one another with scorn. Thus, the sight of them cooperating in this search was a little surprising and was due, I suspected, to Dom's careful cultivation of good relations with all of the island's other law enforcement agencies.

Other state cops were known to consider town officers to be a lesser breed and to cut them out of certain crime investigations, especially those whose profiles were high. This attitude naturally only encouraged the local cops to view the state cops with suspicion and hostility. Much valuable information and talent were thus never shared between agencies supposedly charged with common work.

These small rivalries and their consequences were, of course, only lesser examples of the larger and more famous and infuriating ones among the CIA, the FBI, the NSA, and almost all of the other national and international criminal investigating and intelligence-gathering agencies, rivalries that were almost certainly responsible for the success of many criminal activities.

But Dom Agganis had, for today, managed to assuage island enmities and form a group of searchers who were, at least in part, trained in such work. He took the time to tell them what they were doing and why.

"There isn't much to go on," he concluded, "but the hair in the nest is long, red, and human, and it came from somewhere not too far from here. Work slowly and be patient. It's easy to miss things in the woods, and it's been almost a year since the girl disappeared, so it's hard to guess what you might find. Let's go."

With so many searchers involved, we could work closer together and cover the area more thoroughly. We turned up our collars against the wind and moved slowly through the trees, alert to anything unusual. But the layer of brown, fallen leaves on the ground hid much, and though we discovered the sort of human debris that is found in the wildest of places—pieces of torn plastic, deflated balloons, unexplainable pieces of paper and cardboard, all stuff that escaped its origins and was carried away by the wind—we found no sign of Nadine Gibson.

I was not an experienced searcher and wasn't sure I really wanted to find the remains of the woman. The robin that had found the long strands of red hair so useful when building its nest had had no such qualms, of course.

But I was moved by a sense of duty, so kept my course, wading through the leaves, pushing aside the grasping branches of undergrowth, ducking under and around tree limbs, trying but failing to see anything useful until, at last, we seekers gathered together once again on the edge of the meadow. We were united in both disconsolation and fatigue, and like survivors of a battle, felt the comradeship of shared discomfort.

"That'll do for now," said Dom, as we grouped ourselves around him. "It was a long shot at best. If we give it another try, I hope some of you will help out again." There were mur-

murs of assent as he dismissed us, and the searchers wandered back down the meadow toward the road.

But Clay didn't wander far. Instead, he paused and looked at the ruins of the old farmhouse. Dom and I stopped beside him, followed his gaze, and exchanged glances. Then the three of us walked to the broken foundations and looked down into the debris-filled cellar. Cracked timbers and rotting floorboards vied with fallen foundation stones and weeds for possession of the pit.

Clay gestured toward the rubble and said what I was also thinking.

"If the girl really died somewhere near here, and if she died accidentally or of natural causes of some kind, she could be anywhere. But if she was killed here, the person who did it was stuck with a body he needed to hide in a hurry. It's pretty unlikely he would have carried it farther than we searched just now. That leaves this place."

Dom studied the ruins. "Where were you last March?"

Clay smiled faintly. "Out on the West Coast. My mother will swear to it, if necessary."

"Your mother lives out there?"

"Actually, she lives in Wichita, but she'll swear I was wherever I tell her I was. You know how mothers are."

Dom grunted, but not in surprise. In police investigations, mothers are known liars who will swear that their criminal children were home reading their Bibles when the crimes went down.

"Well," he said, "since I'm the only cop here, I guess it's my job to go down there."

For all of his bulk, he was fairly nimble as he climbed and slid down into the cellar.

Our advice followed him: "Watch out for rusty nails and broken glass."

He nodded, found a steady spot amid the rubble upon which to stand, and looked around. He took hold of a section of fallen floor and tugged at it. It moved a bit, and he shoved it to one side. There were rotting pieces of timber beneath it. He studied them, then pulled one out and put it aside.

"We should get a machine in here to lift this crap out," he said.

Beside me, Clay was studying the cellar.

"If the woman's down there," he said to Dom, "the guy who put her there didn't have a machine to help him. I'm coming down." And before Dom could object, Clay was sliding down to join him. They stood side by side with Clay pointing to the far wall.

"Over there," he said. "See where that section of foundation has fallen in? Most of the rest of the foundation is at least partly in place, but not that section. And it didn't fall too long ago, either. The stones are lying on top of those floorboards."

They picked their way across the cluttered floor and gazed down at the fallen stones that were scattered over the rotting wood. Suddenly Dom knelt and put down a hand, then rose and held out his find to Clay. I couldn't tell what it was, but I could guess.

"We're done here for now," said Dom. "We need a crime-scene crew and a machine to lift off the lumber and rock. Let's go." He and Clay returned across the cellar floor and climbed out where they'd gone in. Dom showed me his find. It was a strand of tangled red hair.

"Bonzo is going to be pretty unhappy," I said.

"Don't talk to Bonzo," said Dom. "I want to talk to him first."

"Is this a good time to discuss my First Amendment rights?"

Dom's big jaw went out a little farther than usual. "You stay away from Bonzo."

"Bonzo wouldn't hurt a fly and you know it."

"He brought the woman here once and maybe he brought her here twice. Who else would have brought her here? It's a stretch to think somebody else would have come here with her."

"How should I know? All I know is that Bonzo didn't do this."

"Maybe not."

"He shouldn't even be on your list."

"Everybody's on my list. Even your pal's mother, the old lady in Wichita."

"I knew I shouldn't have mentioned her," said Clay. "Now I'll have to swear she was on the West Coast with me last March."

"If you guys don't mind doing something useful for a change," said Dom, "you can stay right here and keep stray people and dogs away from the site until I get back with my yellow tape and reinforcements. Maybe I can catch some of the Oak Bluffs guys before they get too far. I shouldn't be long."

"We'll be here," I said.

We watched him walk out of sight.

"Well, well," said Clay. "I've done a lot of things, but I never guarded a crime site before."

"Maybe it wasn't a crime," I said. "It could be that the woman died a natural death or an accidental one, and who-ever was with her at the time panicked and hid the body so he wouldn't be suspected of anything."

"What do you think of Dom putting Bonzo on the suspect list?"

"Not much, but he's a guy Dom has to talk with. Bonzo brought the woman here once to listen to the birds. And if she's under those floorboards, somebody put her there."

The wind was rising and the air was cooling. Clay pulled his cap down over his ears. "Was there a boyfriend? A hus-band?"

I tried to remember the stories in the local papers. "A boyfriend, but he and the woman had broken up and he'd left the island before she disappeared."

"Maybe he sneaked back."

"Maybe."

"It wouldn't be the first time something like that happened."

"No."

We paced about, trying to stay warm.

"She have another guy on the hook?"

"I wouldn't know. She was a pretty girl, so I imagine she wouldn't have been lonely any longer than she wanted to be."

In my memory I could see her: a slender young woman with brilliant blue eyes, a bright smile, and all that long red hair. I imagined that every regular at the Fireside had fantasized about her at one time or another, and I remembered how she laughed and would slip easily away from drunken would-be embraces with jokes that left her admirers feeling almost as good as if she'd fallen into their arms.

And she had treated Bonzo with the same respect and humor as she treated everyone else. No wonder he had been so fond of her, and had been so pleased when she'd accepted his invitation to go birding in this meadow.

Had they come here again?

Had something happened here between them?

If not Bonzo, then who? Why?

If I were Dom Agganis, I'd want to talk with the boyfriend again and check out his alibi, if he had one. And I'd want to talk with all of the regulars at the Fireside, not just with Bonzo.

I wondered if the state police would shake free a few detectives to work the case, or whether a long-dead woman wouldn't merit their energies and time.

Years ago, after taking a bullet, which still rested against my spine, I'd left my police job in Boston precisely because I was tired of trying to save the world. I'd moved to the Vineyard to become a fisherman and to avoid involvement in even the pettiest of island crimes. I'd planned to live a quiet life in the woods, in the old hunting camp my father had bought when I was just a kid, and I'd intended to be content with my own company.

But life doesn't leave us alone. I'd fallen in love with Zee, and after that, living by myself no longer had its old charm. I'd fixed up the house and we'd married and started raising a family, and now I led a life that was not significantly different from that of many other year-round islanders. I didn't have a career but I had a lot of jobs that kept me busy, and I had friends, one of whom was Bonzo.

In spite of myself I was *engagé*. I was involved with life. And now, with death.

After what seemed like a long time, police cruisers crept up through the trees along an overgrown road that once must have been the driveway to the farmhouse. They parked in the meadow and disgorged Dom, his state-police colleague, Officer Olive Otero, and several Oak Bluffs policemen.

"No dogs or people came by," I said to Dom as police officers began to surround the site with yellow tape.

He nodded and went off to make sure his helpers didn't contaminate the site before the detectives and lab people got there. Already a photographer was taking pictures.

"I believe that ringing silence means we can go," I said to Clay.

He nodded and we walked down the meadow and through the woods. At the road we found another police car with an officer standing beside it to ward off curious civilians if any paused to find out what was going on. We went on along the road and as we got to the Land Cruiser, a truck pulling a trailer loaded with a large backhoe stopped behind the cruiser. We watched as the driver unloaded the backhoe and drove it out of sight up the driveway.

I was shivering when I climbed into the Land Cruiser, and not just from the cold wind.

"A hot cider in front of your living-room stove sounds good to me right now," said Clay, reading my mind.

"Yes."

At home I mulled the cider while Clay added wood to the embers in the stove. Seated in front of the flames, steaming cup in hand, I was aware that the warmth of the fire was psychological as much as physical; perhaps because of some prehistoric, genetic memory we'd inherited from our cave-dwelling ancestors, for whom fire meant the difference between life and death.

"Shalom," said Clay, touching his mug to mine. "It's barely noon and I already feel like I've put in a full day, but when I finish this, I'll head back to work some more on the boat."

"The working class makes our country great."

We drank and stared into the fire, and then he left and I was alone, thinking about Bonzo and about Dom Agganis's understandable suspicions.

I was having a second glass of cider when I heard a car coming down our driveway. I looked out a window and watched as a yellow Mercedes convertible stopped in our yard. It had California plates. Two men wearing what looked like new winter coats got out, studied the house, then walked toward the door. They had West Coast tans but didn't look like movie stars.

— 10 —

When I opened the door to their knock, the man in front smiled a friendly smile.

"Mr. Jackson?"

"That's right."

He put out his hand. "My name is Jack Blume. I'm a friend of Clay Stockton. I understand he may be staying here. I'd like to see him."

He was a medium-sized man but his companion took up considerably more space. As I shook Blume's hand, I glanced over his shoulder. The second man wasn't wearing a smile or looking at me but was peering past me into the house with a gaze as cool as the March air.

"Come inside," I said. "It's pretty chilly out."

"Thanks," said Jack Blume, and the two men entered. I waved them toward the fire and shut the door.

"I noticed your plates as you drove up. You're about as far from California as you can get," I said. "What brings you to my place?"

"Like I told you," said Blume, "I'm a friend of Clay Stockton, and I heard he was staying with you. We happen to be on Martha's Vineyard, so we thought we'd drop by and say hello."

I turned to the other man and put out my hand. "I'm J. W. Jackson."

He didn't seem to want to take his hands out of his coat pockets, but it's hard to refuse to give your name when someone offers his, so he pulled out his right hand and shook mine. "Mickey Monroe." I noted a lump in the pocket before his hand returned to it.

"Any relation to James or the Doctrine?" I asked.

Mickey looked perplexed.

"Mickey doesn't read much history," said Blume with a laugh.

My memory banks didn't hold any references to Jack Blume or Mickey Monroe. If Clay had ever mentioned the names, I'd forgotten them.

"Sit down and warm yourselves," I said. "I'm having some mulled cider and there's more on the back of the stove. I'll get you a couple of cups."

"What's mulled cider?" asked Mickey.

"It's a hot drink made of apple juice," said Blume. "They drink it here in the wintertime to warm themselves up."

I got two mugs of cider and handed them to my guests. Mickey sniffed his and took a sip. "Not bad. Be good with some whiskey in it. You got any whiskey?"

"Forget the whiskey, Mickey," said Blume. "Just drink the cider."

"I have whiskey," I said. I got some and poured a slug into Mickey's mug. The smell of bourbon filled the room.

"Better," said Mickey after a gulp of his drink.

"Who told you that Clay Stockton was living here?" I asked Blume.

"I don't think it's a secret," said Blume. "We used to work together out west. He wrote me that he was here."

"That must have been a while back," I said. "He hasn't been here for several weeks."

A frown floated across Blume's face then disappeared. "Where did he go?"

"Didn't he write and tell you?"

Blume's face hardened. "I've been traveling and I probably missed his message. Can you tell me where to find him?"

"Maybe the police can tell you," I said. "The last I heard, he was working with them on a case. Contact the state police.

Their office is up in Oak Bluffs. Talk with Dom Agganis. He's head of the unit down here on the island."

"Clay had his tools shipped here, to you," said Mickey. "He must be staying around here someplace and you must know where." He drank his cider and stood up. The heavy mug looked like a weapon in his hand.

I tried not to appear nervous. It wasn't easy. "I knew Clay almost thirty years ago," I said to Blume. "He showed up a few weeks back. Out of the blue. Said he didn't have a place to stay but wanted his tools and could he have them shipped to this address while he found himself a house. I said sure. He stayed here until his tools came. We talked about the old days, but he said he didn't want me to know much about what he'd been doing and he didn't want me to know where he was living because what I didn't know wouldn't hurt me." I looked at Blume. "I thought that was kind of a funny thing to say. But that's Clay. He always liked to kid."

"What's he doing working with the police?"

"A woman went missing last year. The police think they finally have a lead. Clay's been in the search party for her body."

"Why?"

I shrugged. "I don't know. Clay's a friendly guy. Maybe he and Dom Agganis have hit it off."

"What's he doing with his tools?"

"Clay's always been good with his hands. You've probably noticed all the building that's going on here. Mansions going up everywhere. A guy like Clay can get all the work he wants."

"I don't suppose you know where he's working."

"I don't suppose I do. He mentioned the Chilmark Store a couple of times, so maybe he's up-island someplace."

Blume looked around the room.

"You married, Mr. Jackson?"

"I am."

"Kids?"

"Two."

"I have a family, too. It's good to have a family, but if you're like me, you're always just a little bit worried that something might happen to one of them. You know what I mean? Your kid will fall off a swing or something like that. Get hurt." He smiled and shook his head. "I guess it's the price we pay for being fathers, don't you think?"

I felt my muscles stiffen. "I guess. I try not to worry about things I can't do anything about."

"That's a good philosophy. You sure you don't know where Clay's staying?"

"I'm sure. If I see him, do you want me to tell him you're looking for him?"

"Yeah," said Mickey. "Tell him that. Tell him we want to talk with him."

"All right," I said. "If I see him, I'll tell him. Where are you staying?"

"That big hotel down in Edgartown," said Blume. "Out by the lighthouse. You know the place I mean?"

"The Harbor View."

"That's the place. You ever try their Sunday brunch? Terrific! A raw bar like you dream of. All the oysters you can eat. You're sure you don't know where Clay's living?"

"He's never said. My guess is up-island someplace. There are a lot of winter rentals up that way."

"Well, if he comes by, tell him we'd really like to see him." Blume looked at his wristwatch. "Your kids both in school? I imagine they'll be coming home before too long. Wife'll be coming home, too. Come on, Mickey, we'll leave Mr. Jackson alone."

Mickey looked at me without love and followed Blume out the door. I watched them climb into the Mercedes and leave.

The room still felt chilly after they'd driven away. My impulse was to immediately drive up to Ted Overhill's barn and tell Clay about my visitors, but I decided to wait an hour or more to give Blume and Monroe time to stop watching for me to leave. No need to lead them where they wanted to go.

I had some more cider and put more wood on the fire. I thought about Blume and Monroe. They weren't making any effort to hide their presence, so maybe they were as innocent as doves and just what they claimed to be: a couple of Clay's old West Coast pals who happened to be on the island and wanted to say hello.

But I didn't think so. My guess was that they were being open about their presence because they were so far from California that they figured island police would have no reason to look twice at them.

In any case, they'd given me a problem I could have done without. If Clay weren't my friend, I could simply wander downtown and tell the chief of the Edgartown police that a couple of guys I took for West Coast hoodlums were ensconced in the Harbor View Hotel. I could tell him what they'd said to me, and then he could do what he saw fit: maybe make some calls west to see if Blume and Monroe were people he should be watching or perhaps even arresting.

But Clay *was* my friend and if I told the chief of my visitors' interest in him, it was in the cards that the chief would include questions about Clay when he got in touch with West Coast law enforcement. I didn't want that to happen. I didn't know what had brought Blume and Monroe looking for Clay, but I didn't want the law after Clay, too.

Friendship has gotten a lot of people into trouble, but I could stand a little trouble if I was the only one involved. But Blume had hinted a threat to Zee and the kids, and I didn't like that at all. I wondered what Monroe had had in his coat pocket. Whatever it was, it was heavy enough to make the pocket sag. I didn't think it was a rock he'd picked up as a Vineyard souvenir.

I saw Blume as the brains and Monroe as the muscle, but I could be wrong about that. Just because you talk smart doesn't mean you are smart, any more than looking stupid is the same as being stupid.

Still, if the two were not the nefarious types that they seemed, they were both great actors.

I wondered how convincing my own act had been. Had I come across as the simple guy I hoped they saw? Or maybe by their standards I *was* simple. Could be. I'd always suspected that I wasn't as smart as I thought I was.

When my hour was up, I shrugged into my winter coat, got into the Land Cruiser, and drove into Edgartown. I didn't see the Mercedes parked on any side road or either of the men shivering in the trees and staking out my driveway. If I hadn't watched them when they arrived and then when they left my house, I might have wondered if they'd stuck a tracking device on my truck, but they hadn't done that, so I knew they weren't trailing me at a distance. But maybe Jack and Mickey were better shadows than most. Maybe they had changed cars. Maybe they'd hired somebody else to watch me and let them know when I left home and where I went.

My guess was that they'd just returned to their hotel, but when I got into the village, I drove around some back streets until I was confident that no one was behind me, then, just to be sure, drove out on the West Tisbury road until I got to Metcalf Drive. There, feeling wicked as wicked could be, like the Pirate Don Dirk of Dowdee, I took a right and, ignoring the signs proclaiming this was a private road and not a through way, drove all the way through to the Vineyard Haven road. Criminal acts don't have to be significant to be pleasurable.

No one was following me when I drove down Ted Overhill's driveway and stopped in front of his barn beside Clay's blue Bronco. Inside the barn, progress was being made on the schooner. The spars had been laid out on sawhorses, and fittings were being attached to them. I climbed the ladder that leaned against the boat and went into the cockpit. Clay was alone in the cabin, fitting a piece of teak to a counter. He looked up as I blocked the light coming through the hatch.

"Hey, J.W., what's up?"

"Ted around?"

"No, he's out taking care of a few errands. You want to see him?"

"No, I came to see you."

"Talk away. I'll listen while I make this board fast." He slid a bronze screw into a predrilled hole and began to screw it in. The board was a perfect fit. I could barely see the line where it joined the next board. I admire such skill but am incapable of it. I do all right with two-by-fours, but any carpentry more subtle than that is pretty much beyond me.

I told him of the visitors. When I said their names, he stopped working and listened in silence. When I finished my description of the visit, he rubbed a hand through his beard, then looked at me.

"How long have they been on the island?"

"Not long. I saw Eleanor down at the coffee shop and she mentioned them coming off the ferry. They caught her eye because California convertibles driven by guys in summer clothes don't often show up in the wintertime."

"Describe the guys." I did that and he shook his head. "I don't know them. Stupid of me to have the tools shipped to you. I never should have done that. They must have pressured the guy who was storing them on the coast, and he gave them your address."

"They've come quite a way to find you."

"Yeah. I went to some trouble to drag red herrings across my track, too. Stopped several places as I came across country and left signs that I'd been there before moving on. I was hoping that I'd convinced them I was in Arkansas." He gave me his old smile. "I'm sorry as hell I brought this trouble to you."

"I've lived in a lot of places and done a lot of things and made some good friends," said Clay, looking absently around the cabin of the schooner. "But I never liked anything better than what I have here: a good boat to work on, friends, Elly . . ." He paused. "I thought I might finally settle down, but I guess it's time to move on."

"Maybe not," I said.

He shook his head. "If I stay, some innocent people might get hurt. I don't want that."

"Where would you go?"

He smiled a small, humorless smile. "Arkansas? They don't believe I'm there, even though I tried to make them think so."

I patted the side of the hatch. "You're a cruising man. Arkansas is a long way from salt water."

"Well, there's the Mississippi," he said, with irony in his voice. "Maybe I could build a riverboat. I've never tried that. Or I could change my name to Finn and live on a raft."

I said, "Do you want to tell me what this is all about? If you don't, that's still okay, but if you do, we might have a better chance to neutralize these guys."

He looked up at me. "You're the one I'm most worried about. Jack Blume didn't come here just to take the waters, and Mickey Monroe doesn't teach Sunday school classes. If they think you can lead them to me, they'll do what they need to do to get you to tell them. They think I have something that belongs to somebody else and they're here to collect it."

"Do you have it?"

"I know where it is." He put aside his tools and thought for a moment. "You really don't know much about my life, J.W."

True, but faith is the evidence of things unseen. "I know you," I said. "That's all I need to know. You can tell me as much or as little as you want. How I feel about you won't change."

He said nothing for a moment, then said, "Do you know what the largest cash crop in the United States is?"

I thought of the horizon-to-horizon fields of middle America, the breadbasket of the world, but shook my head. "I'm not sure."

"Marijuana. It must drive the Reefer Madness people and the DEA crazy that in spite of all the money they've spent and all the effort they've made to keep kids from smoking dope, weed is the biggest cash crop in the country. Do you have any idea how much money it brings in?"

"No."

"Well, the pot industry doesn't pay taxes or keep official records, but the best guess is that the crop is worth about thirty-five billion dollars a year. Corn is second. It brings in twenty-three billion. The soybean crop is worth seventeen billion. It's third."

"I can't think in numbers that big," I said, surprised that soybeans were such moneymakers. "Where's wheat on your list?"

"Fifth or sixth," said Clay. "I can't remember which. Hay is somewhere in there, too. I've never worked in the soybean or corn trade, but in my travels I've cut and stacked hay and threshed wheat, and I can tell you that farmers earn their dollars. Ranchers, too. Raising cattle and sheep is chancy business. The industry produces a lot of money, but individually, many a farmer is living on the edge and takes a job in town to make ends meet."

On Martha's Vineyard we have farms, but mostly they're

owned by people who don't have to live off what their land produces. They're gentlemen farmers who love to plant and harvest but often hire professionals to do the real work. My father used to say that it was the only way to farm. He said he'd come north to Summerville and become a fireman so he could eat steadily. Down in Georgia, his parents had a hard-scrabble one hundred acres that included just a scrap of bottomland, which never produced enough to do much more than pay the taxes. The boys had all been hunters and the girls had all married early and moved away because the land didn't bring in enough money to put food on the table for a big family.

My father liked the Vineyard farms, with their painted buildings and nice fences and no junked machinery out behind the barns, and sometimes he'd drive my sister and me around so we could admire them. He'd never expressed an interest in owning such a farm but instead had taught me and Margarite how to fish and how to shoot a rifle and shotgun fairly early in our lives, just in case we ever needed to live off the land.

Now I said to Clay, "Nobody's written a song about amber waves of grass, as far as I know."

He grinned. "I've never heard it either, but somebody may have done it. There's a whole drug culture out there that has entertainments of its own." His grin went away. "As I recall, you used to smoke the occasional weed. We weren't much more than kids, were we?"

I nodded. "A long time ago. I liked dope. It made me feel good and I laughed a lot. I think they should legalize MJ and sell it through liquor stores. The government could control the quality so people would know what they were getting and wouldn't be buying fake grass or weed hyped with more powerful stuff. And it could stop spending all that money on arresting dealers and users and keeping them in jail."

"You aren't worried about people getting addicted?"

I shrugged. "I'm willing to bet that nicotine is more addictive."

"How about harder stuff. You want to legalize that, too?"

"*Decriminalize* is a better word, maybe."

"Are you hedging your bet?"

"Probably. I think people have a right to do whatever they want to do with their bodies as long as they don't hurt anybody else. I think it's stupid for people to shoot up or do other self-destructive things, but I don't think they're criminals if they do."

"Why'd you quit?"

I thought about my experiments with some really good grass I'd gotten hold of when I was about twenty. We called it "one-toke dope" because that was all you needed to have your head go floating up to the ceiling and stay there for an hour or two. We also called it "laughing grass" because it made everything incredibly funny so that we could hardly speak a single sentence without bursting into laughter.

Then, because I am who I am, I tried some tests. I got stoned, but told no one, then attended a party to see if anyone would notice that I was higher than a kite. No one did, so apparently I didn't act differently from normal even though I felt sure anyone could tell I was high by looking at me or listening to me.

Then I got stoned and tried to read but found myself forgetting the beginning of paragraphs by the time I got to the end of them. I read the same paragraph over and over and never understood it.

Finally, I got stoned and sat down to watch television. I discovered that being high was wonderful for watching hockey because I could see the puck moving in slow motion from stick to stick, whereas when I was straight, I could hardly see it at all. However, I also discovered that I was laughing and laughing at the wonderful wit in sitcoms that I normally thought were boring beyond comprehension.

My conclusion was that however much grass improved hockey and made me happy, it kept me from reading and it made me think television comedy was clever. Ergo, it was apparently turning my brain into mush.

So I stopped smoking it. I had no moral objections to other people smoking, but it wasn't for me.

Later, I'd given up nicotine as well, although even to this day when a pipe smoker passes me on the sidewalk, my nose almost pulls me around so I can follow the fragrance of the smoke.

I gave this long answer to Clay in response to his short comment.

He nodded. "Well, you still have alcohol and caffeine, the socially acceptable drugs in American culture."

I nodded back. "I like them both and I think I know enough to use them instead of having them use me."

"I imagine some AA people might doubt that."

I thought he was right, but I also thought that AA people were in a minority on the Vineyard, where drugs of all kinds were popular. We'd come a long way from the time when marijuana first became a hit with middle-class kids and many a user deemed it a plant of peace and a local island guy had proclaimed himself Johnny Potseed and had driven all around the Vineyard scattering and planting seeds from his personal plants in hopes of improving life on earth for one and all.

"Are Blume and Monroe reps for somebody in the business?" I asked.

Clay nodded. "They are."

"They don't seem to be the peaceful types we used to think of as pot smokers."

"We're not talking about smokers. We're talking about businessmen running the biggest cash-crop industry in the United States. They're not running it to lose money, and because they're outside the law, they make their own laws.

They're their own judges and juries and enforcers. Blume and Monroe are two of the enforcers."

I thought of Balzac's famous adage that behind every great fortune was a great crime. "I don't know much about the business," I said.

Clay nodded. "It may work differently in different places, but I can tell you how I got involved. Remember me telling you that I plowed snow on a ranch in Montana? Well, it's a huge ranch, most of it well off the main road, and it had its own little runway and its own very nice Beechcraft. My second ex had gotten my plane in the divorce settlement, and I'd left the state one jump ahead of the posse—remember me telling you about that? I knew a guy in Alaska who knew Mark Briggs, the guy who owned the ranch. Mark's pilot had gotten married and had moved down to San Antonio, and Mark needed a new pilot and my friend recommended me for the job. I needed a job, and Mark and I hit it off and I went to work as a sort of combination ranch hand and pilot. I fixed fences and plowed snow and even played cowboy at branding time. It was a real ranch with cattle, horses, even a few sheep. Evenings, Mark and I and the other guys who worked there would eat together at the big house. Great food, good wine, beer, and some really great dope. Weekends we'd watch the Seattle and Denver games on TV.

"It wasn't long before I realized that the ranch was really headquarters for Mark's marijuana business. Cars and trucks came and went bringing in the local harvest from growers in the area and shipping it out again to other wholesalers. The growers were mostly farming high-powered female plants in labs under grow lights. My flying job was to take people, usually a guy named Larry Jelcoe, and luggage to or from L.A. or Spokane or other places. I never asked questions and kept my mouth shut, and one day Mark called me up to his office and asked me if I'd make a delivery on my own. I said yes and he took me into a back room and showed me suitcases full of money. Hundred-dollar bills in packets, just like you see in the movies. There must have been two or three million dollars there. He wanted me to take it to L.A. and get it to a friend of his who worked at a bank. Something had come up that kept Larry from going with me and doing that part of the job.

"I said, 'That's a lot of money. What if I just keep going, plane and all?'

"He just laughed and slapped me on the back and said he trusted me, so I delivered the suitcases. The MO was for me to leave them in a storage locker, go to the bank and meet my man, give him the key, and leave. No receipt or anything like that.

"So I did that and after that I made that kind of flight alone every two or three weeks, going to one bank or another in one city or another or sometimes picking up satchels from people and bringing them back to the ranch. I don't know what happened to Larry, but after he left the ranch, it was my job. Mark must have had several fortunes stashed away in a lot of banks. He had so much money that he didn't attach much significance to it."

I could understand that. When you don't have much money, it means a lot; when you have a lot, it doesn't mean much at all.

Clay went on. "I worked there for several months and it was a good job. I was making good money, I was flying a lot, and I liked the guys I was working with. Then things changed. Mark decided to get out of the business. More and more DEA people were coming into the area and he figured that it was only a matter of time before they raided some grower and pressured the grower into naming the people he dealt with. None of the growers knew Mark's name, but they could name the guys who picked up their harvest and those guys could name their bosses and some of those bosses could name Mark, so it was a good time to move out. He sold the ranch, Beechcraft and all, for big bucks to a guy named Lewis Farquahar who wasn't afraid of the DEA, and he moved to Palm Springs. Jack Blume and Mickey Monroe are Lewis's muscle.

"Lewis offered me a job, but I figured that if Mark was getting nervous, maybe I should move on, too. My last job was to fly Lewis's payment for the ranch down to San Diego, to deposit in one of Mark's bank accounts. It was a couple of suitcases of bills. I was to bring the Beechcraft back to the ranch afterwards, then be on my way. I was honest with Farquahar. Told him my plan to leave. Told him I knew a guy in Sausalito who was building a boat and who had offered me work. I landed in San Francisco and dropped my tools off with him on my way down to San Diego.

"So far, so good. When I landed in San Diego, I put the suitcases in a storage locker like I always did, but the guy I usually met at the bank wasn't there. A new guy was, but I wasn't sure I should be dealing with him so I kept the key and left. Two guys followed me but I shook them and called Mark in Palm Springs. He said he didn't know anything about the new guy at the bank so I should just bring the key to him in Palm Springs. I said okay but when I got back to the airport, the Beechcraft was gone. I called Mark again but all I got was an answering machine. I kept trying but there was no answer.

"I decided that it was time to leave the West Coast and I figured that two suitcases full of money was probably a good motive for somebody to come looking for me. I didn't know if Lewis Farquahar thought it was still his money or whether Mark thought I had made off with it or whether the Feds thought it was theirs. But I trusted Mark, so I took a bus to Palm Springs. I didn't have Mark's address, but I figured I'd phone him again once I was there and give him the key to the storage locker. But nobody answered the phone and so much weird stuff was going on that I thought maybe somebody had tapped the line. So I finally left a message on the answering machine saying that I'd gone to Las Vegas and I took a bus to Denver.

"There I sent an e-mail from a café to Mark and another to the ranch telling them where I was and saying I'd phone later. But instead I went down to Dallas and stayed there a week before I tried another phone call to Mark and had no more luck than before. I e-mailed the ranch again and said I was going to Little Rock but I came to Boston instead and you know the rest. I didn't figure they'd find me here but I was stupid about the tools. Farquahar's boys must have had to dig a little, but they had enough information to find me."

"Well, we know one thing," I said. "Mark isn't after you. Lewis Farquahar is."

"There's that," agreed Clay. "Of course, there's the Feds, too. I don't think we should leave them out just yet."

I believed he was right, and I felt as worried as he looked thoughtful.

— 12 —

"Why don't you just give Blume the key?" I asked. "Then Lewis Farquahar will have the money and Mark can deal with him directly and it won't be your problem anymore."

"Because I think Lewis may be behind all this bad business. Mark didn't know anything about the new guy I met at the bank and something must have spooked him enough to make him disappear right after I phoned him from San Diego the first time. All he had to do to get the key was answer his phone when I called him from Dallas. But he didn't do that. He's gone underground if he's not dead, and if he's alive, the money's his, as far as I'm concerned."

"So you think Lewis wants his money back now that he's got the ranch? Is that it? He pays Mark all fair and square, but then robs the stagecoach before it can get the strongbox to the bank, like in those old Westerns?"

"If Hollywood can think of that idea, so can Lewis."

"Look," I said, "you may think you owe something to Mark, but you're not working for him anymore, so it still seems to me that you'll be better off if you give Blume the key and step out of the scene. Blume and Monroe will go away, Lewis will be satisfied, Mark can't blame you for a thing, he and Lewis can fight it out, and you can live happily ever after."

Clay shook his head. "Even if I did that, I'd still be the only guy who knew what happened and if Lewis is the man he seems to be, he won't want to leave a loose tongue behind that might flap in a Fed's ear or in Mark's ear, if Mark still has an ear. I might slip away from Blume and Monroe after I gave them the key, but I couldn't stay here any longer and I'd never know how far they might chase me." He looked around the cabin. "I'm getting too old to play cat-and-mouse games."

"About the Feds," I said. "Maybe the new guy at the bank was a Fed. Maybe he wasn't working for Lewis at all. Maybe that's why Mark went underground. Because he smelled the Feds getting too close. After he talked with you the first time, he got to thinking that he'd been doing business with that bank for too long and that it was time to break away from it, take his losses, and drop out of sight for a few years. You said that he had more money than he could count and had it in a lot of banks. He may have had a lot of passports, too, and other plans in case the Palm Springs one didn't work out."

Clay nodded. "That could be."

We looked at each other for a while.

"Blume and Monroe said they were staying at the Harbor View?"

"That's right."

"They're definitely not Feds."

"No."

"I want you out of this picture," he said. "It's bad enough that I'm in it, but that's my own fault."

It always annoys me to discover that I have habits and values I distrust in others and would advise them to alter if they asked me for my opinion. One of the ideals I view with suspicion is loyalty, because even the devil has faithful followers and fidelity has caused as much grief as treachery. So when I find someone sticking to a friend or cause out of simple loyalty, I'm skeptical at best. Yet now, in spite of the logic of his reasoning, I had no more impulse to abandon Clay than I had to abandon Bonzo, thus proving once again that my efforts to be rational were often in vain. The realization almost made me laugh. But not quite.

"You trust Mark?" I asked.

"Yes."

"With your life?"

He hesitated, then nodded. "Sure. I trust people with my life every time I step off the curb when I have a green light."

"Is there any way you can get in touch with him or he can get in touch with you?"

"No to the first, yes to the second. I have a cell phone number and an e-mail address but he hasn't answered any of my messages. Also, Blume and Monroe found me, so Mark probably can, too. I may have mentioned my Sausalito friend to him at some point."

"Yes, if Blume and Monroe left your boatbuilding friend alive to talk to the next guy who asked where he sent your tools. That next guy could be Mark or a Fed, which means we may be getting more visitors soon, if they're not here already."

"That's why you should get out of this business."

The statement made me angry. "What we need to do first is get you to a safe house, someplace nobody knows about, including Eleanor and Ted and Zee. I know a place that will do. Then we have to find out what's going on, and I know a guy who might help us do that."

"I don't like the idea of Elly and Ted being left in the dark."

"You can explain the details to them if you want to. That's your business, not mine. With a little luck, we'll have this situation straightened out before long and you can move back to Eleanor's apartment."

"I don't want Blume and Monroe coming near Elly or Ted."

"And I don't want them coming near Zee or my children," I said, feeling a tingle of fear as I spoke those words. "The best way I know to stop it from happening is to keep you under cover while we decide what to do, and the quicker we do that the better."

He nodded and looked around the cabin. "All right. I don't want to abandon what I have here. I've abandoned too much in my life already. I just wish we had a few more things going for us."

"We have local knowledge. They're strangers in a strange land. That should even things up. In the *Code Duello*, the challenged party got to choose the ground, as you no doubt recall."

"Actually," he said, "I've never read the *Code Duello*. I don't believe it was included on the Five Foot Shelf."

"No matter." I stepped back into the cockpit of the boat. "Blume and Monroe won't be coming around today unless they're a lot smarter and luckier than I think they are, so you may as well stay here and get some work done during the rest of the afternoon. I'll go get your safe house ready, then come to Eleanor's apartment later and take you to it. That'll give you time to tell Eleanor and Ted whatever you want them to know."

I climbed out of the boat and briefly allowed myself a fantasy that consisted of Blume and Monroe arriving next fall instead of now and finding that Clay, Eleanor, and Ted had sailed over the horizon in the schooner and were forever beyond their grasp, somewhere on the far reaches of the sea. It was a pleasant fancy but one I set aside as I drove out to the highway, made sure no yellow Mercedes convertibles were in sight, and went home.

I got the keys to John Skye's farmhouse and drove there. John taught things medieval at Weststock College and wouldn't be coming down to the island until May, when he and Mattie and their twin undergrad daughters would arrive for the summer. One of my jobs was to close the place in the fall, tend to it through the winter, and open it in the spring. It was just the right place to put Clay. He'd be out of sight and comfortable, but with ready access to Eleanor and the schooner.

I parked in the yard between the house and the barn and corrals, circumnavigated the house, and walked through the outbuildings making sure everything was more or less as it had been when I'd made my last inspection, then went inside.

March could be pretty chilly and we could even have snow; I kept low heat in the house all winter so the pipes wouldn't freeze even if we got an unusual cold spell, and all I had to do now was turn up the thermostat. There was dry firewood stacked on the back porch and I brought some in and laid paper, kindling, and logs in the fireplaces. I turned on the water heater and checked the toilets and faucets. Upstairs, in the guest bedroom, I made the bed, using sheets and blankets from the linen closet. When I was sure that everything was as it should be, I drove into Edgartown and bought a week's worth of groceries, a bottle of rum, and a gallon of cider. Back at the farmhouse I stored the provisions in the kitchen, noted that the house was already warming up, and indulged myself with a visit to John's library, my favorite room in the house.

The library was walled with books and had a triangulation of épée, foil, and saber on the wall, a tribute to John's long-ago athletic career in college as a three-weapon man. His desk was a heavy old carved table and there was a large, worn Oriental rug on the floor, upon which were gently distressed leather chairs, reading lamps, and small tables. A fireplace interrupted the bookcases on one wall, and on its mantel was a small bust of Beethoven and another of Socrates. Often during the winters when I was making sure that all was well in the house, I'd sometimes lose myself in the library, so that when I returned home, Zee would wonder where I'd been.

I found it hard to imagine that Clay wouldn't love the library. Not everyone is drawn to books as bees are drawn to nectar, but I liked to imagine that my friends were, even though I knew perfectly well that some of them read nothing but scandal sheets and the sports pages.

Driving to Eleanor's house, I wondered how serious she and Clay were about each other. They'd been seen together in enough public places for gossip to continue to thrive in the slow winter months, when the year-rounders had less to do and could concentrate on rumor and romantic speculation. Ted, too, had been free in his public talk about how well the

schooner was coming along and how pleased he was with
Clay's work, so I didn't think it would be long before Jack
and Mickey heard the talk and came to see Ted and Eleanor.

At Eleanor's house I found her and Clay together in the
apartment. His gear was already in the old blue Bronco. Her
face was unhappy and her eyes were damp, so it was clear
that he'd done his best to explain his plan to move and that
she didn't like it. She didn't like me, either, for having suggested the move.

"No one needs to know you're staying here," she said
angrily to Clay. "I won't tell anyone. It's nobody's business
anyway!"

"Did you tell her about Jack and Mickey?" I asked him.

He nodded, and I turned to Eleanor. "Jack and Mickey are
not nice guys and they work for another guy who apparently
doesn't mind hurting people, including people like you and
Ted. You've never met people like these men, but I have. If
you know where Clay is, they'll make you tell them whether
you want to or not, so it's best that you don't know."

"I'd never tell them!"

I didn't want to describe what they might do to her to get
the information, so I said, "Not even if they put a gun to
your brother's head and give you ten seconds to talk before
they pull the trigger?"

"They wouldn't dare!" But there was fear in her voice.

Clay put his hands on her shoulders. "I'll be on the island.
You just won't know where. You can't tell what you don't
know."

She hesitated until I said, "Half the people on the island
have seen you two together, and the other half have heard
Ted talk about Clay working on his boat. Jack and Mickey
have ears for gossip so they could be here anytime. You
want to be able to say Clay heard they were on the Vineyard
and moved out right away. You can show them through
your house and the apartment to prove he's gone." Even if
they hurt her, I thought, she wouldn't be able to tell them

anything. But I didn't say that. Instead I said, "You can tell them you think he flew to Nantucket."

She flashed her eyes up into his. "Do you think you might go to Nantucket?"

He put on a smile. "It's not a bad idea."

"Go! You'll be safer there!"

"If things get tight here, I'll do that. But it may not be necessary." He brushed at her hair with a gentle hand.

After a moment, she stepped back. "All right," she said. "Do what you have to do."

"The first thing we're going to do," I said, "is go to Ted's place and tell him what we've just told you. Then we'll put Clay's tools in the Bronco so Jack and Mickey won't find them if they go looking in the barn." I looked at her. "With luck this will all be over soon and things will get back to normal."

She pulled a handkerchief from a pocket and blew her nose. "Good," she said.

I followed the Bronco to Ted Overhill's house and we replayed our scenario while we loaded Clay's tools into his truck. To his credit Ted didn't bluster about his ability to take care of himself. Instead he said, "Tell you what. Tomorrow morning at the coffee shop I'll start bitching about Clay taking off with hardly a word except something about Nantucket, leaving me with jobs half done and summer getting closer by the day. I'll keep it up whenever I get the chance. That help any?"

"That will help a lot!" Clay smiled grimly. "If Jack and Mickey have their ears up, they may decide I really have pulled out."

Ted put a hand on his arm. "I hope you don't. Elly would be pretty sad, and so would I."

"Me, too," said Clay. "Maybe we'll be lucky."

All three of them deserved to be lucky, I thought, but as Bill Munny said, "Deserve's got nothing to do with it." Sometimes it's a blessing when we get what we deserve, but just as often it's a blessing if we don't.

I led the way to John Skye's farm and we parked with the house between the road and us.

"You can put the Bronco in the barn, if you want a little more security from prying eyes," I said.

"I may do that." Clay's eyes flowed around the house and farm yard.

I showed him where I sometimes hung the key, behind a shutter on a kitchen window, and we went inside.

"Nice," he said, after I showed him around.

"Don't tell anyone where you are and don't show yourself in the usual places," I said. "Buy gas and groceries up-island, where they don't know you. If you need anything, give me a call, but don't use the phone to call any of your friends out west because their lines may not be secure or they may have caller ID. You have a cell phone, so use that if you need to.

"I'll come by tomorrow morning and take you for a ride."

"Where are we going?"

"To Aquinnah to talk with a friend who may be able to help us find out what's going on."

His blue eyes were bright. "You have interesting friends."

I felt a smile on my face. "You're evidence of that."

— 13 —

I rarely tell anyone everything, so that evening I told Zee about my encounter with Jack and Mickey and how I'd warned Clay about them, but I didn't tell her about the rest of my day because if Jack and Mickey came by before she learned otherwise via gossip, she could tell them that Clay was living in Eleanor's apartment and was working for Ted. If the gossip about his departure reached her before Jack and Mickey did, she could pass that bit of disinformation along instead. I asked her to tell Jack and Mickey what she knew and to have the children do the same, so there would be no reason for Blume and Monroe to feel any need for threats or violence.

She looked up at me with her great, dark eyes. "Do you think there's any danger of that?"

"I don't think there is but I want you to be careful."

She glanced across the room at the gun cabinet, where we kept our weapons locked up tight. I guessed she might be thinking about the deadly little .380 Beretta 84F she'd used when she first learned to shoot. It was easier to conceal than the big .45 she now shot in competition.

The trophies stored in the closet of our guest bedroom spoke to her skill but not to her paradoxical dislike and disapproval of firearms in general. I, on the other hand, lacked her magical abilities with a pistol but had no theoretical objections to the existence of guns or their use in hunting or self-defense as long as the hunting was for meat and the self-defense could stand the test of reason. I don't like trophy hunting, and in practice, I rarely feel so endangered as to go armed, unlike a few islanders I know, who feel quite naked without a pistol on their person and are, therefore, always dressed.

I thought that Mickey Monroe was such a pistol packer, although I hadn't actually seen what he carried in his coat pocket. But if Jack Blume was another one, he hid his weapons more successfully and was, if my first impressions were correct, less inclined to use brute force as anything but a last resort. Even his threats had been indirect. Maybe he'd studied to be a psychiatrist before abandoning that career for one of crime.

Now, as we sat before our fire after the children were in bed, I put my arm across Zee's shoulder. As an ER nurse she had no illusions about violence in the world and had devoted her life to tending to its victims. Her gentle heart was accompanied by a cool head that forbade her to ignore truth, so I had no doubt that she would now accept the reality of Blume and Monroe and I trusted her to act appropriately. If she decided to carry the Beretta, that was fine; if she didn't, that was fine, too. But I hoped she didn't feel that she had to.

Zee leaned against me and repeated something she'd said before: "I'm glad you're not an adventurer."

It wasn't the first time that tension roused passion in us. "You're all the adventure I can handle," I said, feeling a familiar electrical charge pass between us.

I could sense her siren smile. "Oh? Can you handle me?"

I pulled her toward me and cupped her breast in my hand. "Sometimes I seem to have you under control. But maybe you're just pretending."

She put her hand over mine. "Sometimes I am," she said. "But not always."

Her fragrance filled my nostrils and my free hand drifted to the buttons of her blouse. As my hand entered her clothing, I heard her breathing change. When my own breathing seemed so loud that it filled the room, we got up and went into the bedroom. Blume and Monroe faded into a mist.

They were back in my consciousness again the next morning, though, along with Nadine Gibson, whose officially unidentified body had been found, according to the morning news on the radio. The reporter of this news, however, took note of the corpse's strawberry hair and reminded his audience of Nadine's disappearance just a year before.

The poet thought that April was the cruelest month, but March seemed to wear the crown this year.

"Be careful," said Zee, as she prepared to depart for work after we'd seen the kids off on the bus for school.

"You, too."

I watched her drive away in her little red Jeep, known lately as Miss Scarlet because we'd been playing Clue with the kids. My old Land Cruiser was the wrong color to be given any of the names in the game, although I thought its rust might qualify it to be Colonel Mustard. When Miss Scarlet was gone, I called Joe Begay to learn if he was home. He was and I told him I wanted to talk with him and that I'd be right up. Then I drove to John Skye's farm, where I found Clay in the library reading a copy of the *Code Duello*.

"After you mentioned them, I thought I should catch up on the latest rules," he said, "but this book was published more than a hundred years ago. Duels seem to be out of fashion these days."

I believed the French still had them occasionally, remembering reading a story or seeing a photograph of an outraged pastry chef and somebody else having at each other with sharpened épées. Drawn blood was usually enough to settle passions and balance the demands of honor sufficiently for the participants to embrace and go off together to share a few glasses of wine.

"In America the killing rules have always been a little shaky," I said. "Back in the days of the Wild West, people popped away at each other with smooth-bore pistols now and then, but mostly they preferred to shoot their enemies from ambush or catch them unarmed before they blazed away.

Nowadays that's how the gangs and angry lovers do it in the wild Eastern cities. Better by far to shoot somebody in the back or from a moving car. Fair fights are too dangerous."

"Disputed honor seems to have been important in the old days," said Clay, putting his book down on a reading table, "and I guess it still is, if you take dissing as the modern equivalent."

I thought that it was and that the idea of honor has probably caused more grief than most notions. "If you'd like to come along, I'm visiting a friend of mine. He may be able to find out what's going on out west."

"No more ignorant armies clashing by night?" Clay shrugged into his coat. "That would be nice. Who's your friend?"

I told him as we drove toward Aquinnah. How Joe Begay had been my sergeant in a long-ago war and how we'd been blown up by a mortar along with the rest of our patrol but had survived and met again years later right here on the Vineyard, where he had married and now lived with a Wampanoag woman he'd met in Santa Fe. How since our war days, he'd worked for some unnamed agency in Washington and still occasionally disappeared in that direction for a few days, although he was officially retired.

Clay listened and then said, "You trust him." It wasn't a question.

"He saved my life in Nam."

"Does he subscribe to that old Oriental notion that if you save a man's life you have to take care of him from then on?"

"It hasn't been mentioned, but he's helped me out several times in the past."

"What does he do in Washington?"

It was a question I'd considered more than once but had not voiced. "I've never asked. Maybe that's why we're still friends. I met a woman once who'd seen him in Europe at some bigwig international political function, and I know he was overseas another time as part of a trade mission when some bad guys got killed. He knows a lot of people and he's got a lot of contacts with a lot of agencies."

"That's a lot of lots."

"I'm going to ask him to use some of those contacts to find out what's going on with your friends Mark and Lewis and whether the Feds are on their case."

"If the DEA is interested in them, it may be interested in me, too," said Clay. "Even though I was mostly just a pilot, I was part of the gang."

I'd thought about that. "We can ask Joe to look into that possibility, too, but only if you okay it. We'll talk with him together and you can decide whether you want your name mentioned if he noses around. It'll be hard to get the answers we need if we don't tell him about Jack and Mickey looking for you."

We came to West Tisbury and took South Road past the field of dancing statues and the general store. In the summertime the farmers market would be spread out in the yard of the old Ag Hall, but now the yard was empty and brown. West Tisbury is farm country, defined by fields and meadows, quite unlike Menemsha and the coastal down-island villages, where beaches, fishing, and yachting establish the ambiance. A lot of artists live there, and like the citizens of many other parts of the island, they socialize among themselves. In that respect the Vineyard is akin to large cities: a place made up of small neighborhoods quite separate from one another and from the whole, where people know one another and may live out their lives feeling little need to expand their horizons. I sometimes thought of the island's towns as little mouse nests shoved together in a box, the mice eyeing one another carefully and rarely entering a neighboring territory.

When we got to Beetlebung Corner, we took a left past the Chilmark Store, home of some of the best sandwiches on the island. If you blink as you drive through Chilmark Center, you'll miss seeing it, which means, alas, you'll also miss Chilmark Chocolates, makers of deluxe candies that have destroyed many a diet. Summer people who are customers never lose weight in spite of their intentions to go home slim and fit and tan in the fall.

In time we fetched Aquinnah, once known as Gay Head, which is famous for its colorful clay cliffs and, to fishermen, for its excellent bass fishing. On the other hand, it's infamous to me because of the No Parking and even No Pausing signs that line its roads and make it hard for would-be fishermen to wet their lines on Lobsterville Beach, and also for its pay toilets, which require elderly tour-bus passengers to come up with fifty cents each to relieve their bladders and which are, like all pay toilets, an abomination in the eyes of God. I consider Aquinnah to be an unfriendly town and I bad-mouth it regularly. A pox upon its No Parking signs and its pay toilets, I say.

However, I do like to fish there and manage to do that without contributing to Aquinnah's money-grasping hands by parking for free at the homes of friends, of whom Joe Begay is one. Joe and Toni and their children live in a house just north of the cliffs. A path leads from the house to the beach where, back in January 1884, frozen bodies from the *City of Columbus*, wrecked on Devil's Bridge, washed ashore hour after hour in spite of the heroic efforts of the Wampanoag lifeguards, who rowed out in the storm and managed to save twenty-nine people from the stricken ship. Even now, in March, you wouldn't last long in the cold waters surrounding the Vineyard.

In Aquinnah I took a right onto Lighthouse Road, then a left into the sandy Begay driveway and pulled to a stop in front of the house. Joe's car was there but Toni's was not, probably because she was up at her shop on top of the cliffs, getting a jump start on organizing things for the summer trade. Toni sold American tribal arts and crafts, scorning the term "Native American" as being even more nonsensical than "Indian," since the latter was based on a simple geographical error while the former was a conscious effort to name a whole continent and its many cultures of people after a tardy Italian explorer. She sold no Taiwan- or Chinese-made bows and arrows, but stuck strictly to genuine American tribal rugs, pottery, carvings, jewelry, and knickknacks.

As we got out of the car, Joe Begay stepped out onto his porch. He was a tall man with most of his weight above his belt. He had a broad chest, wide shoulders, and a face that looked like the one on the old nickels. His wife claimed that when they'd first met in Santa Fe, where she was on a buying trip, she'd been instantly smitten because he looked more like an Indian than anyone she'd ever seen.

We shook hands and I introduced him to Clay. Each of them took in the other with what seemed to be a casual glance. "Come in," Joe said to me. "I'm inviting you even though you're impolite. Out on the rez you stay parked in your car for a while so whoever's inside can size you up before deciding how to deal with you."

"Is that the Navajo rez or the Hopi rez?" I asked, since Joe was about half one tribe and half the other.

"Either," said Joe as we went inside. "Be a good tradition for these parts, too, but around here people are in too much of a hurry. Sit down. I've got coffee going. Too early for beer." He looked at Clay. "For me, at least. How about you?"

"Coffee's fine."

Joe waved us into chairs at the kitchen table and brought coffee and the makings. "Been a while since you came out here to Indian country," he said to me. "There are no fish around, so it must be something else."

"It's something else. I'm looking through a glass darkly and I want to see face-to-face."

Begay smiled. "I think Paul was saying that would happen only after death. Is that what you have in mind?"

"No, I just want some light and I'm hoping you can shed some for me."

"Some off-island light, I presume. If it was local light, you'd know more than I do about how to shed it."

"It's off-island light that I need." I glanced at Clay, who was looking into his coffee cup. "Here's the situation," I said, and I told him about my encounter with Jack Blume and Mickey Monroe. When I was done, I added, "I want to know who sent them and what they want with Clay. If we get that information, we may know what to do about them."

"Maybe you should be thinking about what they'll do to *you*," said Begay. "You haven't given me much to go on." He looked at Clay. "You want to add anything to this story?"

"J.W. says he can trust you," said Clay.

"Did he, now?" Joe lowered his cup from his lips. "He trusted me once in Nam and I led us right into a mortar attack. Got several men killed and damn near got us killed, too. He saved my ass. I'm the one who trusts him."

"J.W. told me it was you who saved his ass." Clay seemed amused, but Joe's remarks also seemed to lead him to a decision. He flicked a glance at me, then took a drink from his cup and told Joe everything he'd told me about his work with Mark and the events that had brought him to the Vineyard. He concluded by telling how he'd departed from Eleanor and her brother and where he was staying now.

"Now you know everything that I know," he said.

Begay looked at him for what seemed a long time. Then he looked at me. "You want me to find out what's going on. I'm not sure I can, but I can probably find out a few things." He turned his eyes to Clay. "I'll need the telephone numbers and the e-mail addresses and any other addresses you have and I'll see what I can do. No guarantees." He paused, then added, "I'll try to keep you clear of things."

Clay considered that, then nodded and dug a worn address book out of a buttoned shirt pocket. He tossed it onto the table in front of Joe. "When you're through with that, I want it back. It's got all the information you want and a lot more that you don't want. It's one of a kind. If I lose it, I'll be out of touch with everybody I know."

Joe picked it up and thumbed through it. "This will help," he said. "And don't worry; you'll get it back."

When we finished our coffee and Clay and I were headed out the door, Joe said, "If you think of anything or learn anything else that I might use, let me know."

"Will do."

Clay and I went out to the truck and drove back downisland.

— 14 —

"Is this a typical March on Martha's Vineyard," asked Clay, "or do you always have bodies and mob muscle turning up?"

"Atypical. Normally we have a lot of wind and rain, mud and cold weather, and some snow. It's usually too miserable for criminals to be out working."

"I feel naked without my address book. Tell me more about Joe Begay, since I've just put my life in his hands."

"You know about as much as I do," I said, but told him how Joe grew up in Arizona near Second Mesa, in Oraibi or close by. That his people are mostly Hopi and Navajo and still live out there. How we'd been blown up in Nam when our patrol got hit with mortar fire. How, after we got out of the hospital, he'd disappeared from my life until he showed up on the Vineyard married to Toni Vanderbeck, of the Gay Head Vanderbecks, who was a friend of my wife, and how he was supposedly but not really retired from whatever he'd been doing in Washington and elsewhere. "That's about all I know about him," I concluded. "I usually don't ask people much about their work."

"Why not?"

"It lets me see them better if I don't know what they do for a living. If I know somebody's a doctor or a minister or a truck driver, I make assumptions that I shouldn't make. Actually, though, it doesn't make much difference whether or not I ask them what they do, because most people tell you that right away. They define themselves by their jobs."

"'Hi, my name is George Smith. I'm a diamond smuggler.' Like that?"

"Usually it's not quite that straightforward, but sooner or later it slips out, especially if the person is proud of himself. I prefer to talk to him awhile before finding out what he does."

"What do you say if you don't say, 'What do you do when you're not talking to me?'"

"Sex, politics, and religion are always good subjects of conversation."

"Taboo topics are the best topics, but most people don't get to them until they know each other better."

"Actually, I usually ask them where they live, how long they've been there, what they do when they're not working, that sort of thing. What people do for fun tells a lot about them."

"So you're nosy even though you don't want to know their professions?"

"I'll make an exception for Jack and Mickey. I'd like to know more about their work."

"Maybe Joe can find out about that. I don't think you'll get the information from Jack and Mickey."

For variety I took Middle Road down to West Tisbury. It's my favorite island road, winding between fields and woods and stone fences, having fine views of the Atlantic off to the south, and passing the pasture that's home to the long-horned oxen who've been photographed almost as much as the rebuilt bridge on Chappaquiddick.

Clay admired the longhorns. "Impressive. I haven't seen horns that long since I left Texas. Back when I had my own plane, I did some flying down around the border. I made pretty good money flying cargo through canyons under the radar. It was sort of like the job we had bringing the *Lisa* back to West Palm. Remember?"

"I remember."

"If you don't know what's in a box, you can't testify about it if you get squeezed. So I rarely asked what I was carrying. Well, what next?"

"I've been thinking of escape routes. There are only two

ways off the island: by sea or by air. You still have your pilot's license?"

"I do. Why?"

"If need be, you can rent a plane. I doubt that'll be necessary, but you should keep it in mind. Have you been to either of the airports since you got here? The big one, where the commercial planes land, is in West Tisbury—we came by it today—and the little one is at Katama—grass runways for small planes."

"I haven't been to either one."

"You might want to drop by and let the regulars see you a few times so they'll know who you are if you decide to rent a plane."

"Good idea."

"Nobody's at the Katama airport this time of year, so I'll take you to the big one now, if you want, so you can see what the place is like."

"Forward the light brigade!"

The Dukes County Airport is right off the Edgartown–West Tisbury road, and is only a hop, skip, and a jump from the long driveway at the end of which then president Joe Callahan took his summer vacations. Huge cargo planes full of cars, Secret Service personnel, and other materials had landed there before, during, and after the presidential holidays, and the airport was getting busier every year as more and more mansion builders landed in their private jets. It was an attractive place, but I preferred the little Katama airport and enjoyed watching planes land and take off on the grass runway that paralleled Herring Creek Road. I had even given thought from time to time to getting a pilot's license of my own, but nothing had ever come of it because my days were already full of things I liked to do, such as fishing and sailing and hanging around with my wife and children.

We parked in the approved lot and walked into the Plane View restaurant, where the coffee is always hot and the food is good and also cheap by island standards. On the field there were many parked planes, including a couple of commercial jets. Not there were the glider and two biplanes, one white, one red, that flew out of the Katama airport during the tourist season.

All summer long, one or both of the planes could be seen flying around the island, carrying sight-seeing passengers. Sometimes the red one entertained with loops and slides and rolls and spins, and I wondered what it must be like to be in the cockpit while all that was going on. But I never wondered enough to hire the plane and pilot to take me up and do those things. I'm acrophobic enough to get the shakes on high buildings; I don't need to be upside down in an open-cockpit airplane.

We sat down and had coffee and chatted with the few people who were there. They were friendly to Clay when I introduced him but were mostly interested in talking about the girl with the strawberry hair.

"I hear the cops are saying it's murder."

"I ain't heard that. All I heard is that they found the girl's body."

"Well, she sure as hell didn't bury herself in that old cellar hole. Somebody else did that."

"I hear the Oak Bluffs police and the state cops are asking all kinds of questions along Circuit Ave."

"Well, they got a body now. They didn't have that before. All they had was a missing person, and people leave the island all the time without telling anybody."

"I don't know about that. They may leave, but they tell somebody. They don't just run off."

"This Gibson woman didn't tell nobody nothing. And now we know why."

"You ever see her, up at the Fireside? Good-looker. All that long red hair. Nice, too. Always a smile."

"I hear the cops are talking with that fella they call Bonzo. You know, the one that pushes a broom and cleans tables. Sort of a half-wit."

"We got our share of those on this island." Laughter and nodding heads.

"Yeah, well, I guess that this Bonzo is what the cops call 'a person of interest.' That's somewhere between being innocent and being a suspect."

"They don't have enough on him to arrest him, but they've got him under a magnifying glass. You know him, J.W.?"

"I know him," I said. "He's a friend of mine."

"Oh." There was some quiet coffee drinking.

"Bonzo wouldn't hurt a fly," I said.

"I don't think the cops are so sure of that," said a gray-haired man, screwing his courage to the sticking point.

I felt a little flicker of anger. "The police are interested in anybody who might have known the girl. They might want to talk with you, for instance."

"Me! What for?"

"You just said she was good-looking and you mentioned her long red hair and her smile. The police might wonder how you know she was nice and just how much she interested you."

"Now just a damned minute! What the hell are you saying?" He pushed himself away from his table.

I waved him back into his chair. "Take it easy, Rod. I thought she was pretty, too, and so did everybody else who saw her. The point is that the police are interested in anybody who might have known her, including you and me. They're not just interested in Bonzo. As for me, I know you didn't kill her and I know Bonzo didn't, either. Let's wait for an official statement about cause of death before we decide who did it."

Rod sat down and drank some coffee.

"Hell of a note," he said, almost to himself. "Man says something nice about a woman, next thing you know he's a damned murder suspect."

"You're not a murder suspect, Rod," said the man sitting across from him.

"Hell of a note," said Rod.

"I seen her up there at the Fireside, myself," said his companion. "She brought me and the wife beer and burgers where we was sitting in a booth. I thought she was pretty, too, and nice, but that don't mean I'm a suspect. You neither. Drink your coffee and take it easy."

"Let's change the subject," said someone. "How about them Sox?"

Normally that would have been a topic worthy of argument, but I had chilled the room and voices didn't rise again until I was shutting the door behind me as Clay and I left.

"If you don't mind some friendly advice," said Clay as we drove away, "I think you should give up your plans to become a politician."

"Wise words. I'll imitate Udall. If nominated, I'll run to Mexico. If elected, I'll fight extradition."

"Smart. What's next on our agenda?"

"Let's drive by the Harbor View. The parking lot is out back. We can check and see if there's a yellow Mercedes convertible with California plates parked there."

"Why should we do that?"

"Because if Jack and Mickey are at the hotel, they aren't someplace else. Like at Ted Overhill's house, for instance. So if you feel like going there and parking behind his barn so nobody can see your truck, you can probably get some work done on the boat without risking your neck. I advise you to avoid power tools, so you'll be able to hear a car if one drives in, and have time to scat."

"I'm doing a lot of scatting lately, but I would like to get back to work on the boat. Another few weeks and she'll be ready to launch."

"You're ahead of schedule."

"Ted's got his arm back and works evenings after he gets home from landscaping. Two men get a lot more done than just one."

We circled the Harbor View once just to make sure no yellow convertibles were parked in front of the hotel. None was, so I drove into the parking lot where, lo! the Mercedes, looking a bit garish amid staid New England vehicles, was right where I had hoped it would be.

I drove out the back way to Fuller Street, where I pointed out Manny Fonseca's woodworking shop. "You might get on with Manny when you finish the schooner," I said. "He usually works alone, but if he sees what you can do, he might make an exception."

"This is the same Manny Fonseca who's coaching Zee how to shoot and wants her to try out for the Olympics?"

"The very same. He can't get over how she took to pistol shooting. He says she's a natural and is getting even better than he is even though she doesn't have his experience and doesn't approve of guns."

"I don't approve of them either, but when I was a kid out in Wichita, my dad made sure I knew how to shoot. Incidentally, while I was nosing around the house last night I found a box of shotgun shells but no shotgun."

"That's because John's guns are in my gun cabinet so none of the local thieves will sneak into his house and steal them while I'm not looking."

"You have local thieves?"

"We have all the perps you'll find anywhere else, in about the same population proportion. This may be Eden but it has rocks with snakes living under them."

"My, my," said Clay. "Does the Chamber of Commerce know about this?"

"I've never seen it advertised."

We drove to John Skye's farm and Clay got out of my truck.

I opened my window. "Do you want a shotgun to go with those shells? Would that make you feel better?"

He hesitated. "No . . . yes . . . maybe. Sure. You know what the NRA says about it being better to have your trusty six-gun by your side and not need it than to need it and not have it."

That phrase would probably be the NRA's principal contribution to the next edition of Bartlett's.

"Would you rather have a pistol?"

"No. Some gunslinging magazine I read a long time ago asked a bunch of shootists what weapon they'd choose if they could only have one. A shotgun won hands down. You can hunt big game or little birds, or you can shoot people with a fair chance of hitting them. They didn't have shotgun guards on stagecoaches for no reason, you know. Not many bad men liked the idea of going up against a double-barreled twelve-gauge. That's probably still true."

"Well, I have my father's old double-barreled Browning but you'll be getting a Remington pump that'll hold three shells. Massachusetts, in its wisdom, believes that limiting the size of the magazine makes civilization safer."

He waved a dismissive hand. "Three should be more than enough. I don't plan on shooting anybody. The gun will be just like a pacifier. It'll make me feel loved."

"As another sign of love, I'll follow you to Ted's place."

"No need, but okay."

He got into the Bronco and drove to Ted's barn, where he parked in back, out of sight.

I turned around and drove home. I didn't see any yellow convertibles of any make.

— 15 —

I fed Oliver Underfoot and Velcro, answered their questions about where I'd been and what I'd been doing, then got out my own Remington 12-gauge pump and a couple of boxes of shells and took the weapon and ammo to John Skye's house. No need, I thought, to insert one of John's weapons into the game we were playing; I'd use my own.

At John's house I put the gun and ammunition in Clay's bedroom closet, then drove to the Edgartown library, where, since it was March and not July, I found a convenient parking place on North Water Street. Bonzo was on my mind. I needed to help him, and the library was a good place to start.

I'm very fond of libraries because they're full of books and are run by people who are smart, who like their work, and who, unlike many public employees, welcome customers. Our family computer can produce all sorts of information, but a library has charm and warmth, two characteristics the computer lacks. Besides, I wanted information I couldn't get, or at least couldn't find, on the computer, being an antigeek with regard to both talent and temperament, to say nothing of my age. Already my ten-year-old son, Joshua, could run computer rings around me, and his little sister, Diana, was not far behind. Both of them, however, were in school that day, so to the library I had come.

Amelia Samson was at the desk. "What can I do for you, J.W.?" she asked.

"A year ago a woman named Nadine Gibson disappeared from Oak Bluffs. There was some newspaper coverage of the case. I'd like to see the local papers from that period."

"Oh," she said. "The radio says they've found her body. I remember the original stories. For a few days she was news, but then she wasn't anymore. I guess the police decided there wasn't any reason to pursue it further at the time. Now they will."

"Yes."

"It's not like that Brazilian man who disappeared. His roommate cleaned out his bank account and went back to Brazil. The police are still interested in the roommate even though they've never found the body of the missing man."

I nodded. It was a recent case, but since the United States had no extradition treaty with Brazil and since there was no body, the chances were that the crime, if there was one, would never be officially solved and the perp would live happily ever after.

"Anyway," said Amelia, "we have old copies of the *Gazette* and the *Times* on microfilm. Do you know how to use our machines?"

"I think I can figure them out."

I could and did. Sharing the front pages with reports of a March snowstorm were stories of the missing woman. They were brief since no crime had ever been proved and no body had ever turned up. Still, they contained information I'd forgotten, some part of which had been gained from local people who knew her. The *Gazette* reporter was wise enough to include her sources in her story.

Nadine Gibson was twenty-two years old, five seven, and about one hundred twenty pounds. She was considered pretty and personable, and was notable for her long, strawberry red hair. She had lived for a while in the Boston area, had attended Tufts University for a time, and had come to the island the summer before her disappearance, along with several thousand other young people about her age, looking for work. She'd first found a job waitressing in a restaurant where the tips were good and then, after the summer ended and the restaurant closed, had found a winter job bartending and waitressing in the Fireside, where she was a favorite of the mostly male customers who were the regulars there. Her boss liked her and said she was a good, dependable worker.

She had a boyfriend by then, a Harvard student who aspired to be the next Howard Roark and who was taking a year off from his studies to work as an apprentice in a Vineyard Haven architect's office. The two young people lived together in a year-round rental at the west end of the Camp Meeting Grounds, not far from Dukes County Avenue.

She and the boyfriend had a spat and broke up before she disappeared, and the boy had packed his bag and gone home to Newton to lick his wounds. When Nadine disappeared, naturally he was high up on the list of suspects but had a perfect alibi: his sympathetic mother, who was glad to have him free of the grasp of the redheaded bartender, had flown with him to Scottsdale for two weeks so his heart could mend while he visited Taliesin West and other notable architectural sites of interest between rounds of golf with Mom.

A woman neighbor in the Camp Meeting Grounds who was friendly with Nadine had noticed that after the snowstorm there were no footprints leading from the girl's house and, after a couple of days, had inquired at the Fireside and learned that she'd missed work for those days. Alarmed, the neighbor had contacted the police, and not much later, Nadine had officially become a missing person.

She'd last been seen leaving the Fireside after closing hours. She'd been in good spirits and was presumably planning on walking home through the narrow, winding Victorian streets of the Camp Meeting Grounds to her own little gingerbread cottage at the far end. It was her habit to do that, and no one gave it a thought.

And, at the time the stories were written, no one had seen her since.

The police had gotten her landlord to open the door of her house, wherein their most suspicious finding was what seemed to be most of her clothes and goods. No signs of foul play were seen.

The Oak Bluffs police had contacted the Newton police, who had gone to the boy's house and learned from his father that the boy had gone out west several days before and wouldn't be home for several more. The OBPD had then tracked down Nadine's family, using her employment forms as a guide, and learned that they lived in Rhode Island and thought their daughter was still on the island but, because she had an independent streak and didn't always keep them informed about her travels, couldn't guess where she might be now.

The police had gone up and down Circuit Avenue and through the Camp Meeting Grounds asking if anyone knew anything, but no one admitted to seeing the woman that night or had useful information. The owner and employees of the Fireside similarly knew nothing. The girl with the strawberry hair had walked into the March night and had disappeared.

Until now.

I sat back in my chair and thought about what I'd read. I wanted to see the police reports but didn't think I could get my hands on them since the case was now officially open and I didn't have a friend in the department who might be persuaded to slip them to me for a few minutes unofficially.

That left the reporters who had written the stories and who certainly had learned more than had appeared in print. The reporter for the *Gazette* was someone I knew pretty well, although not as well nowadays as I had before I'd met Zee. Susan Bancroft and I had been an item for a while long ago and, though a lot of water had flowed under the bridge since then and both of us were now married to other people, we were still friends.

I got up and walked out of the library. As I passed Amelia Samson, she asked, "Did you find what you were looking for?"

"Some of it. Thanks."

Too lazy to walk to the *Gazette* office, I drove there and parked on Summer Street just beyond Davis. Two parking spots right where I wanted them in a single day. It must be winter on Martha's Vineyard.

Susan was at her desk, which was piled with papers stacked around her computer. She stopped pecking at the keys when I appeared.

"We've got to stop meeting like this," I said. "People will start to talk. How can you find anything in this mess?"

"It may look like chaos to you, but everything is in perfect order. And who cares if people talk?"

"Not me," I said. "It might be good for my reputation, in fact. I'm becoming known as a hopeless, stay-at-home fuddy-duddy. The bartenders all over the island have forgotten my name."

"That's what you get for being married and having kids. It happened to me, too; it happens to us all. What brings you here to the inner sanctum of the fourth estate?"

"Information. You heard about finding that red-haired body up in Oak Bluffs?"

Her antennae went up immediately. "The presumed remains of the Gibson girl? I've heard. I've also heard that your friend Bonzo is a prime suspect. Do you know anything about that?"

"A little, but I want to know more."

She pointed at a chair piled with papers. "Put that stuff on the floor and sit down. You must think I know something you don't. I'll trade you what I have for what you've got, which is . . . what?"

I sat down. "I just came from the library, where I read last year's accounts of the search for the girl. I want to know what you know that didn't get into the stories."

"You're in luck. I've been going over that material myself as background for the story I'm writing this week. Before we get into that, though, what have you got for me?"

Ever the reporter looking for an edge on her rival writers. But I wanted her information, so I told her about the call from Bonzo's mother and about what had happened after that. As I talked, she scribbled notes the old-fashioned way. When I was done, she said, "You're pretty sure it was Nadine Gibson's hair in that bird's nest?"

"The lab will determine that, but I'd say it's a pretty sure thing. Not many people have hair like that."

"And you don't think your pal Bonzo had anything to do with her disappearance?"

"Not in a million years."

"Mrs. Capone probably had a high opinion of little Alphonse, too."

"A lot of people say that she did, but she was wrong; I'm right. Now it's your turn. When you were covering the disappearance last year, did you learn anything that didn't get into your stories?"

She dug under some papers and brought out a spiral notebook. She flipped it open and scanned a page or two. "These are my notes. I got a lot of stuff that didn't turn out to be relevant. You always get that, because you can't be sure until later what was important, so you collect the chaff with the wheat. What do you want to know? Or do you even know what you want to know?"

"Who was the neighbor who called the cops?"

"An elderly woman who'd gotten friendly with Nadine. If you think she's a suspect, think again. She's about eighty years old."

"Was she nosy? Did she see anything suspicious?"

"Not a thing. At least nothing she told me. Her house is full of books and she said she reads a lot. I believe her. She didn't strike me as the type with her face in the window keeping track of her neighbors, but she did notice that there seemed to be no one home at Nadine's house."

"Did you interview the landlord? What was his name? What was he like? What did he say when you talked with him?"

"You think he did the girl in? I doubt it. He's a guy in his sixties, the grandfatherly type, but not too old to give women the eye, even me; name's Gordon Brown, lives with his wife a couple of houses away from the one the Gibson girl and her boyfriend were renting. Been there for years. Member of the Camp Meeting Association, I think. Used to be a plumber."

"What's he look like?"

"Not Charles Atlas, if that's what you mean. Going bald, average height and weight, bit of a potbelly. You'd never look at him if you passed him on the street."

"Any criminal record?"

"Not that I know of. If the cops knew of one, it wasn't important enough for them to ask him more than a few questions: When did he last see the girl? Did he hear anything when she and the boy had their spat? That sort of thing."

"Did you talk with the boy?"

"No. He never came back to the island."

"Did you phone his parents?"

"Yes. I talked with his father. He told me his wife and son had gone out to Arizona shortly after the boy had come home and that they were still there."

"Did you believe him?"

"I talked with a guy on the OBPD who told me that they'd called Scottsdale and the story checked out. The boy and his mother really were there and had definitely been there since their arrival. No quick trips back to the island."

"What was the spat about?"

"Who knows? There was no one for me to ask. The boy and girl were both gone."

"People knew they'd had an argument and that he'd left the island. That means she talked about it to somebody. Who?"

She looked at her notes. "She mentioned it to the bartender and to some of the other help. The bartender asked if she planned to leave the island, too, and she said no."

"That must have made people wonder what happened to her."

"You'd think so," said Susan, "but young people can change their minds in a hurry, so nobody thought of foul play until later."

"She tell the bartender what the fight was about?"

"He said she told him they were just tired of each other."

"Do you think there was another man in her life?"

"She was twenty-two and beautiful, so it would be a surprise if there wasn't at least a wannabe beau or two."

"Do you have any names?"

"Yes. Do you want them?"

"Yes."

She gave me three names I'd never heard of and addresses to go with them.

"Are these guys still on the island?"

She shook her head. "I haven't the slightest idea. I interviewed them almost a year ago."

"Tell me about them."

She looked at her notes again. "Three guys in their twenties, two working in the construction business, putting up these mansions people are building everywhere. Both college grads who told me they were making more money as carpenters than they could as schoolteachers or bottom-level execs. I think they were probably right."

I thought so, too. When Joshua gets older I'm going to try to get him to learn how to be a plumber or an electrician while he's going to college. It always pays to have a trade, and on Martha's Vineyard it pays a lot. I'm not sure it's really a joke when people say there are more millionaire plumbers on the island than there are millionaire doctors.

"What about the other guy?" I asked.

"Oh," said Susan, "he's a deputy sheriff. You may remember him. A couple of years back he was a cop in New Bedford who shot a kid holding up a liquor store. The kid was unarmed and he was shot in the back. Cop said it was self-defense and he was cleared but resigned anyway because of the uproar. Came over here and now he works for the County of Dukes County. He was hot for Nadine and when they interviewed him, he said the feeling was mutual."

"I presume the cops talked with these guys."

"I didn't ask them, but I'd presume that, too."

"What did you think of the deputy when you talked with him?"

"I thought he looked like a straight Rock Hudson. My little heart went pitty-pat. If Nadine had the hots for him, I could understand why."

"Did he strike you as the murdering sort?"

"Ask the people in New Bedford."

"Did any of these guys have run-ins with the boy who went to Scottsdale?"

"If they did, they didn't tell me."

"You know anybody else I might talk to?" I asked.

"Well, you might sit there awhile and talk with me."

"Sorry," I said, rising. "You married another man and hurt my feelings. I'm still getting over it."

She laughed. "What a fraud you are. I don't know how Zee stands it. Get out of here."

I got.

— 16 —

At home I got out our phone book and looked up the names Susan had given me. Two of the three wooers were listed as living in the same places they'd been the year before. If nothing else, that meant that those two, at least, hadn't been spooked away by the attention they'd gotten from the police. I figured the young men were probably at work, but there was a good chance the landlord and the woman who'd called the cops were at home, so I drove to the Oak Bluffs Camp Meeting Grounds.

The Camp Meeting Grounds is owned by an association, so the colorful, privately owned houses all stand on leased land. It's a charming place of small parks, walkways, and narrow, winding streets built around a tabernacle that was originally only a large tent. The camp meeting area was established in 1835 during the Methodist revival when preachers expounded from stumps and believers came from the mainland to combine religious joys of the spirit with vacation joys of the flesh.

The tents that were the first habitations of the congregations were gradually replaced by prefabricated gingerbread cottages brought over from the mainland, and the large tent that served as a church was replaced by the wood and metal tabernacle that is still the center of the neighborhood and provides a stage for musical, religious, and other summer events. The Island Community Chorus officially opens the tabernacle season with a concert in early July and activities don't taper off again until September. Principal among these is Illumination Night, which takes place in mid-August when, following a community songfest in the tabernacle, thousands of Chinese lanterns are lit and hung from the porches of surrounding cottages to be ogled by mobs of admirers who parade past them.

The houses are mostly empty in the winter but are quick to fill in the summer. They're brightly painted, often in four different colors, the most famous and most often photographed of them being the Pink House on the corner of Butler Avenue and Jordan Crossing, which looks like it belongs in a fairy tale. The community is often studied by students of Victorian architecture because, though there were many such meeting grounds built up and down the East Coast at about the same time, none is so well preserved as the one in Oak Bluffs.

Gordon Brown lived out on Clinton, about as far from the tabernacle as you can get and still be in the Camp Meeting Grounds. At that end of the community the houses aren't painted as brightly as those closer in and are set a little farther apart. The house that Nadine and her beau had rented was not far from Brown's, and the lady who had notified the police lived only a bit farther on.

As was true everywhere else on the island, you could get a good deal on a winter rental in the meeting grounds as long as you didn't move in until after Labor Day and got out before Memorial Day, but Nadine and her companion had gotten themselves a nice little house in which to hunker down year-round. Their landlord's house was larger and well kept. Its cedar shingles were in good shape and its well-painted trim was deck gray, a popular Vineyard color from the times when most islanders also owned boats. There was an elderly van parked in the driveway. It bore the logo of a plumbing company.

I parked and saw a window curtain fall as I walked to the door. The man who answered my knock was much as Susan Bancroft had described him: sixtyish, of medium weight and height, losing his hair, bit of a belly pushing at his sweater.

"Gordon Brown? I'm J. W. Jackson."

He smiled, showing teeth that were too even and brilliant to be real. "Yes. What can I do for you, Mr. Jackson?"

"You've heard about the body they found . . ."

His smile was replaced by a frown. "Yes. Terrible thing. The Gibson girl, they say. She was renting a house of mine, you know." He waved an arm toward the house. "Nice girl. I'd hoped she'd just left the island, but I guess she didn't."

From inside the house came a woman's querulous voice, "Who is it, Gordon? What do they want? Don't buy anything!"

"My wife," he said apologetically. "She doesn't trust me to repel salesmen. Says I'll buy anything from anybody who comes to the door."

"I'm not selling anything," I said. "I'm investigating the Gibson case."

He turned his head and shouted, "It's just a man, Gertrude! He's not selling anything!"

"Don't let him fool you!" came Gertrude's voice. "It's not hard to do! I saw him coming up the walk. Looks like a salesman to me!"

Brown smiled without humor. "My wife doesn't leave her room much anymore, and she doesn't trust me out of her sight. Good thing I'm retired and can stay home most of the time."

"Is that your van outside?"

"Yep. Had my own company for years, but no longer. I should probably take that logo off and sell my tools, but I've just never got around to it."

"It's been a year, but can you remember whether Nadine Gibson changed her routine in any way just before she disappeared? Whether anyone was visiting her or whether she was staying away from home more than usual? It looks like someone took her or went with her to the place where they found her body."

"The old Ormstead place, I hear. That's not too far away."

"The Marshall Lea Foundation owns the land now. Not

many people go there. There are No Trespassing signs all around it. They found the body in the basement of the old farmhouse, under some fallen wreckage. She didn't get under that material by herself."

Brown pulled the door shut behind him and buttoned his sweater against the chill March air. "I don't want to upset my wife," he explained. "She didn't like those two young people living together without being married. You know what I mean? She's religious. She was glad when they broke up and she wasn't sad when the girl disappeared."

"What does she think about the body being found?"

"She wasn't surprised and she wasn't sad. The wages of sin, she said." He shivered.

I repeated my questions about the girl's last days, but he only shook his head. "I think that after the boyfriend left, some other young fellas may have come by, but I don't snoop and I wasn't keeping track. I'm not like Gertrude. Live and let live, I say."

"Nadine Gibson liked birds. Did you ever see her go off birding with someone?"

"She told me she went off with that weak-minded fellow that works at the Fireside. What's his name? Bonzo? I think they maybe went off together once or twice. She told me they'd gone looking for birds."

"You talked to her?"

He shrugged and then nodded. "Sure. Not regular or anything like that, but when we happened to meet or when she brought over the rent."

"She never mentioned going birding with anyone else?"

"No. No, she never did."

"Do you know the names of any of the young men who visited her after her boyfriend left?"

"No. No, I don't." He looked at his watch. "I'd better get back inside. Gertrude will be wondering where I am." He grinned a faint grin and his teeth gleamed. "Sorry I can't be more help." He backed into his house and shut the door.

I walked up the street, glad that I wasn't married to Gertrude.

The woman who had called the police was a widow named Loretta Aldrich. When she opened her door to my knock and got my name she, unlike Gordon Brown, waved me right in.

"Come in out of the cold. It gets into my bones and it doesn't want to come out." She shut the door behind me and waved me toward a rocking chair in front of a gas heater with fake logs aflame. "I wanted a fireplace but settled on this. Works just fine. Made in Sweden. You like some tea? I'm having a cup to warm my innards. I'm having a splash of rum in mine. How about you? Good. Sit right there and I'll be back." She disappeared through a door leading to the kitchen.

She was what, in my childhood, I would have called a skinny old lady. Her hair was white and tied in a frizzy bun at the back of her head, and she wore a comfortable-looking old housedress and floppy slippers. Her glasses were small and round and set about halfway down her nose. Since she had looked at me over the top of them I guessed they were for reading and that she had been reading the book now lying facedown on a small table beside a comfortable chair next to the one I was now seated in. I leaned over and twisted my head to read the title. *The Prince,* by Machiavelli. Was Loretta serving as advisor to the Oak Bluffs selectmen? It seemed possible, considering O.B.'s arcane politics, which were the subject of much head scratching and laughter in other towns

There were many other books in the room; in a bookcase, on top of the bookcase, on a shelf of knickknacks, on the coffee table in front of me, under the coffee table, and on a chair in the corner. I recognized one cover as belonging to *The Sibley Guide to Birds,* an excellent book, a copy of which I had at home but never read as studiously as I probably should. I had a lot of books like that—on mushrooms, trees, butterflies, fish, animals, and edible wild plants. I'd read some of all of them but not all of many of them, which accounted for the large gaps in my knowledge of the natural world.

Loretta Aldrich came back from her kitchen and put cups of tea on the coffee table. They smelled of rum. She sat down in her reading chair and looked at me with sharp blue eyes. I thought she must have driven men wild sixty years ago, and perhaps still did.

"Now, Mr. Jackson, what brings you this way?"

I told her, including my concern for Bonzo.

"Ah," she said. "You're afraid your friend Bonzo may be accused of a crime, eh? I presume you want to know if I saw anything last year that might prove useful in clearing him of suspicion."

"That's right. And whether you saw anything that might suggest who the real perpetrator is."

"The police interviewed me shortly after the girl disappeared," she said. "I didn't have any information of use to them then, and I don't have any more now."

She sipped her tea and so did I.

"If you added honey and lemon juice to this," I said, "you'd have my favorite cold medicine."

She nodded. "A very traditional remedy. If you don't actually cure anything, you feel better anyway." She grinned. "In the old days, most of the pink pills and potions for pale people contained good percentages of opium or alcohol. No wonder the ladies always felt better."

"Circumstances have changed since the police interviewed you last year," I said, guiding the conversation back to the subject. "Last year the police were just inquiring about a young woman who had gone missing. Now they're looking for a murderer."

"Are they? I hadn't heard that. I heard they found her body, but the news didn't mention a murderer."

"I think it will soon. Things that may not have seemed important last year may be important now."

She cocked her head to one side. "I haven't had much experience being a witness. What sort of things might those be?"

"Well," I said. "You may not have seen or heard anything at all. I've been told that you're not the snoopy type."

She gave an amused snort. "Is that what you were told? You mean I'm not one of those old hens who spend all their waking hours peering through their lace curtains spying on their neighbors?"

"Something like that."

"Goes to show what your informant knows! I may not be glued to the window like Gert Brown, but I'm as nosy as most people. This is my neighborhood and I like to know what's happening in it. I try not to miss too much. What interests you?"

"I'm told you were friendly with Nadine Gibson. What was your impression of her?"

"I liked her. Lovely girl. All that red hair! A very decent young lady, very independent. Not one to let someone else make decisions for her."

"What did you think of the young man she was living with?"

"Perfectly nice young fellow. I called him Adam the Architect. That was his name: Adam Andrews. I never understood what she saw in him, but that was her business, not mine. He was more interested in architecture than he was in her, as far as I could tell. When they broke up I thought it was for the best."

"What caused the split?"

"I think she was just ready for someone new. Adam always had his head in some book or in some plans he brought home from the office where he worked. She wanted a little more from a man. I knew just how she felt. He didn't put up much of an argument, he just left."

"Was there someone new? I've been told that several young men were trying to make time with her."

My hostess nodded. "After Adam left, I noticed some young fellows come by her house. Don't blame them a bit, either. More tea?"

"Why not?"

She left and came back with refills.

"Did you see or hear anything that looked or sounded like an argument between Nadine and any of these would-be boyfriends?"

"Nope, can't say that I did."

"Do you know any of their names?"

"Never knew any of their names. Just young guys driving pickups. They brought her home from somewhere or other a couple of times. The movies, maybe, or maybe a bar."

"They go inside the house?"

"I saw a pickup there one morning, if that's what you mean."

"That's what I mean." I nodded toward her *Sibley.* "Are you a birder?"

"Used to get out more. Now I mostly watch them from my front porch. I haven't added to my list for a long time."

"Did you hear where they found the girl's body?"

"I did. Up on the old Ormstead farm."

"Do you know the place? I know the girl went up there at least once to go bird-watching."

Her little white-haired head bobbed up and down. "Did she now? I used to go birding up there before the Marshall Lea Foundation bought it and put up all those damned No Trespassing signs they like so much." She waved in the general direction of Gordon Brown's house. "Went up there a lot with Gert Brown when she and Gordy first bought here. That was before she went queer in the head, of course. Back then, she was just a young woman who liked birds, so I showed her around, took her on bird counts and that sort of thing. Took Gordy, too." She sipped her tea and shook her head. "Now there's a sorry story. Some screw goes loose in her brain and she's hardly been out of the house since. Still strong as an ox, but loose in the flue. I visited her a few times, but pretty soon I quit that. She was too miserable to be with. Un-Christian of me, I'm sure, but I can only take so much whining and vitriol."

"He seems used to it."

When she again tipped her head to one side and looked at me, I was reminded somehow of a little white hen. "I guess he is. Tell you one thing, though. He misses having a real, healthy woman around. I see him watching women passing by in the summertime and he has that lonesome look on his face. I imagine he's remembering Gert when they were first married. She was a pretty woman then, big and full of life and energy." She drank some tea. "Those days are long past. Now she gives him grief just for going shopping. Too bad. Like the kids say these days, sometimes life sucks."

"Sometimes it does," I said. "Did Gordon try to spend time with Nadine? When he collected the rent, for instance? Or maybe when she was going to work or coming home?"

"Sure, he talked with her when he could. She was a beauty and he's a man. But if you're thinking Gordy Brown might have done her in, you're wrong. I've known him for over twenty years and he doesn't have a mean bone in his body. You're too young to remember Caspar Milquetoast, but that's Gordy. He makes Caspar look like Charles Atlas. As nice a man as you'd want to meet, too. Takes my trash to the dump when he goes, for instance. Good neighbor."

I drained my cup. "The police may be by to talk with you again. You might think back on Nadine and the people she associated with. Maybe you'll remember something you forgot the first time you talked with them."

When I left I had a glow in my belly from the tea. I was glad to have it because the air was getting colder and the wind seemed to be coming up, chilling things even more. I turned up my coat collar as I walked to the Land Cruiser.

I didn't know where two of the three young men Susan Bancroft had mentioned were working, but I thought I could find the deputy sheriff. I drove to Edgartown and parked by the County of Dukes County Jail, which also houses the sheriff's office.

The County of Dukes County is the legal name of the county that consists of Martha's Vineyard and Cuttyhunk. Normally, one would think, the title of the county would be, simply, Dukes County, and originally it was. But because an act passed by the legislature in 1695 gave the county name as Dukes County, the legal name thus became the County of Dukes County and continues to be that to this day. Thus the Vineyard sports the County of Dukes County Courthouse, the County of Dukes County Jail, the County of Dukes County Airport, and, officially, the County of Dukes County sheriff and sheriff's deputies. Tourists are sometimes perplexed by this nomenclature, but natives are mostly just amused.

The deputy I was looking for was named Reggie Wilcox and, according to Susan Bancroft, looked like Rock Hudson. Rock had been dead for quite a few years by then, but I thought that Susan was probably referring to his appearance when he'd been a movie star, before he'd been brought low by AIDS. I figured somebody in the sheriff's office would know where I could find Wilcox if he was on duty, so I went in.

At first glance the county jail looks like a nice private residence on Main Street, but if you look twice you can see the barred windows in front, and if you drive down Pine Street you'll see the caged area in back where the inmates sometimes loll in the summer sun, working on their tans. There have been a number of jail breaks over the years by huddled inmates yearning to breathe free, but none of them has ever come to much because there's really no place to run or hide once an escapee makes it out the window. Each has been quickly recaptured and returned to his cell to serve out an even longer term than before.

Reggie Wilcox, I learned, was at the County of Dukes County Courthouse, where he was part of the security at a trial that was taking place. I drove down to the courthouse, parked behind it in the lot, and, as I approached the door of the building, encountered Sergeant Tony D'Agostine of the Edgartown police coming out. Tony wore a look of mild disgust and I had no trouble guessing why.

"Have you given your testimony?"

"I have."

"Is His Honor letting the perps return to the streets faster than you can take them off?" I asked.

"As always," said Tony. "They're back at work before we are."

"Who are the innocent victims of false arrest this time?"

"Oh, just some of the local druggies. The judge doesn't want to ruin their future lives by finding them guilty of anything, so he's doing the usual: continuing the cases with the promise of dismissing them if the perps stay clean for such and such a time. The accused are wearing borrowed neckties and they've cut their hair so the judge won't have any reason to think they're scumbags."

"Is it Walking Sam?"

"It is."

Walking Sam was the name by which His Honor Judge Wigglesworth was known because of his propensity to let everyone go unless it was practically impossible not to do so. He was not the cops' favorite judge, but the perps and their lawyers loved him.

"Well, maybe the wheels of justice are just grinding a little slower than they're supposed to."

"With Walking Sam on the bench, the wheels aren't turning at all," said Tony. "What are you doing here?"

"Looking for Reggie Wilcox."

"I believe you'll find him holding up a wall inside."

"While I've got you at my disposal, what do you think of Reggie?"

Tony looked up and down the street, as though searching for a crime that might be taking place outside the courthouse. "What do you mean?"

"I mean he shot a boy over in New Bedford, then got this job as a deputy. What do you think of him?"

"The official verdict was that the shooting was justifiable. As far as I know, Wilcox has been doing his job over here. Cops don't have a lot of time to decide whether or not to shoot, as you know as well as anybody, and Wilcox said the boy made a gesture that looked like he was reaching for a weapon."

"He was shot in the back."

"Wilcox said the boy turned just as he fired."

Things can happen fast in dark alleys. I had an extra belly button and the bullet that had made it still resting near my spine from a shooting in Boston when I'd been on the PD there. There was never a time when I wasn't a little worried that it might move.

So I wasn't ready to put the Bad Cop flag on Reggie Wilcox, although I knew that there were a few police officers who used their badges and weapons to bully and brutalize other people.

"You spend any time with Reggie?" I asked.

"I've run into him down at the wharf a couple of times. Had a beer. That's about it. Seemed like an okay guy. Didn't talk about New Bedford. I think maybe he wants to forget what happened."

I thought that was understandable.

"Is he married?"

"I heard his wife left him after the shooting," said Tony. "He didn't say so, but that's the scuttle."

"Does he have a girlfriend?"

"I think he may be going out with a woman named Joyce Something-or-other. Lives up in Vineyard Haven."

"Did you hear that he and Nadine Gibson were hot for each other?"

Tony looked at me with more interest. "No. Were they?"

"So I hear. That's what I want to talk with him about."

"Well, like I say, you'll find him inside, holding up a wall so the ceiling won't fall on Walking Sam."

Tony went on out to the street. I entered the building and passed through security and into the courtroom.

There were several people in the room, including the judge, the lawyers, the accused and their friends and families, and people for whom watching trials, continuances, and dismissals was free entertainment. Reggie Wilcox, or Rock Hudson (Susan was right!), was standing near a side door trying to look interested in the mostly inaudible conversations between participants in the proceedings. He looked as tall as a tree.

After a time Walking Sam announced a short adjournment and I caught up with Reggie in a hallway. I gave him my name and told him I was investigating the Gibson case.

"You a detective?" he asked in a cool voice.

"No. I was a cop for a few years, but I got through a long time ago."

"Where?"

"Boston."

"Why'd you quit?"

"I killed a woman. I didn't like it, so I decided to let somebody else save the world. I came down here and went fishing."

His handsome lips flickered in what might have been a brief, bitter smile. "You kill her in the line of duty, or was it a private fight?"

"Line of duty. She shot me first, but I had a lot of time in the hospital to think things over, so when I got out I retired and moved here."

"How'd it happen?"

"Robbery. It was night. I chased her down an alley that dead-ended. She came running back out, blazing away. It wasn't until afterward that I found out she was a woman. Nineteen years old."

"Justifiable use of force?"

"That was the finding. I think it was right." I added, "My wife stuck around until she knew I was going to be okay, then left me."

Wilcox seemed to relax a bit. "I been in those shoes," he said. "But I like the work, so I got on down here." He studied me, then asked, "How long does it take you to get over killing somebody?"

"I don't know," I said. "It doesn't bother some people at all, but time helps the rest of us. It comes back to me sometimes but I try to keep it out of my mind. I'm married again and that makes it easier. I've got a family to think about."

"We have a few things in common," he said. "What can I tell you about Nadine Gibson? I hear they think she was killed."

"They found the body in an old cellar up in Oak Bluffs, under some lumber. She didn't put herself there; she had help. It could have been murder or it might have been an accident that scared whoever was with her enough to hide her there. I've talked with her landlord and with the lady who reported her missing. Now I'm talking with other people who were with her not long before she disappeared. Your name came up."

He nodded. "I talked with the OBPD after she disappeared. She and I seemed to hit it off even before her boyfriend took off, and afterward we went out a couple of times. I was just beginning to feel good about our prospects when she dropped out of sight. I was a cop long enough to know I'd be questioned. Hell, I'd have put the new boyfriend on the top of my list if I'd been in their shoes."

"But you couldn't tell them anything."

He shook his head. "She never said a word about going away. In fact, she and I were going to the movies the next week. That's what made the whole thing weird."

"Did you ever argue?"

"We didn't know each other long enough to argue."

"A couple of other guys were interested in her. You know anything about them? You ever meet them?"

He nodded. "Yeah, I know who they are. They hang out up at the Fireside, where she worked. I couldn't blame them for carrying the torch for her and we never got tangled up over her. We all kidded her and told her to get rid of her architect so the rest of us would have a chance. She didn't nix that idea completely. She and I had a couple of beers at the Newes, and she may have gone someplace with one of those other two guys, or maybe both of them, even before she finally sent the boyfriend on his way."

"It sounds like the split wasn't a sudden thing."

He shrugged. "People don't usually break up all at once. It happens because of the straw that breaks the camel's back. When my wife left me it wasn't only because of the shooting I was involved in. That was just the last thing that went wrong between us. If it hadn't been that, it would have been something else. Nadine and her boyfriend had been slipping apart for weeks. She worked a lot of nights and he worked days, so they didn't see much of each other. Maybe that had something to do with it."

My ex left me because years of worrying whether or not I'd come home in one piece had finally gotten to be too much for her. It was a common problem in police marriages, where the divorce rate is high. My getting shot was just that last straw that Wilcox had mentioned.

I said, "Are you telling me that three young guys scrambling for the affections of one pretty woman never got nose to nose over her?"

Not many people can look down into my eyes, but he could and did. "No," he said. "All I'm telling you is that I never did that. I avoid trouble. I had enough of that in New Bedford. Maybe the other two guys met under the oak tree at dawn, but I didn't."

"Not even for Nadine?"

"Not even for Nadine. I figured she was a big girl who could make up her own mind about who she wanted to be with."

"Did either of the other guys try to discourage you from hanging around?"

He stood up straight, and I had to tip my head farther back to meet his eyes. "Would you pick a fight with me?"

"I don't pick fights," I said.

"Neither did either of them," said Reggie.

"How about Nadine?" I asked. "How was she treated while all of this romancing was going on? A lot of domestics have the woman getting beat up."

His eyes hardened. "If anyone had tried that, I'd have visited the guy who did it."

"I thought you avoided trouble."

"I'd have made an exception." His voice was grim.

About then a voice announced that the judge was returning to the bench. Reggie Wilcox went toward the courtroom and I walked out of the courthouse into the chilly March air. I thought about what Reggie had said and was pleased that my ploy had worked: by telling him of my woes in Boston I'd gotten him to speak more freely than otherwise might have been the case. Still, I wondered if I should believe what he had told me.

What had Nadine looked like that last day of her life? Had she been beaten and bruised by someone's hard hands? Had that been what had killed her? Had one of the men in her life become so enraged by her refusal to be his alone that he'd struck her down? The motive for many a murder is jealousy.

I looked at my watch and saw that I should be going home if I wanted to be there when the children got out of school. Still, I had time for one exploratory journey. I drove back to the Harbor View Hotel's parking lot and saw that the yellow Mercedes convertible was gone.

— 18 —

I tried to imagine Jack and Mickey's mode of operation, and figured that since they were looking for Clay but didn't know where to find him, they'd be looking for information in places where they thought he might be known.

They knew enough about Clay's interests and habits to have found his friend in Sausalito and traced his toolbox to my place. That no doubt meant that, at the very least, they knew that he was fond of building wooden boats, and they probably guessed that, being single, he liked a beer now and then. Putting all that together, they'd most likely be spending time in the island's bars, boatyards, and building sites, pretending to be old friends of his and asking questions.

At least that's what I'd be doing in their place.

Or they might decide to question Zee or the kids to find out what they knew. That thought was an unpleasant one since the men wouldn't know for sure that they were being told the truth and might use force in an attempt to extract the information they wanted. They would not be the first to have irrational confidence in the power of torture, as evidenced by intelligence agencies both here and abroad. I felt a small red flame rise and flicker somewhere deep in my psyche, and drove home.

No yellow Mercedes was there ahead of me. I went into the house. No one was inside except Oliver Underfoot and Velcro. I listened to their arguments for food, agreed that they merited a snack, and gave them one. The flame within me sank and became an ember but still glowed sullenly in the darkest recess of my consciousness.

I had been wondering about the Mercedes. Why had Jack and Mickey driven it all the way from California when it would have been much faster to have flown to Boston and rented a car?

And why had they arrived in chilly New England wearing California clothes? Why hadn't they brought winter jackets? When I'd seen them they were wearing new coats, probably bought on the island.

It was a puzzler.

Where were they now?

They'd been on the island only a few days, so they couldn't know their way around too well, but they'd probably learned that Edgartown and Oak Bluffs were the only two wet towns, so that's where they'd be barhopping. They might also have heard about Gannon & Benjamin, properly famous builders and repairers of wooden boats, and may have made inquiries, assuming that Clay might be working there.

It would be hard for them to miss all the house construction that was going on all over the island, because mansionizing was the Vineyard's principal industry during the winter, so maybe they were also checking those projects. I had hinted that Clay might be living and working up-island, so maybe that's where they were focusing their efforts.

As I prepared supper, I wondered what Joe Begay would come up with. I had confidence that he'd find out something, at least. Maybe quite a lot.

Supper was red beans and rice with kielbasa, and I used a recipe we'd stolen from a visiting professor friend of John Skye who'd come up to visit him from the U of Kentucky. The Kentucky prof had gotten his recipe in New Orleans, a town famous for its food and one that I had never visited.

He'd served the dish at John's house when we were guests, and when Zee had fluttered her eyelashes at him, he passed over the recipe without hesitation. Another triumph for sex appeal.

The kids got home first and I fed them hot cocoa and cookies to keep them alive until supper. When Zee arrived and had switched into her civvies, I plied her with vodka on the rocks. We sat on the sofa in front of the stove and watched the flames dance while we told each other of our days.

"You've been a busy bee," said Zee.

"I'm not through yet," I said. "After supper I'm going up to the Fireside to see if I can find one or both of the two other guys who were interested in Nadine. I want to talk with them. Maybe they know something."

"You're a married man," she said in a faux-tart voice. "You're supposed to be past your days of hanging around in bars and hang around at home with me instead."

"Home is where the heart is," I said. "You can come, too, if you don't trust me alone."

"Someone has to stay with the children. Remember the children? We have two."

"Bring them along. They're old enough to learn what a bar looks like. They can have soft drinks if you think they're too young for beer."

"You're a danger to society, McGee. How about another wee dram?"

I poured her another Luksusowa and stirred the beans. They smelled delish, as always, and tasted just as good when we ate them a half hour later. Vanilla ice cream was dessert. The little people had theirs with chocolate sauce and the big people had theirs with blackberry liqueur. Simple pleasures are the best. Since I was the cook, Zee was the dishwasher, in accordance with our traditional division of labor. While she was washing the plates and stacking them in the drainer, I kissed her, suggested that she lock the doors while I was gone, and drove to Oak Bluffs.

Bonzo was on duty at the Fireside and the place was about half full of regulars, mostly young guys but with a mixture of middle-aged men. There were even a few women: girlfriends and wives and wannabes. The place smelled of spilled beer and illegal cigarettes, both hand rolled and packaged. Since the sixties, the management of the Fireside had always been lax in its enforcement of Massachusetts's laws against smoking in public places, as long as the sinners were discreet, and the Oak Bluffs police were happy to ignore the transgressors as long as no one complained. Like all police, they had better things to do.

Bonzo gave me his happy child's smile. "Hey, J.W., good to see you! Whatcha doin' here? You don't come so much at night anymore."

I had been married more than ten years but to Bonzo time was always new. He was just as surprised now as he'd been when I first stopped being a steady customer a decade earlier.

"I'm a married man, Bonzo." I found an empty booth, sat down, and ordered a Sam Adams. When Bonzo brought it, I said, "I'm looking for a couple of young guys. You may know them. Jimmy Calhoun and Al Verdi."

He beamed. "Yeah, sure I know them. They come in here almost every night for beer and burgers. I guess they don't like to cook like you do. Lookie. See that booth? That's them eating together. They're pals."

I looked across the room at the two young men. They were chewing hamburgers and chatting. I'd seen them both before but had never known their names. There are fifteen thousand year-round people on Martha's Vineyard and I don't know almost all of them.

"They live together or just eat together?"

Bonzo thought that hard one over, then nodded as though to himself and said, "They just eat, I guess. Al said once he lives in a house in the winter and a tent in the summer, but Jimmy's got a year-round house someplace. I think they're working on the same job this winter. You can ask 'em."

Al wasn't the only islander who summered in a tent. The secret was to have it out of sight of people who were afraid such primitive accommodations would lower their property values. Many a native family once earned a good portion of their yearly income by renting their house in July and August and camping out until fall.

"I heard that they both liked Nadine," I said. "Do you know anything about that?"

He immediately became sad and rubbed nervous hands on the bar towel he had across his shoulder. "Yeah, I remember that. They liked to talk with her all the time. She was beautiful, so a lot of people liked to do that. She talked back, too. She was nice, you know. She talked and smiled at me and everybody else."

"Did either of them ever get mad? At each other or at her?"

He thought hard and shook his head. "Gee, I don't think so. How could you get mad at Nadine? Nobody could get mad at Nadine."

Saint Nadine. Actually, Bonzo was probably the saint.

"I mean did Al and Jimmy ever get mad at each other? You know, the way men do sometimes when they both like the same woman."

Another head shake. "I never seen it. Not ever. They're pals." He leaned closer to me. His voice was conspiratorial and touched with fright. "I hear that they found Nadine dead up there on that Marshall Lea land where we was the other day. They say that was her hair in my bird nest and that Dom Agganis may be wanting to talk with me some more about her and me going up there last year. My mom is scared and I don't feel too good myself. I don't like people thinking I'd do something bad to Nadine. You don't think I would, do you, J.W.?"

"No. I know you wouldn't, Bonzo. Dom Agganis has to

talk with everybody who knew Nadine. I already told him that you've never hurt anybody in your life."

"Thanks, J.W. I'm glad you think that, because it's true. I never would hurt Nadine or anybody else. Not ever." He patted my arm with his thin hand and went back to work, wiping tables, returning glasses and bottles to the bar, and serving customers.

I drank some of my beer and kept an eye on Jimmy Calhoun and Al Verdi. When they finished their burgers and were having dessert beers, I got up and went over to their booth.

I gave them my name and asked if I could talk with them. They couldn't see why not and made room for me in the booth.

"What can we do for you?" asked Calhoun. "You have a building project in mind?"

"If you do," said Verdi, "we won't be able to get at it for a while because we're working on a job already and we won't be done with it until May or so."

It was a familiar tale. People with small construction jobs such as a porch roof to be repaired or a garage to be built had a hard time finding anybody to do the work because all of the carpenters were busy building mansions.

"No," I said, "I'm not here about a job. I want to talk with you about Nadine Gibson."

They instantly became cautious.

"They say they found her body," said Verdi, twirling his beer bottle. "What's that got to do with us?"

"I'm talking with everybody who might have been close to her," I said. "I'm trying to find out what happened. A year ago people figured she probably just left the island, but now we know she didn't."

Calhoun glanced at Verdi, then back at me. His eyelids had lowered. "You a cop of some kind?"

"This is preliminary and off the record," I said, dodging the question but putting on the cop face I'd learned to wear in Boston. "The investigation will get official when the state police come to talk with you. I've talked with Reggie Wilcox already, and with Nadine's landlord and the woman who first noticed Nadine was missing and called the cops. Now I'm talking to you because you were two of the people who were interested in Nadine and you may know something that will help find her murderer."

Calhoun sipped his beer. "Murderer? Are you saying she was murdered?"

"It's not official yet, but that's how it looks. You don't seem surprised."

He paled. "What's that supposed to mean?"

I looked at him. "It means you don't seem surprised."

"Why should I be?" he asked in a low, angry voice. "They find a body, what's the first thing you think of? That it's either an accident or a murder."

"I don't like this," said Verdi. "Are you here because we're suspects? Is that why you're here?" He looked at Calhoun, then back at me. "We don't know anything about what happened to her."

"You both went out with her, didn't you?"

"So?"

"So how did the dates go? She argued with Adam Andrews, the guy she'd been living with, and threw him out. Did she argue with you, too?"

"Not with me," said Verdi. "Hell, I was only out with her a couple of times."

"You get inside her house? Into her bed?"

"None of your business!"

"The police will ask you the same thing."

He rubbed his mouth with the back of his hand. "Okay, so I spent a night with her once. Two, three days after the boyfriend left. So what? She was a nice girl."

I looked at Calhoun. "Did you know about this?"

I don't know if he heard me but he was staring at Verdi with an expression that gave me my answer. I raised my voice.

"How about you, Jimmy? You dated her. Did you make it with her, too?"

He glared. "What are you, anyhow? One of those jerks who gets his kicks talking about sex?"

"I don't make it a habit," I said, keeping my voice deliberately low now. "I'm trying to find out what might have happened to her. You two are supposedly pals, but if you were both bedding the same girl, it's not hard to imagine you getting mad about it, either with her or with each other. Maybe mad enough to get violent."

They exchanged looks, then shook their heads.

"That never, ever happened," said Calhoun. "She was as nice a woman as you'd ever want to meet. Maybe she liked more than one guy at a time, but she never gave me any reason to be mad at her."

"You never made it to her bed."

"I don't make it to a lot of beds, and I was never mad at her."

"Neither was I," said Verdi. "She was beautiful and she was sexy but she was sweet, too."

"Did she ever say anything about anyone who was giving her grief?"

They both thought, then Calhoun shook his head. "No, not really."

"And you two never tangled over her?"

"No. Never."

Roland and Oliver.

I sat back and drank the last of my beer. "Did you ever see her with anybody else? Besides Reggie Wilcox, that is."

"A lot of people liked Nadine."

"Anybody you can name?"

Calhoun waved an arm in a gesture that took in every customer in the room. "Take your choice," he said.

"Not everybody loved her," I said. "Somebody killed her."

Calhoun looked at Verdi. "Now that I know Al got into the bed I was after, maybe I'll kill him."

"You're scaring me," said Verdi, looking at his empty bottle. "Tell you what. I'll buy you a beer if you spare my life."

"Oh, all right," said Calhoun. "That should make us square."

I thanked them for their time and went home.

The next morning I drove to John Skye's farm and found Clay putting breakfast dishes in the dishwasher. We don't have a dishwasher at our house, though I'm not sure why since they seem handy things to have. Maybe the reason is the same one that accounts for me driving a rusty forty-year-old truck: I'm too cheap to buy anything I don't really need. As long as my old Toyota Land Cruiser keeps passing inspection and running, I'll probably keep driving it. Why not? If we need a fancier vehicle—if we're ever invited to a presidential ball, for instance—we'll use Zee's little red Jeep, Miss Scarlet.

"Did you find the shotgun?" I asked.

"I did. I loaded it with buckshot."

"Wyatt Earp always loaded buckshot."

"I'm not Wyatt Earp, but I thought buckshot was appropriate under the circumstances."

I told him about my musings concerning Jack and Mickey's car and clothing, and wondered what he made of them.

"All I can guess," he said, "is that they left California when the weather was warm and drove cross-country trying to catch up with me."

"If they knew where you were, why didn't they fly, then rent a car?"

"Maybe they didn't know where I was when they left. Maybe they drove to Palm Springs first, then went on from there one step at a time, following those fake clues I left on my way here."

That made as much sense as anything. But if that was what had happened, when and how had they learned from Clay's friend in Sausalito that he'd shipped Clay's tools to the Vineyard? If they'd gotten that information before they came east, they'd have known that Clay's false trail was false and would have flown directly to Boston and then rented a car. But they hadn't done that; they'd driven east in a convertible and summer clothes.

"Ergo, what?" asked Clay, when I put this issue before him.

"Ergo, maybe they have someone else working with them. A pal who stayed behind and caught up with your Sausalito friend after Jack and Mickey were already headed east. Their West Coast guy gave them the information about the tools, and since Jack and Mickey were already halfway here, they just kept coming."

"That would explain why they didn't stop in Arkansas," said Clay. "Lewis sent Jack and Mickey east and had somebody else on the coast check out my friends there."

He shut the dishwasher door. The machine was far from full and he made no move to add soap since, like most dishwashers, this one served most of the time as a storage space for dirty dishes. When it finally was full, it would be turned on to do its duty. At my house we washed up after every meal and stacked the clean dishes to dry in a rack by the sink.

"I wonder where Mark is," said Clay. "The money I left in the locker is his, but he hasn't contacted me about the key. Lewis seems to want the money more than Mark does, so why did he give it to me to take to Mark in the first place?"

"Maybe Mark is dead," I said. "He was in a dangerous profession."

Clay frowned. "It's possible, but I doubt it. Mark was a careful guy, and he always treated people fair and square so I never heard of anybody who was mad at him. Whoever tried to get that money I was carrying is more the double-dealing type."

"Lewis Farquahar?"

He nodded. "That would be my guess, although I can't be sure. I only met him a few times, but my gut told me I didn't want to work for him. Of course, Jack and Mickey could be working for somebody else entirely by now. It's a byzantine business and there are a lot of people who'd like to get their hands on three or four million dollars."

"But you think it's probably Lewis and that he probably figures that you have money he wants to retrieve."

"It belongs to Mark, if it belongs to anybody."

"If Mark is dead, it doesn't belong to anybody. Was he married? Did he have children or kinfolk?"

"I never heard about them."

"Have you tried to contact Mark since you got here?"

He nodded. "The problem is making contact without revealing my position, but I've given it a shot. I know a woman in Vancouver. She's an old friend, and she's smart. I sent her money and had her buy a cell phone, then go to one of those online cafés and send an e-mail to Mark telling him I wanted to get in touch with him and that he'd get a phone call in Palm Springs at a certain time. Then I had her make the call for me on the cell phone. But all she got was the same answering machine I got, so she hung up. I haven't tried contacting him since."

"Did you tell the woman where you're living?"

He shook his head, smiling a small, ironic smile. "No. She probably looked at the postmark on the letter I sent her, and if she did she knows it was mailed from the Vineyard, but she doesn't know more than that. She's a good friend."

He'd had a lot of women in his life and not all of them had ended up friends. I hoped he was right about this one. I remembered the book Loretta Aldrich had been reading and thought that Machiavelli would have advised Clay to be less trusting. I saw no point in mentioning that cynical diplomat's views on faith and, instead, told Clay of my guesses concerning Jack and Mickey's search pattern.

"Well," said Clay, "they can certainly find people who know

I used to be here on the island, but there aren't many who can swear I still am, and you're the only one who knows where I'm living, so I don't expect to have to use your shotgun."

"How do you feel about working on the schooner? I told Zee and the kids to tell the truth about what they know if anybody asks."

"I'd go wacky if I wasn't working. I take roundabout routes to get there and I don't go to the barn until I'm sure nobody's on my tail. I do the same thing coming home to this house. I park behind the barn at Ted's and I try to avoid using power tools so I'll hear anybody driving into Ted's yard. If Jack and Mickey ever show up, I should hear them in time to hide in the loft or cut and run through the back woods. I feel like some kind of character in a B movie."

"The hero, I hope. The heroes in B movies always survive and get the girl."

"That's my plan: to be a star." He slapped me on the back and got his coat. "Speaking of work, it's time I got to mine. You can follow me if you want to, just to make sure I get there."

I did that and saw no sign of anyone showing the slightest interest in Clay's blue Bronco as it turned down Ted Overhill's driveway. I drove on into Edgartown wondering just how big a gang was after the suitcases Clay had carried to San Diego and whether Jack and Mickey were just the tip of the iceberg. I parked in front of the police station on Pease's Point Way. To get into the station these days, thanks to Homeland Security policies, you have to punch a button beside the door and have someone at the desk admit you. The someone that day was Kit Goulart, the 250-pound wife of a similar-sized husband. When the two of them walked hand in hand, as they often did when she was in her civvies, they never failed to remind me of a team of draft horses.

"What brings you to this citadel of law and order?" she asked.

"I'm trying to catch up with Tony D'Agostine."

"Well, you won't find him here. He's off duty today. Try his house."

"Can I use your phone instead?"

"Since it's you."

I phoned the house and Tony was actually there. I asked him if he knew the last name of the woman Reggie Wilcox was seeing. "You called her Joyce Something-or-other, but I don't think that's in the book."

"Smithwick, I think," he said. "Joyce Smithwick. Or something like that. She lives out on West Chop someplace. Works in a jewelry store on Main Street. My wife likes the store. Wait a minute." He was back in less than that. "Yeah, that's right. Rita says it's Smithwick. There can't be too many Smithwicks in Vineyard Haven." He gave me the name of the jewelry store, in case I couldn't find her house.

I thanked him, hung up, thanked Kit for the phone, and asked if I could now borrow her phone book. She said yes and in it I found a lone Smithwick telephone number and an address. I thanked Kit again and left. Outside, the sun was trying to break through a high, gray overcast as March was deciding whether to be warm or cold that day. Someone once told me that the weather was always perfect in San Diego, where Clay's suitcases were parked, but the same could not be said for New England. I drove to Vineyard Haven.

Vineyard Haven is the only town on Martha's Vineyard where you can still buy most of the things you need. Oak Bluffs still has a couple of practical stores, but Vineyard Haven has more. The jewelry store where Joyce Smithwick worked, however, was not one of them.

I actually found a parking place on Main Street, a difficult thing to do in Vineyard Haven even in the wintertime, and went into the store, past windows full of gold and wampum bracelets and earrings. Inside was more of the same. A young woman was the only clerk and I was the only customer. She was tall and slender and was decorated with mostly silver jewelry, which she wore well. She gave me a nice smile.

"May I help you?"

"I'm looking for Joyce Smithwick."

"That's me."

I couldn't fault Reggie Wilcox's visual taste in women. She was a beauty. I told her my name and said I was talking to people who might know something about Nadine Gibson, the girl whose body had recently been found in Oak Bluffs.

"Oh," she said, and her smile disappeared. "I heard about that on the radio. But I don't think I can help you because I never knew her."

"Actually, I want to talk with you because you've been dating a man who did know her. Reggie Wilcox."

"Reggie?" Her eyes widened. "Did he know that girl? He never mentioned it."

"Have you seen him since they found her body?"

She shook her head. "No. I haven't seen him since last weekend. Did he really know that woman?"

"They dated a few times, apparently. I talked with him yesterday and I'm interested in your impressions of him."

"I don't know what you mean. What impressions? Why are you asking me about my impressions?"

I raised a hand in what I hoped was a calming gesture. "There's going to be an official investigation about the woman's death because it was probably either a murder or an accident that someone tried to cover up. Everybody who knew her, especially during the last days of her life, is being interviewed. The hope is that someone can help the police figure out what happened and who, if anyone, is responsible."

"Reggie didn't kill anyone!"

Reggie apparently hadn't told her about his life as a policeman in New Bedford. I was tempted to mention it, but didn't. I'd leave that to Reggie himself, or to someone else.

"How long have you been dating?"

Her face had become unhappy. "About six months. Since last fall."

"What sort of person do you take him to be?"

Her chin lifted slightly. "I don't know what you mean. He's very nice, very thoughtful."

"Who decides where you go and what you do?"

"Are you trying to find out who's the boss? Well, neither of us is. We decide things together. If one of us really wants to do something, the other one agrees. We don't fight about anything."

I thought but didn't say there'd be time enough for that later, if their relationship continued. Was I becoming a cynic? Should I write *The Return of the Prince*?

"So he doesn't boss you around?"

"No. He told me he was married before and he didn't want to make any of the mistakes he'd made in the past."

"Did you take that to mean that he'd tried to boss his first wife around?"

"No. I think he meant he wanted to be different in a lot of ways. He's very gentle and that's always a surprise to me because he's so big and strong. It would be easy for him to use power to get his way, but he never does."

I remembered how he'd looked down at me. He was at least four inches taller than I am and about fifty pounds heavier. And he'd looked very fit in his deputy sheriff's uniform.

"Women must find him attractive," I said.

Her face became happier. "Who could blame them? Not me. But I'm the one who's dating him. The others are just looking and wishing."

"Does he ever lose his temper?"

"Never."

"Does he ever hold you too tightly?"

"No! What sort of question is that?"

"You mentioned his strength."

"And I told you that he never uses it!"

I thought I'd learned whatever Joyce Smithwick could tell me.

"The police may come by to ask you similar questions to the ones I've asked," I said. "Meanwhile, I think Reggie is fortunate to have met you. Thanks for your help."

I went out and noticed that the sun had won the battle with the clouds. The day was warming and there was a faint promise of spring in the air. But nature is always indifferent to the woes and joys of men. The sun may shine on murder and lovers may reap the whirlwind.

— 20 —

I had talked with everyone I could think of and I hadn't learned much other than that Nadine Gibson had been beautiful and nice and liked men as much as they liked her. Her flaming hair had been a wonder, and she had smiled and kidded with everyone in the Fireside. Everybody liked her. She was young and vibrant and independent.

And now she was dead, dead, dead.

Since I was already in Vineyard Haven, I stopped at the state police offices on my way home, to get the latest news about her. Officer Olive Otero was at the desk. There was a pile of papers near her elbow and an open file cabinet behind her. Her eyes were going from her computer screen to a piece of paper in front of her and back again.

"One of these reports is wrong," she said as I sat down. "The problem is, I don't know which one."

"Information overload," I said. "The curse of the electronic age. Back when there was less to know we didn't get as confused."

"The theory that confidence is a sign of ignorance. I've heard of it." She pushed her chair back from the desk as though to put some psychological distance between her and it. "What brings you here? Let me guess. You want to know if the ME has found a cause of death. Am I right or do I owe you a beer?"

"No beer for me this time."

She leaned forward and glanced at a sheet of paper she took from the pile. "Blunt trauma to the head," she said.

"Homicide by person or persons unknown. Probably with a piece of pipe or a tire iron or some such thing."

"Definitely not an accident, then."

She shrugged. "Not according to the ME. There were multiple blows and signs of defensive efforts on the part of the victim. A broken arm and broken fingers."

"Any leads? Did you get any evidence from her house after she went missing?"

"You mean a diary naming some stalker who had been threatening her? No, nothing handy like that. The most suspicious thing we found was her clothing. There was no sign that she'd packed anything for a trip. Aside from that, we didn't have any real evidence that a crime had been committed, so we didn't take her stuff and keep it in storage. The landlord collected it and he probably still has it in his attic or someplace if he hasn't sent it to her family. If he still has it, we'll take a closer look at it in case we missed something the first time."

"Was the body clothed?"

"She was fully dressed and wearing a green loden coat and she was wrapped in a sheet. No sign of attempted rape. We'll see if anybody at the Fireside remembers what she was wearing when she left work that night. If the clothes are the same, we can be pretty sure that she was killed that night, maybe before she even got home."

"Can you trace the sheet?"

"I doubt it, but we'll try."

"What kind of a night was it? March can be warm or cold."

"We'll check the records for that night, but my recollection is that it was cold for most of that month. I know there were about six inches of snow on the ground when we went to her house, and that it didn't melt for a long time. That might explain why she was buried under those boards."

"Ground too frozen to dig a grave?"

"That's the idea."

"If you're right about that, it probably means the killer knew about the cellar when he killed her, and put her there because he couldn't think of a better place."

Olive nodded, and her voice was wry. "I never heard of that old farm until this happened, but now it seems almost like I'm the only one who hadn't. If you listen to talk around town, you'd think every birder on this end of the island used to go up there before the Marshall Lea outfit closed it off. And some of them, like your pal Bonzo, snuck in after that. There must be more to looking at birds than I ever guessed."

"Hamlet would probably agree. Birders are a passionate bunch. Maybe it would spice up your life if you became one. All you need is field glasses and a bird book."

"My life is spicy enough already. We'll be talking with birders. Maybe one of them saw something."

"I doubt if there were many birders wandering around Oak Bluffs in the middle of the night when Nadine left the Fireside."

"We don't need many," said Olive. "We just need one."

"I've been talking with some of the people who knew her or wanted to," I said. "Do you want to know what they told me?"

Olive frowned. "You just can't keep your nose out of our business, can you?"

"I don't like the idea of Bonzo being in your sights."

"Everybody is in our sights right now. Him, too. All right, tell me what you have."

I did that and when I was through Olive said, "That's not much."

"No, but it's all I have so far."

"So far? Are you planning to do more? Why don't you go home and leave this investigation to us?"

"When you decide to take Bonzo off your list, I'll go home."

"We can't do that, and you know it."

"I do, so I'll keep going. I won't interfere with your investigation, and if I learn anything I'll let you know."

Olive placed her strong hands flat on her desk. "Don't get under our feet, J.W."

"I'll try not to."

"Don't try. Succeed."

I left and drove to Circuit Avenue. The Fireside had just opened for the day, and I went in. The bartender was putting beer bottles in the cooler behind the bar, and I caught a glimpse of Bonzo going down into the cellar, where the beer and booze were stored. I was the day's first customer. I took a stool and ordered a Sam Adams and a hamburger, and the bartender passed the food order back to the kitchen through the service window behind him.

"I just learned that Nadine Gibson was murdered," I said. "Were you on duty the night she left here that last time?"

He paused in his work. "Murdered? Are you sure? Jesus! Well, I can't say I'm too surprised, because that's seemed possible ever since they found the body. Still . . ."

He shook his head and I waited for him to tell me that you read about these things but you never expect them to happen to people you know.

"You read about these things," he said after a moment, "but you never expect them to happen to people you know."

"Isn't that the truth," I said. "Were you here that last night?"

He shook his head again. "No. Clancy O'Brien was on. He's talked about it a lot since they found Nadine's body. People treat him like he's an expert on the subject and he's beginning to think he is. You want to see Clancy, you come back this evening. He'll be here about six."

"Do you have his address?"

"Sure." He looked at a tattered piece of paper tacked to the wall behind the bar, and read an address and a phone number to me, adding, "He worked last night, but he's probably up by now."

"One more thing," I said. "I ran into a couple of friends of Clay Stockton. Have they come by looking for him?"

"Yeah, they did," he said. "Just a couple nights ago. I told them he hadn't been in for a while. They wondered if I knew where he lived or was working but I couldn't help them out."

Clancy lived in Vineyard Haven, wouldn't you know? So when I finished my beer and sandwich, and had a brief chat with an uncharacteristically somber Bonzo after he brought a case of beer up from the cellar, I drove there for the second time that day. I was glad that the owner of the Fireside kept Bonzo on year-round. It was about as demanding a job as Bonzo could handle and it brought in some money to supplement his mother's income from teaching. She and her eternal child were all the family either of them would ever have.

Clancy O'Brien lived in an apartment in the basement of a house near the Stone Church on William Street, a one-way street that stops at Woodland, skips a block, then starts up again on Greenwood as North William Street. I've often wondered why it skipped that block, but have never been enlightened.

Clancy came to the door chewing on a grilled cheese sandwich—lunch for the single male. When he heard that I wanted to talk with him about Nadine Gibson, he waved me right in.

"Want a beer? I'm having the first of the day."

"No thanks. I just had one at the Fireside. They said you were working the bar the night Nadine disappeared and told me where I could find you."

We sat at his kitchen table and he talked around bites of food and swallows of Rolling Rock. He didn't actually have much in the way of information, but he spread what he had over quite a bit of time. The usual crowd had been there, and when the place closed, several of the guys had invited Nadine to go home with them as they always did and she'd laughed and said no as she always did and the guys had laughed and left and a little later Nadine had said good night and left, too.

When he was through I said, "Was Bonzo still there with you?"

"Yeah. Him and me. We always stay and clean things up a little more, just to make sure we're ready for the next day."

"Did you leave together?"

"Yeah, like always. I drove him home, like I do sometimes. It's pretty much on my way."

"When Nadine left, did you happen to notice if anybody was hanging around waiting for her?"

"No. Could have been, though, because I wasn't watching. I just let her out and locked the door so nobody would come in looking for a nightcap. That was the last time I ever saw her. It's a weird feeling. You hear about these things but you never think it'll happen to somebody you know. You know what I mean?"

"I sure do. Do you remember what she was wearing that night? Do you remember her coat? Was she wearing a hat?"

"Nobody ever asked me that before," he confessed with a frown. But then he beamed when he suddenly realized that he knew the answers. "You know why I remember the coat? Because it was a new one she'd just got. Made in Germany, I think she said. Sort of a green color. Looked good with all that red hair."

"A loden coat?"

"Yeah, I think that's what she called it. Something like that, anyway."

"What sort of night was it? It was a cold month, mostly, as I remember."

He was back on familiar ground now, answering a question he'd been asked before. "It was chilly, but what I remember most is the moonlight. It was almost a full moon and

everything had that sort of silvery look to it. You know what
I mean? It was chilly but it was a bright night with a lot of
stars. I almost didn't need to turn on my headlights to drive
home."

"I thought there was snow on the ground."

He shook his head. "That didn't come until the next day.
There was a ring around the moon the night she left the bar.
It was bright, but there was a ring around it, and the next
day the storm came. March weather. You never know what to
expect."

"Did Nadine ever mention any problems she was having
with anyone? Anybody who was giving her grief? A would-be
boyfriend, for example. A jealous woman. Somebody who
thought she owed something and wasn't paying. Anybody
like that?"

He gave me a confidential look. "You know, I've thought
back a lot about that. Her and me had a lot of little talks and
made jokes and like that, but you know what? She never
mentioned anything."

"She broke up with a boyfriend. Did she mention that?"

"Sure, but she never said he was threatening her or anything like that. She just said they'd grown apart. And I guess
they had, because the next thing I knew was that he'd gone
back to America and she was living alone."

"At least three customers of yours were dating her. Did she
ever talk about any of them? Were any of them giving her a
hard time or fighting over her?"

He shook his head. "No. You'd think that at least one of
the guys would get possessive or jealous, but she never let
that happen. She was an independent girl who made up her
own mind about who she dated, and she never let anybody
get the idea that they could boss her around." He thought
back. "I liked her for that. All the regulars did."

"Somebody didn't."

His brows drew together. "I know. I'd like to get my
hands on that guy."

"It'll be harder to find the killer now than it would have been a year ago," I said. "If there's still evidence, it won't be fresh. But the police won't stop looking, because murder cases are never closed until they're solved."

"Good!"

I thanked him for his time and left. I saw no point in telling him how many murder cases were never solved. There's a popular slogan that crime doesn't pay, but conviction rates in homicide cases suggest otherwise. When the Shadow noted that the weed of crime bears bitter fruit, he didn't add that often the victims were the only ones who had to eat it.

I went back to Oak Bluffs and drove through the winding streets of the Camp Meeting Grounds trying to guess what route Nadine had taken on her last walk home. Was she followed through the moonlight? Did another shadow overtake her shadow in the silver night and strike her down before she could cry out?

Or did she get home only to encounter a waiting killer? And if so, did she wrongly deem him friend, or recognize him instantly as foe?

I drove around Butler Avenue, went right on Victorian Park, fetched Clinton, and passed the houses of Loretta Aldrich and Gordon Brown and the now empty house where Nadine had lived. Brown's old van, his business logo still painted on the side, stood in his driveway. He, like me, apparently didn't mind driving an old truck.

I pulled out onto Dukes County Avenue, thence to Wing and Old County, and finally to the Edgartown–Vineyard Haven road, which I followed to the side road that led to Ted Overhill's driveway. There, I took a left and drove to Ted's house. When I turned off my engine I heard no sound. It was a silence that felt heavy. I got out and, feeling spooky, walked into the barn, unsure of what I'd find.

— 21 —

At first I found nothing. The building seemed empty. Then, because I didn't want to use Clay's name in case Jack or Mickey were somehow, magically, waiting for me to make just such a mistake, I called, "Anybody home?"

And someone was home. Clay peeked down at me from the hay-filled loft and said, "Only us chickens." He climbed down and brushed a few stalks of alfalfa from his clothes. "I heard you coming but discovered too late that there's no way for me to see the driveway from the boat, so I skedaddled up yonder and pretended to be a bale of hay. I can see that I'm going to have to figure out a way to identify visitors if I plan to work here."

I noticed for the first time that neither of the two windows on the driveway side of the barn was on a line between the schooner and the drive. Dumbness. Together, Clay and I studied the situation.

"What we need is a fair-sized mirror," I said. "We can set it up so when you're in the boat you can see what's happening outside."

He nodded. "That'll work. You happen to have one on you?"

"No, but we can probably find one at a thrift shop or the Dumptique."

I eased his small frown by explaining that the Dumptique was a shop at the entrance to the West Tisbury landfill. It was run by some fine women who glommed on to good stuff before people could throw it away, and made it available for recycling. The price was right, too. Everything was free and came with a money-back guarantee. The little shop was the last echo of the long island tradition of dump picking, when every dump served as a shopping center for whoever wanted to hunt there for what he needed.

"The golden days of yesteryear," said Clay.

Golden, indeed. Whole houses were built and furnished with free materials. At the Edgartown dump there had been a lumber area where you could find just the boards you needed for a job, as well as doors and windows, a hardware area where whole bathroom sets were commonly available or you could get repair parts for stoves or refrigerators, and a furniture store where you could trade in your old sofa for a better one.

Now, of course, thanks to environmental and public health zealots, only the Dumptique offered such treasures.

"If you want to keep on working, I'll go see if I can come up with a mirror," I said. "Or you can come with me if you're so inclined."

"I've never seen the Dumptique," he said, "and I think it's time I did."

"It's not a popular tourist site," I said, "but it should be."

I drove to Vineyard Haven and took a left at the intersection with State Road, the site of one of the island's three worst traffic jams in the summer but no problem in March. While I drove west on State Road I told him about my day. When I was through he said, "I didn't hear anything that gives me a clue about who might have killed the girl. Did I miss something?"

"No. Everybody I've talked with so far has told me the same sort of thing. She was beautiful and a lot of men were chasing after her. A couple of them may have scored a night in her bed, but no one replaced the architect boyfriend after he left. I never heard one bad word said about her by anybody."

"But somebody killed her with a blunt instrument."

"With a lead pipe in the conservatory. Yes."

"I wonder if she did anything to deserve it."

"Deserve has nothing to do with it."

"I remember that line. You're probably right, but some-body thought she deserved it. Your cop friend said the guy didn't hit her just once. He hit her over and over. He wanted to make sure."

I thought that, too. There had been nothing sophisti-cated or professional about the killing. It had the earmarks of a lot of amateur homicides, when the instrument is what-ever is handy and the act occurs in a moment of intense pas-sion that the killer may regret an instant too late.

Or maybe not. Maybe the pot had simmered for a long time before boiling over. Maybe the beating was methodical and cold, like the doom of Fortunato after the thousand injuries and final insult.

We came to North Tisbury and I explained to Clay how West Tisbury was actually southwest of Tisbury, and how North Tisbury was north of West Tisbury but west of Tis-bury.

"It there a South Tisbury or an East Tisbury?"

"No, and it's probably a good thing."

At the Dumptique, off North Road, the fates smiled. There was a large mirror that had some missing silver behind the glass but was plenty good for our purposes. We loaded it into the back of the Land Cruiser and headed back down-island.

There was no one ahead of us at Ted Overhill's barn and it didn't take us long to rig the mirror so it would reveal the driveway to anyone in the cockpit of the schooner.

"Nifty," said Clay. "When I was in Egypt I went down in some tombs in the Valley of the Kings, and way down inside there were walls covered with pictures and writing. The guide said they lighted the shafts with a series of mirrors that caught the sunlight and bounced it from mirror to mirror all the way down. I was impressed. You ever been to Egypt?"

"No. The farthest east I've ever been is Nantucket."

"You'll go someday. You'll like it."

"What were you doing over there?"

He made a dismissive gesture. "Oh, it was just a job. A guy in Cairo needed a pilot and I needed work, so we got together for a while. I did some low-level flying across borders and saw some interesting things, including a couple of tank carcasses left over from World War Two. Would you believe that? Still there after all these years. When I wasn't flying I went sightseeing. I'd go back to Egypt in a minute if it wasn't for a few people there who are mad at me."

"What were you carrying?"

He spread his hands. "Crates and boxes. The usual. I never opened one."

"Who's mad at you?"

"I don't know, but somebody killed the guy who hired me, and my landlord told me that some people came to my room looking for me while I was out, so I decided it was time to leave. I got to Alexandria and went from there to Italy and kept going until I was back in the States. Egypt's ruins are amazing. You could hide the Parthenon in the Temple of Karnak. Well, I guess I'll get back to work, now that I can see who's coming for a visit."

"You have much more to do?"

"There's always more to do on a boat, but you could launch this girl right now, and if she was ballasted and rigged, you could sail her away. I'm doing mostly finish work. It'll make her look a lot better and it'll make things easier for whoever sails her, but it doesn't have anything to do with her seaworthiness. I think Ted will have her in the water earlier than he thinks."

I left him there and drove back to the house, running things through my mind and wondering if I'd heard anything that didn't seem important but was. Some little tidbit of data was fluttering around in the distant recesses of my consciousness like a tiny bird angry about being in a cage, but I couldn't make it out other than that it was annoyed at not being recognized and freed. If, previously in my life, all such fuzzy mental disturbances of mine had eventually turned out to be significant, I might have treated this one more seriously. But such was not the case; my past experience showed that often my tiny irritating ill-defined thoughts, when finally brought forth for examination, turned out to be of no importance whatsoever.

I wondered if Joe Begay had learned anything useful about Clay's situation and when I'd hear from him. Soon, I hoped. I hoped, too, that somber Bonzo and his mother weren't too worried about the investigation into Nadine Gibson's death. I didn't think they should be, but I wasn't sure they weren't. In their place I would probably have been worried, too, since the law, like rain, falls on both the just and the unjust.

At home I discussed these issues with Oliver Underfoot and Velcro and in reply got their usual feline wisdom: This too shall pass. How about something to eat?

There are dumber creatures than cats.

I doled out cat snacks, then checked the leftovers in the fridge. There weren't enough for all of the Jacksons so I thawed out some of last fall's scallops and put together a Coquille St. Jacques for supper. It's a meal that takes some prep time, but I had that time and I knew the results would be worth it. By the time the kids got home from school, it was ready for the oven.

Joshua came in with downcast eyes and a discolored cheekbone. Uh-oh.

I said nothing but hello and he mumbled a reply as he went on into his room. Diana lingered.

"Pa."

"What, Diana?"

"Joshua got in a fight."

Her tone was that of an honorable informant possibly in search of a reward.

"Did you see it?"

"No, but my friend did. Mr. Hobbs made Joshua go to the principal's office."

Not just to Patagonia but to the principal's office. "Who else was involved?"

"Jim Duarte. He had to go to the principal's office, too."

"Well, thank you, Diana. You can go change out of your school clothes now."

"He's not supposed to fight, is he, Pa?"

"It's usually better not to fight. Now go change. Your mother and I will talk with him when she gets home."

"Pa?"

"Yes?"

"I never get in fights."

"That's good. Now go change clothes."

She went and I remembered that Joshua and Jim had shoved each other around before and that Zee was teaching Joshua to box. He clearly hadn't learned well enough to keep from getting hit, though. Maybe after Jim went home with a bloody nose his mother had decided to teach *him* the manly art.

Joshua was still in his room when Zee came home. I waited until she was in her civvies before telling the war story.

"Oh, dear," she said. "Jim's his best friend, too."

"Joshua is hiding out in his room," I said, "but we should talk with him. He and Jim aren't old enough to be fighting about some girl, are they?"

"You tell me. You were a boy."

"I haven't been that age for almost forty years. I don't remember much about it."

"We'll ask him. I don't want people hitting him, but I don't want him to be a bully, either."

We knocked politely on his bedroom door and heard his voice telling us to come in. Nurse Zee looked at his bruise and said it didn't look too bad. I asked him to tell us how it happened.

It had happened at the noon recess after lunch. He and

Jim were kidding around with some other boys when somebody shoved somebody into Jim and Jim thought Joshua did it and shoved the other boy into Joshua, and before you knew it, the laughing stopped and Jim had hit Joshua in the face and Joshua had hit him back and the other kids were all watching, and then Mr. Hobbs was there between them. And then he took them to the principal's office.

"And what did the principal say?" asked Zee.

"He said we were disruptive and on probation until the end of this week and if we did anything bad again we would be sent home. Here." He pulled a note out of his backpack and gave it to us. It was from the principal and said, among other things, that Joshua was indeed on probation and that if we had any questions to come into his office.

"I think we should do that," said Zee. "I thought Jim was your best friend, Joshua."

Joshua nodded. "He is."

"Then why did you fight? This happened before, not long ago. You hit him on the nose."

Joshua shrugged unhappily. "I don't know why."

I wondered if his hormones were acting up a little earlier than in most boys. In any case I wasn't surprised that he didn't know quite how the fight had started. Push had come to shove had come to hit. A lot of fights are like that. Afterward you don't know how they happened.

"How's Jim?" I asked. "Is he okay?"

He nodded and looked on the verge of tears.

"Well," I said. "You'll have to serve out your probation, but the past is past. Nobody got hurt. That's the important thing. From now on, though, you have to keep an eye on yourself so you don't accidentally get into more fights. You know now that they can get started for no real reason, so you have to keep that from happening to you. Are you still taking boxing lessons from your mother?"

He nodded and I glanced at Zee before putting my hand on his thin shoulder. "That's good," I said, "because knowing how to box may keep you out of trouble. Did I ever tell you the story about John L. Sullivan when he was in a bar and a little drunk man came up to him and challenged him to a fight?"

He shook his head, eyes still down. "No."

"John L. Sullivan was the heavyweight boxing champion of the world. He was in a bar having a beer when a little drunk guy challenged him to a fight. Everybody in the bar thought that John L. would knock the little drunk flat with one punch, but instead John L. said, 'No, I'm not going to fight you.'

"The little drunk man was furious and called him all sorts of bad names, but John L. just ignored him and drank his beer until finally the little man gave up and left the bar. When the other people asked John L. why he hadn't just flattened the guy, John L. said, 'Because I didn't have to.'"

There was a silence for a long moment, then Joshua nodded. "I understand," he said. "John L. didn't have to prove anything so he didn't get in a fight."

I rubbed his head. "That's right. Supper's in the oven. It'll be ready in about half an hour. Do you have any homework?"

"A little."

"You'd better get at it. I'll call you when it's time to eat."

Zee kissed her damp-eyed son and we went back to the kitchen.

"Is that a true story?" she asked.

"I don't know. I heard it a long time ago."

"Well, it's a good one and I hope it helps."

After supper, as Zee was washing dishes, the phone rang. It was Joe Begay. "I have some information for you," he said. "Some of it's kind of interesting."

22

The next morning I picked up Clay and we drove to Aquin-nah. "Jeez," said Clay, as we shivered our way up-island. "You need either a new truck or a new heater."

"I thought you were going to fix it. You're the one with the magic hands."

"Icicle hands are more like it this morning."

"You've been spending too much time in warm climates," I said. "Truly manly men are impervious to the cold."

"Spoken like a guy wearing gloves."

We fetched Joe Begay's house in time to wave good-bye to his wife, Toni, who was turning out of the driveway as we were turning in. Inside the house, Clay curled his hands appreciatively around a hot cup of coffee as we sat at the dining room table. Joe plucked a doughnut from a plate that he then pushed toward us. "I've made a few calls," he said. "Maybe what I learned will interest you; maybe it won't." He pulled a small notebook from his shirt pocket and gave it to Clay. "This is yours." Then he looked at some scribbles he'd made on another sheet of paper. "Here's what I've been told. I think it's probably true, but you can't be sure because people don't always know the truth or tell it if they do know it. My sources mostly work for federal agencies, for what that's worth. Anyway, here's the scoop:

"First, a guy named Mark Briggs, who used to own a fair-sized spread in Montana before he sold it to a guy named Lewis Farquahar and moved to Palm Springs, seems to have disappeared. Those in the know think he's in Rio, which is not a bad place for him to be since the U.S. doesn't have an extradition treaty with Brazil. Not that he needs to be worried about being arrested because our narcs don't have any proof that he ever did anything to deserve jail time. They have their suspicions and they worked pretty hard over the years to nail him, but he outfoxed them. The smart money says he's really there to get away from the people who took over his business."

"I thought that Lewis Farquahar took over his business," said Clay, chewing on a doughnut.

"That's apparently what Lewis thought, too," said Joe. "He supposedly paid Mark Briggs cash money up front for the ranch and the connections that went with it. That would be the cash that you took down to San Diego, if it really existed. Did you ever actually see what was in those suitcases you flew down there?"

"Actually," said Clay, "no. I saw other money in other suitcases at other times, but those two were already closed when I got them from Farquahar. Are you telling me that there was no money inside?"

Joe shook his head. "No, but since you didn't see the contents, we're only guessing that the money was there. I think it probably was, mind you, but we can't be absolutely sure. Now, about the guy in the bank. You said he wasn't the guy you usually did business with. His name is Rodriguez. He replaced the usual clerk about a week before. You should be glad you decided not to deal with him because Rodriguez is a narc. If you'd handed over the suitcases you'd probably be in jail now instead of here enjoying the pleasures of a winter on Martha's Vineyard. He was one of the agents following the money trail, hoping it would lead back to your friend Mark, whose bank account, by the way, was in the name of Johnson. The idea was that they'd arrest you and you'd tell them about Briggs and that they'd nail Briggs and his network and thereby help save America from reefer madness. But you left the bank before you handed over the suitcases and never came back, and since Mr. Johnson had a policy of transferring earlier deposits to other banks and finally overseas, they didn't even get their hands on very much of his capital. All they had was a bank clerk who was trying to stretch his salary by accepting cash deposits, no questions asked, for a guy named Johnson, first name Jeremiah, and getting a medium-sized fee for his efforts."

"Jeremiah Johnson, eh?" Clay smiled. "Mark had that movie on a disc. We used to watch it in his living room. He had one of those big-screen TVs."

"The real Jeremiah probably didn't look like Robert Redford," said Joe. "They called him Crow Killer because he hated the Crows for killing his wife, and Liver Eating Johnson because he supposedly ate the livers of the men he killed."

"Crow livers?"

"So they said back then in the Wild West. You boys ever eat liver up there in Montana?"

"Only beef. No Crow."

"On with my story, then. The narcs missed getting you and the money you supposedly had. How did they know you were coming with a deposit? The best guess is that somebody in either Briggs's or Farquahar's outfit told somebody who told somebody who tipped off the narcs. It was only a rumor but it was enough for them to put Rodriguez in the bank."

"I thought the guy was probably working for Farquahar," said Clay.

"No," said Begay. "He wasn't working for Lewis. In fact, about a week later nobody was working for Lewis because Lewis was dead. Shot in Billings by person or persons unknown, along with a couple of guys presumed to be his bodyguards. You never heard about it because it was local news in Billings. Big news, but local."

"Lewis dead? Who did it?" Clay seemed more interested than surprised.

"The smart guys think it was somebody who wanted his business. I'd guess that's probably right. I remember when pot smokers and dealers were making love not war. No longer, at least not on the big-business end of things."

"The times they are a-changing."

"Which brings us to your would-be visitors here on the Blessed Isle: Jack Blume and Mickey Monroe. You said they worked for Farquahar, but they don't anymore, and they know you and they know about the suitcases."

"Who are they working for now?"

"They're a couple of fairly small-time West Coast hoods who don't seem to be working for anybody at the moment. It's my contact's guess that they knew about the money shipment going wrong. Probably because when you told Mark about it, Mark called Lewis to complain and Lewis told Blume and Monroe to get their hands on the missing money if they could. He may even have told them about you leaving your tools in Sausalito, or maybe they learned that later, after they'd set out on the road trip. The rest, as they say, is history."

"So," I said, "Blume and Monroe are working for themselves now. Their old boss is dead and they're out of a job, but they think that Clay has two suitcases full of cash, so they followed him here in their California car and their California clothes." Then I had another thought. "Or do you think they're working for whoever kacked Lewis Farquahar?"

"There's some disagreement in narc circles about who did Lewis in. The favorite is a local grower who aspires to rise in the trade, but no one can prove that yet. I doubt if he's even heard of Blume and Monroe."

Clay made a small sound indicating thought and nibbled pensively on his second or third doughnut. "Interestinger and interestinger," he said. "Is the law after Blume and Monroe for anything?"

"They're what they call persons of interest in L.A. but there aren't any warrants out."

"And they're not working for someone a lot bigger? A Mexican cartel or some such thing?"

"Not that my people know of. But, of course, they don't know everything. If they did, Blume and Monroe and you might all be in jail."

Clay smiled agreeably. "If I'd been caught doing some of the things I've done, I'd have been in jail instead of junior high. But I wasn't."

I thought the same thing was true for a lot of us.

"That's about all I can tell you about your West Coast friends," said Joe. "Anything else you want to know?"

"If you can find out how I can get in touch with Mark Briggs, that would be nice."

"I imagine I could, with time. But then I'd owe a lot of people more than they owe me."

"Do you know who's at the ranch these days?"

"I believe the ranch is unoccupied at the moment."

"Who's taking care of the livestock?"

"That I cannot say."

"Does Mark still have his place in Palm Springs?"

"I believe he still owns it but that it's been empty for some time. Since shortly after you phoned him from San Diego, in fact."

"Do you know who swiped the plane in San Diego?"

"I believe the authorities determined that it was parked in a spot that endangered other air traffic, so it was removed to a hangar."

"It was parked where I always parked it."

"All I can tell you is what I was told. Now, perhaps you'll tell me something."

"What might that be?"

"Are the suitcases still in a San Diego storage locker?"

"Of course." Clay glanced at his fingernails. "Who wants to know?"

"A lot of people," said Joe in an amused voice. "More coffee?"

Before we left we'd finished both the coffee and the doughnuts and I was feeling full and good. I had no intention of telling Zee about my midmorning snack since she had, of late, made a few comments about my weight. *Winter fat* was the phrase she'd used, and I didn't want to hear it again.

Beside me as we drove back to Edgartown, Clay was deep in his thoughts and I was soon trying to organize my own. Joe's report had altered my perception of the situation involving Clay, Jack Blume, and Mickey Monroe, and as I followed the narrow, winding road out of Aquinnah and past the Chilmark Store, a plan began to form in my mind. As we approached Abel's Hill, the plan took shape.

At the top of the hill, on South Road, you can turn north into the cemetery and, without getting out of your car, view the gravestone that is the Vineyard's second most popular tourist site, the grave of a once famous comedian who died of an overdose of illegal chemical additives. In the years since his death, aficionados of both his life and his mode of passing have made pilgrimages to the site and left behind mementos of their faith and respect in the form of empty wine bottles, beer cans, roaches, needles, and flowers. The cemetery workers patiently clean the area every now and then, but always have to return before too long.

Across the road from the cemetery a number of driveways lead south, down toward the ocean. Along these sandy byways are houses great and small. Once, there were only a few, mostly modest homes, but increasingly mansions are being erected, some by people who are quick to make it clear that they want nothing at all to do with their neighbors. There was a time when such snobbery was rare on the Vineyard but that is no longer the case, as thousands of new No Trespassing signs give clear indication.

Down one of these narrow drives is a house owned by a friend of mine who uses it only in the summer and who pays me a reasonable sum to close it in the fall, open it in the spring, and care for it during the winter. When we came to his driveway, I took a right and drove down into his yard.

It was a pleasant summer cottage with a wide porch on the

ocean side and a balcony on top of that where many a cock-
tail had been drunk (some by me) as the sun settled over
Aquinnah. Between the house and the ocean was a narrow
section of one of the many brackish ponds that line the Vineyard's southern shore, separated from the sea by a thin barrier beach. Between the pond and the house was a grove of
evergreens and oaks. Between the front of the cottage and
South Road was a tree- and brush-covered hillside that gave
the place a feeling of splendid isolation. The nearest house
wasn't really too far away but could barely be seen even
through the largely leafless winter undergrowth. Besides, it
was, like many of the homes in the area, inhabited only
during the summer.

I led Clay up onto the balcony and waved my arm at the
ocean. "The next land if you sail south is Hispaniola."

"Beautiful view," he said. "Haiti is beautiful, too. I knew a
girl from there once. Too bad about the politics."

"I have a key to this place," I said. "Let me show you
around."

We went down and I showed him through the house. It
was simple and clean and, once the water and electricity were
turned on and there was food in the pantry, it offered everything a half dozen people would need for a pleasant stay.

"Not bad at all," said Clay. "It wouldn't take much to win-
terize it." He ran a hand over the carved wooden mantel.
"Maybe I'll buy it." He grinned.

"It'll probably cost you one of those suitcases," I said.

"No problem. I have two."

"I've been thinking about what Joe told us," I said.

"Me, too."

"And I have a plan."

"What is it?"

I told him.

He thought for a while, then said, "How far away is the
nearest neighbor?"

"Maybe a quarter of a mile."

He thought some more and then said, "You're pretty sure Mickey is dressed?"

"I'm pretty sure. He had something fairly heavy in the pocket of his coat."

"How about Jack?"

"I don't know about Jack. Just to be on the safe side, I guess I'd think he was carrying, too."

"When do you want to do it?"

"The sooner the better, but it's up to you. You're the one they're interested in."

He stared out a window at the ocean. Its far horizon was dark against the pale winter sky. "It would probably save everybody a lot of grief if I just moved on."

"It wouldn't save Eleanor any grief, but it's your decision. I think we should end it here and now."

"You'll be taking a chance you probably shouldn't take."

"I don't like those guys prowling around my island."

"It's not your island. Tell you what. If you can bring Dom Agganis in on this, I'll do it. You need a license to carry in Massachusetts and I doubt if Jack and Mickey have the paper. He can nail them for that if for nothing else. Come to think of it, I can't carry, either."

"That's one problem. Another is if we bring Dom in, you'll have to tell him why you're here."

Clay frowned. "I take it back. Let's not bring Dom in." He looked around. "You sure your friend won't mind us using his place?"

"What he doesn't know won't hurt him."

"That being the case, let's take another look around so I'll know the battlefield."

So we walked and looked and talked and when we were back in the truck Clay said, "You're sure you want to do this?"

"It's my idea but it's your decision."

He nodded. "Okay, let's do it."

23

The next morning I ate breakfast early, then phoned the Harbor View Hotel and asked to speak with Mr. Jack Blume. A voice answered sleepily on the fourth ring.

"Yes?"

"Mr. Blume?"

"Yes?"

"This is J. W. Jackson. Remember me?"

"Yes?"

"When you came by my place, you were looking for Clay Stockton. I ran into him yesterday and he told me where he's working."

"Ah," said Jack, thus proving he had more than a one-word vocabulary.

"If you're still interested in seeing him, I think he'll still be there today."

"Nice of you to call. Yes, I'm still interested. Like I said, he's an old friend."

"He's working alone on a house up near Abel's Hill. Do you know where that is?"

"No, I don't. Is the place hard to find?"

"It's up in Chilmark. I can tell you how to get to Abel's Hill, but the house is on a side road."

Jack seemed to be waking up. "Did you find out where he's living?"

"He told me but I'm not sure I got the directions right. Turns out I know the guy who owns the house he's working on, though, so I know where that is. You go up to the top of Abel's Hill and . . . Do you know where the graveyard is?"

"No."

"Okay. Well, you go up through West Tisbury and take South Road to Chilmark. . . . You have a map of the island?"

"I have a map, but . . ."

"Okay, you look at your map and you'll see the Edgartown–West Tisbury road. You see that?"

"Wait a minute! I have to get the map." His voice became more distant. "Mickey, where's the map of this island? Where? Damn!" The voice returned to the phone. "The map is in the car."

"Oh. Well, maybe you don't need it. You have a pencil and paper? All right, when you drive out of town, you take the Edgartown–West Tisbury road right there by Cannonball Park. When you pass the mill pond in West Tisbury, you go left on South Road. When you get to the Chilmark line you keep going until you come to that curve where people used to walk down to Lucy Vincent Beach—maybe they still do, for all I know. Anyway, you go up the hill and—"

"Wait a minute!"

"What?"

"I can't keep up with all that."

"I'm probably talking too fast. You know how it is when you know something; you think everybody else must know it, too. Okay, I'll slow down. Let's start over. This time I'll start from your hotel. First—"

"Wait!" he interrupted. "This isn't going to work, I—"

I interrupted back. "Tell you what. Why don't you go down and get your map and you call me back when you get it. Clay's not going to be up there this early anyway, so there's no rush."

"Now, just hold on, Mr. Jackson," said Blume, in a voice of reason. "I've got a better idea. Why don't you show us how to get there? You come here, and then we'll follow you there."

"Well, I don't know. I've got some work I'm supposed to be doing . . ." I let my voice fade off as though I were thinking.

"Can't it wait? It can't take too long to get where we're

going. This island is only twenty miles or so long. You show us where the house is and you can be on your way."

"Well . . ."

"You'll sure be helping us out. Hate to miss old Clay when we're so close to getting in touch."

"Well, all right, then," I said. "I'll be down right after breakfast. Say nine o'clock in the hotel parking lot? That'll give you time to eat before we go."

"We'll see you there."

So far so good. Jack even figured it was his idea for me to lead the way to Clay.

I got my old Smith & Wesson .38 out of the gun cabinet, loaded it, put some extra bullets in my pocket, and stuck the weapon in my belt. I'd carried it when I'd been a cop, before the time when the police started carrying higher-powered semiautomatics, and it was still good enough for me. Then I took my father's old Browning double-barreled 12-gauge, loaded it with buckshot, and carried it and a box of shells out to the Land Cruiser.

I drove to John Skye's farm, told Clay about my conversation with Jack, and gave him the Browning and its extra shells. He took the gun and said, "How come you've brought out this old blunderbuss now when a Remington pump was good enough for me before?"

"Because we have a plan now but didn't before," I said, "and because this one is scarier. Like you said when you talked about stagecoach guards, nobody likes to be at the business end of a double-barreled shotgun. I want you to stand this behind the front door, so it'll be hidden when you open it and we go in. I'll snag it as soon as we get inside and we'll take it from there."

"Just make sure they don't snag it first."

"We'll probably get there about nine-thirty. You be up on the balcony like we planned and then you'll come down and open the door."

He looked at his watch. "I'd better be on my way, then, so

I can get things squared away." He looked at me, smiled a crooked smile, and put out a hand. "I hope this works."

I took the hand. "It'll work. If it doesn't, run as fast as you can. I'll be right behind you."

We put both shotguns and their ammunition into the Bronco and he drove away. I had a few minutes to spare so I walked around and checked out the place. Everything was fine. Clay was a neat housekeeper, as many sailors are, because on a small boat you have to be if you're going to live comfortably. There's no room to be sloppy.

When the time was right, I drove to the Harbor View Hotel and into its parking lot. Jack and Mickey were waiting in their idling yellow Mercedes. I guessed that their heat had been on for a while and wished that my own worked better.

I pulled alongside them and rolled down my window as Jack rolled down his. "Good morning," I said. "Just follow me. I'll drive slow so you won't lose me."

"Drive as fast as you want," said Jack. "I won't lose you."

"I'm going to take you all the way to the house," I said.

"You don't need to do that," said Jack, frowning. "Just get us close and point the way."

"It's no problem," I said. "Besides, you can't really see the place until you get there."

Before he could argue some more, I fluttered my fingers in a good-bye gesture and drove out the back entrance to Fuller Street, leaving him no choice but to follow me.

I led the way at a steady forty miles an hour, which is about as fast as my old truck likes to go, and the speedy Mercedes was obliged to dawdle in my wake.

On Abel's Hill I turned down the proper driveway and soon fetched the cottage. I could see Clay on the balcony. He had turned from whatever he was pretending to do and was looking at us as we parked our cars in the yard. I was pleased to see that he had a hammer in his hand. It was one of those small details that make a scene believable.

We got out of the cars and Clay waved his hammer and

called, "J.W.! I'll be right down!" He disappeared from view.

"Thanks for playing guide," said Jack. "We can take it from here." Mickey said nothing, but stood with his hands in his coat pockets.

"I'll go in with you," I said. "While I'm here I'm going to find out where he lives."

Turning my back on them, I led the way to the front door, unzipping my coat as I went, and when Clay opened it I led the way in, shook his hand, and stepped aside so Blume and Monroe could follow. "Brought a couple of your old friends with me," I said.

"We're not exactly old friends," said Jack as he and Mickey entered and Clay moved back toward the middle of the room. "More like we have friends in common." He and Mickey stepped apart, glanced at me, then looked back at Clay. I reached behind the door and brought out the Browning. When I kicked the door shut behind them, both of the Californians turned and saw the leveled shotgun. Their faces changed.

"Take your hands out of your pockets," I said. "Right now."

They hesitated but by then Clay had moved to the right and come up with the Remington that he'd stashed behind a handsome sideboard holding summer chinaware. The sound of him jacking a shell into the firing chamber whipped Jack's and Mickey's heads back toward him.

"Last chance," I said. "Get your hands out of your pockets."

"What the hell's going on?" snapped Jack, feigning innocence but not surprise.

"You got your warning," I said. "Shoot them, Clay."

"Wait!" yelled Jack, and he and Mickey jerked their hands out of their pockets. Clay tried not to look astonished at my command to shoot.

"Take off your coats and drop them on the floor," I said. "Be very careful."

"What is this?" Jack blustered as he and Mickey unzipped

their new winter coats and let them fall. Mickey's thumped as it hit.

"Shut up," I said. "Both of you get over against that wall and spread your legs. I think you know the routine. If you don't it's too late to learn."

They knew. They spread their hands against the wall and spread their legs. I kicked their feet farther back like I'd done a time or two, long ago, when I'd been a uniformed cop, and frisked them, coming up with two pistols, two pocketknives, and two wallets.

"Stay right there," I said, stepping away and taking a look at the contents of the wallets. They didn't have much money, just as I'd guessed, but I took what they had and took their credit cards and driver's licenses, too. I got a third pistol out of one pocket of Mickey's winter coat and a switchblade out of another. I gave the pistol to Clay, then kicked the coats toward their owners and threw the empty wallets after them.

"I don't want you to catch your death of cold, so put those coats on and sit down over there."

They sat in overstuffed chairs and looked into their wallets.

"What the hell are you doing?" asked Jack. "What do you want?"

"You talk again before I tell you to and I'll knock your teeth out the back of your head," I said. "You own that car, or is it a rental?"

"It's mine." His voice was sullen.

"You have the title with you?"

"It's in the glove compartment."

"You're lucky. You're broke, but at least you can sell the car."

"What!"

"Shut up." I looked at Clay, who was listening to this exchange with interest. "Go out and bring in that title."

He frowned. "You'll be all right here alone with them?"

"I have a barrel of buckshot for each of them. That should be enough. If it isn't, I have all these pistols."

The shotgun was enough. Clay went out and came back, title in hand. It was, as I expected, one of those titles that allow a transfer of ownership to be recorded.

I took the credit cards and cut them in two with Mickey's switchblade.

"Hey!" cried Jack.

"I told you to be quiet," I said and started toward him, lifting the shotgun like an ax. Jack cowered back into his chair and lifted defensive arms.

"Hold on, hold on," said Clay. "I don't want any blood here if we can help it. Take it easy, J.W."

I stopped and looked daggers at Jack, then shrugged and stepped back. I took a deep breath as though to calm myself, then glared at Jack again. "You say another word before I tell you to, it'll be your last, Clay or no Clay."

Jack stayed sunk in his chair, staring at me with large eyes. Mickey hadn't changed expression or pose.

"Here's your situation," I said. "Your boss, Lewis Farquahar, is dead and you two don't have jobs anymore, so you thought you'd find Clay and get the money Lewis paid to Mark Briggs. You knew Clay didn't turn it in at the bank in San Diego because Clay contacted Mark and Mark contacted Lewis and Lewis told somebody who told you, so you figured Clay still had it and you traced him here.

"You drove because you already had the Mercedes and you were low on cash. It was cheaper to drive than to fly, and besides, if you flew there'd be a record of it and you didn't want that if you could help it. Am I about right so far?"

Jack started to say something but instead just nodded.

"Fine," I said. "I just emptied your wallets and you don't have much cash, which means you've been living on credit cards. I just took your cash and destroyed your credit cards so now you're really broke. You have a hotel bill you can run out on, but you still need money to get home, which is where you're going, starting today.

"You're going for two reasons: Because I don't like you and I don't want you on this island any longer, and because you made a big mistake." I lifted the shotgun and sighted down the barrels at Jack's face. He lifted his hands as though they could stop the buckshot.

"Don't!" His voice was shrill.

Even Mickey's eyes got wide.

I lowered the shotgun and said, "Look at me, Jack."

He peeked through his fingers, saw that the shotgun was lying across my left arm, and lowered his hands.

"The mistake was thinking that Clay still has the suitcases. He doesn't. The Feds have the money. Clay sent the locker key to the bank when he couldn't locate Mark and Lewis got himself killed. The money was too dangerous to keep. The Feds have had it for weeks, since long before you two got here. You made the trip for nothing. Isn't that right, Clay?"

"Absolutely," said Clay.

"So here's what you're going to do," I said. "You're not going back to your hotel. We're going to put you and your car on the first ferry to the mainland. You have about enough cash here to pay for a one-way ticket, but when you get to America you're going to have to sell your car to get enough money to go home. Out there on the coast, where the living is easy, you can probably find another boss and get back to work. But don't ever come back here. Do you understand?"

Jack and Mickey exchanged looks. Mickey looked disgusted, but both of them nodded.

24

Jack drove the Mercedes to the ticket office with Mickey in the suicide seat. I sat behind them with a couple of pistols. Clay followed us in the Bronco. At the office Clay went in and got a reservation for an early afternoon boat, an impossible task in the summer but no problem in March. Jack then drove to Vineyard Haven and put the convertible in the boarding line. None of us said a word to one another. I stayed in the backseat until the car was on the boat, then leaned forward and said, "Don't come back. There's nothing here for you but grief."

"Don't worry," growled Mickey. "I never want to see another island." He used a familiar adjective to emphasize his point and gave Jack a disgusted look. "This was the dumbest thing I ever got talked into."

"Remember that," I said. "So far, all it's cost you is some time and money. Next time it'll cost more, if there is a next time."

"There won't be, but you better stay out of California."

I got out and went back ashore, where I stayed until the boat left. Then I walked to the parking lot, where Clay waited in his truck.

"Gone where the good doggies go," I said.

We drove back to Abel's Hill, where my old Land Cruiser waited. We put our firearms into its backseat.

Clay said, "You're pretty scary."

"Image is everything."

"Would you have knocked his teeth out?"

"I don't think so, but I was glad when you spoke up."

"I'm a born thespian. You think they'll be back?"

"Your crystal ball is as good as mine. I can't imagine that they're so mad about being sent home broke that they'll swear revenge, but I guess it could happen. I doubt it, though." I told him what Mickey had said.

Clay laughed. "I guess Jack will be coming alone, if he comes at all." He looked at his watch. "I think I have just about enough time to go to the farm, pack up, and move back over the garage. I feel like celebrating, so I'm going to invite Elly to supper."

"Good idea. I'll follow you to the farm and close the place up after you're gone."

"Why don't you and Zee come to dinner? It's on me. I'll make reservations at Le Grenier."

He'd named my favorite island restaurant, but I shook my head. "No, but thanks. I have leftover Coquille St. Jacques at home, and it's always better the second night. Another time."

I followed him to John Skye's farm, and after he'd loaded his gear into the Bronco and driven away, I checked the house and grounds, lowered the thermostat, locked up, and went home. I felt like someone who'd just been let out of jail.

That evening, when the kids were in their rooms and Zee and I were sitting in front of the stove looking into the flames and sipping after-dinner brandies, I told her about my day.

She shook her head. "Sometimes I don't know about you, Jefferson. You could have been killed or you might have killed those other guys."

"I had the drop, and I didn't think they'd be stupid enough to go up against a double-barreled shotgun. And they weren't."

"But what if they had been stupid enough?"

"But they weren't. And they're smart enough not to come back."

There is no end to what ifs, and Zee knew the futility of

going down that road, so instead she said, "I love you, Jefferson. I just wish you wouldn't do these things. I worry."

"That's why I didn't tell you till the game was over. Now there's nothing to worry about."

She whacked me and said, "Oh, yes, there is. Now I have to worry that you'll do it again and won't tell me until later."

"You don't have to worry about that. This was a onetime thing."

"Sure."

"I mean it."

"That's something else to worry about: you actually believe what you're saying."

I put my arm around her. "I really mean it."

She snuggled close. "Now I'm really worried." She turned her face to mine and I kissed her perfect lips. They tasted faintly of cognac. Delish.

The next day was Saturday, and March, just for a change, offered us a day that belonged in June. The sky was clear, the sun was bright, and the air was warm, thanks to a southwest wind that brought balmy Carolina temperatures to New England. They dropped a bit when they crossed over the still-chilly ocean waters to the Vineyard, but were still a taste of summer and roused within us thoughts of gardening. Those thoughts, in turn, enticed us to drive to Cape Pogue for another load of seaweed.

"Pa?"

"What, Joshua?"

"Can I invite Jim to go with us? I don't think he's ever been to Cape Pogue."

A lot of islanders have never been to Cape Pogue since you can get there only by boat, helicopter, or four-by-four vehicle, and there are many Vineyarders who have none of the above. I thought about the fights between the two boys.

"Yes," I said. "And if his parents aren't sure, tell them I said it was okay and that we'll pick him up in about half an hour."

Joshua ran to the phone.

"Pa?"

"What, Diana?"

"Can I have a friend come, too?"

Fair is fair. "Who do you have in mind?"

"Mary Alvarez."

I wasn't going to have too much room for seaweed, if this kept up.

"Yes," I said. "When Joshua is off the phone, you can call Mary and invite her. Tell her we'll come by in about forty-five minutes."

Zee, with whom I was packing a lunch basket, said, "Can I bring a friend, too, Pa?"

"Who do you have in mind?"

"Robert Redford?"

"Why not? When Diana gets off the phone, give him a call."

"I guess we'd better make a couple more sandwiches even if Robert can't join us."

We did that, then I put rods on the roof rack because you never know when some starving fish might be going by just as you get a yen to cast, and a bit later we were off to pick up Jim and Mary, whose parents had raised not a single objection to the trip to Cape Pogue.

I drove down to Katama, then took a left onto South Beach and headed for Chappaquiddick. I was pleased to note a catboat in the center of Katama Bay, its skipper and crew taking advantage of the lovely day. It might be time for us to put bottom paint on the *Shirley J.* and hang her on her stake between the Yacht Club and the Reading Room. I wasn't a frostbite sailor like some, but it wouldn't hurt to get a jump on summertime.

On Chappy I fetched Dyke Road, crossed the bridge and turned north, and drove beside the lagoon up to Cape Pogue Pond. There, because the tide was low, I drove close to the water all the way to Simon Point, then crossed the little drainage creek and went out to the jetties. The beach sand there was soft, as it often is, but my old Land Cruiser was up to the challenge and carried us to the point and around onto the rocky north side of the elbow. Miles to the north we could see East Chop jutting into the sound and beyond that the low, dark line that was Cape Cod. There were gulls both in the air and on the water.

At the crossover, I cut to the inside of the elbow and there, just where we'd found it in January, was a good supply of seaweed. We all got out and felt the warm sun and air fill us with good sensations.

"Pa?"

"What, Joshua?"

"Do you need us to help fill up the bags?"

"I guess not."

"Can Jim and me go to the lighthouse?"

"That's Jim and I."

"Can Jim and I go to the lighthouse?"

"Do you know how to get there?"

"Sure. We just follow the road." He pointed.

"Pa, we want to go, too!" Diana looked up at me with eyes like Zee's.

"Do you know how to get there?"

"Sure. We'll just follow Joshua."

"What if you lose sight of him?"

"We'll follow the road!"

Zee said, "All right, but be careful. Stick together and don't do anything foolish. Joshua?"

"Yes, Ma."

"Be careful and keep an eye on your sister."

"Aw, Ma."

"She's younger than you are. You don't have to be a babysitter, but you're her big brother. Go on, now. You have time to get there and come back before lunch. If you're late there may not be any left for you."

The four children walked along the beach toward the

narrow sandy road that led over the sand dunes and on to the lighthouse. Looking at them I remembered adventures I'd had at that age. I'd been a pretty careful kid but had come home a few times with cuts and bruises I hadn't had when I'd left. My father had been interested in my travels but hadn't ever made a big issue out of my injuries, contenting himself with applying Band-Aids and iodine to my wounds until I was up to telling of my adventures. I hoped I would be as wise.

We filled bags with seaweed and stuffed them into the back of the truck, only leaving room for the four kids, us, and the lunch basket. When the truck was packed, we spread the old bedspread that we use for a beach blanket on the sand on the sunny side of the truck and flopped down side by side.

"I believe this is the way it's supposed to be," said Zee, lying on her back with her eyes shut behind her dark glasses. "This is why people pay thousands of dollars to vacation on Martha's Vineyard."

"Would you like a beer?"

"Not yet. I feel like I have too many clothes on."

"I feel like that, too."

"That you have too many?"

"No, that you have."

"I suspect that if I shed what I'm wearing I'd actually be a bit chilly. I have an idea. Why don't you get naked and then lie there awhile and let me know if it's really warm enough for nude beaching. I'll lie here like this and wait for your report."

We lay in the sunshine and listened to the gulls and the sound of small waves slapping the sand at our feet.

By and by I heard children's voices. From their sound I concluded that no one was dead or seriously wounded. I rose and got the lunch basket and put it on the bedspread.

When the four children rounded the truck and spied us, they looked happy.

"How was your adventure?" I asked.

"Excellent," said Joshua.

"We went all the way to the lighthouse and back," said Diana.

"I forgot to tell you to be careful of cars."

"We didn't see any cars, and besides, we know what to do. You just step off out of the way."

"My dad says just to remember that there are a lot of idiots driving cars," said Jim.

"A good thing to remember. If you guys are ready for lunch, lunch is ready for you. Find places to sit on the blanket."

There were sandwiches and potato chips for all, pickles and olives, soft drinks for the kids, and Sam Adams for Zee and me. For dessert, an apple apiece.

When lunch was over, all of us spent some time casting lures into the empty sea, just in case something was there. Then we put the rods back in the roof rack, put all of the paper and empty containers back in the lunch basket, put it and the bedspread and ourselves in the truck, and went home.

As we waited on the Chappy side for the little On Time ferry to pick us up and carry us over to Edgartown, I was glad to have observed that Joshua and Jim seemed to have totally forgotten that they'd ever punched each other. I didn't think that I'd ever had any fights at their age, but maybe kids were maturing faster these days. In any case, the two of them seemed to be as close as ever. Perhaps it was because their battles had ended in a draw, leaving neither a winner or a loser, so that a balance was maintained between them.

It had been a good day, but as I thought of the combative friendship between the two boys and of how love and hate often seem two sides of the same coin, I found myself wondering if the latter was what had led to the death of Nadine Gibson.

The On Time arrived and carried us across to the village.

I dropped off Mary and Jim at their homes and drove on to ours.

A lot of people had loved Nadine. Had something flipped the coin in one of the people I'd interviewed? Or was there another lover-hater out there, as yet unknown to me?

The sun was sinking and the air was cooling. As I emptied our bags of seaweed out by the garden, I wondered if Nadine's killer had had as lovely a day as I'd had.

— 25 —

Are murderers as happy as other people? There's a notion that they're not, that somehow they are doomed to suffer from their killings. Raskolnikov certainly did, as did Shakespeare's Richard III and Lady Macbeth, although I wasn't persuaded by Bill's dramatizations. Hamlet, on the other hand, didn't seem to mind the blood he shed in the last act. My suspicion was that guilt may not be as common as some would like to believe and that killers probably laugh as often as anyone else.

I thought such thoughts on Sunday, as Zee and I worked in our garden and got our peas planted, refilled the bird feeders, and performed other yard tasks. Joshua and Diana, meanwhile, did spring cleaning in the tree house in the big beech, tossing out leaves and broken branches. When you own property, there's always work to be done, and I liked doing it most of the time. Sometimes, in fact, it seemed to me that my few acres and my family constituted a whole planet and its occupants, and that I needed nothing more from life and had no obligations to any larger universe.

But Donne was right, of course, and the outer world rightly or wrongly demanded attention from all of its inhabitants, including me, especially when it was out of joint. Some groups of people living out in the western deserts believed, I'd read, that crimes were committed by people out of touch with themselves and the world; that they could be cured by being put back in harmony with the universe; that crime was a manifestation of a sickness of the soul best dealt with by curing rituals rather than by penalties. It was a notion not unfamiliar to psychiatrists, some of whom saw evil as a manifestation of mental illness, not sin.

The victims of killers were, of course, just as dead, whatever the cause.

While we cleaned our yard and our little fish pond of winter debris, I mentally reviewed the conversations I'd had with people who had known Nadine and the observations I'd made while talking with them. I hoped I wasn't forgetting anything and that I wasn't attaching too little significance to some detail that seemed inconsequential. I wondered whom I should interview that I hadn't already interviewed, who might know something important, whom I'd managed to overlook.

Who had hated Nadine? And why?

Into my thinking appeared two people I hadn't considered before. They were lean and gray-haired and neatly coiffed, and were wearing expensive, informal clothes. Justin Wyner and Genevieve Geller, Marshall Lea stalwarts, conservationists, and birders, people who were more familiar than most with the old Olmstead farm where Nadine's body had been found. They knew of the old drive leading into the place. They knew of the fallen house and the debris-filled basement. Had they known Nadine?

Had Justin Wyner, aging but still hale, and rich enough to perhaps buy the attention of a young working woman, ever spent time in the Fireside, where he, like many others, had seen and been enchanted by the girl with strawberry hair? Had she flirted with him, then spurned him? Had he struck her down in a rage, then buried her in one place he knew well, since the ground was too frozen for him to dig a proper grave?

Or had Genevieve, a firebrand for conservation, found them out and done the girl in out of fury and jealousy?

Such a scenario seemed unlikely but not impossible. In affairs of the heart no act is impossible.

So the next day, when my wife and children had gone off

to the lives they led when I wasn't with them, I drove back to Oak Bluffs and knocked on the door of Bonzo's house. His mother was at work, teaching, but Bonzo had not yet left for his job at the Fireside. He seemed glad to see me.

"J.W. Whatcha doin' here so early? Come in where it's warm. I'm having some cocoa with marshmallow on top. You can have some, too. It's really good!"

I went in and sat down and he bustled around and brought two steaming cups to the table. The cocoa tasted sweet and good and the marshmallow reminded me of when I was a kid.

"Bonzo," I said, "I wonder if you can remember something for me."

"Gee," he said, furrowing his brow. "I can remember some stuff real good, but not everything."

"Nobody can remember everything," I said. "What I want to know is whether Justin Wyner or his wife used to come in to the Fireside. Can you remember ever seeing them there? Justin Wyner and his wife are the two people who went with us up to Olmstead's farm when we first went looking for Nadine. Do you remember them? They belong to the Marshall Lea Foundation. Two lean, gray-haired people? She knew about how far robins go to get material to build their nests."

His dim eyes brightened, and he smiled with the pleasure of recollection. "Oh, yeah. I remember her. And I remember him, too."

"Good. Now try to remember if either of them used to come into the Fireside back when Nadine was working there. Think hard."

He frowned and rolled his eyes up toward his forehead and then to one side and then the other. Why do we do that? I wondered, as I watched him, knowing that I did the same thing myself.

"Gee," he said finally. "I don't remember whether they was ever there or not. A lot of people come in there, you know.

We got regulars but we get a lot of other people, too, and I don't remember them all." He shook his head. "I don't remember them, but maybe they came in when I wasn't working. That could happen because I don't work there all the time, you know. Sometimes I get time off."

"I know you do, Bonzo. Well, I was just wondering. Are you working today?"

"I sure am. This isn't a day off for me. I got things to do." He looked at the watch on his wrist. "In fact, I got to go there as soon as I finish my cocoa because I got work to do before the doors open."

"I'll drive you. Do you know who's tending bar today?"

"I think it's Jake, but sometimes Helen comes on for the noon shift."

Either would do. When we had drunk our cocoa, we drove into town and I parked in the lot off Kennebec, behind the bar. Bonzo rapped on the back door and Jake opened it.

"J.W. Afraid we aren't open yet." He stepped aside as Bonzo ducked past him.

"I'm not looking for a drink," I said. "I'm after information. Do you know a man named Justin Wyner? Sixty-five or seventy, maybe, gray hair, slim and straight. Belongs to the Marshall Lea Foundation, and looks like he has money. Wife called Genevieve Geller."

Jake said, "We don't usually get Marshall Lea types in here." The tone of his voice indicated that he, like me, was not a Marshall Lea fan. He didn't look like a bird-watcher, so I guessed him to be a shooter who'd been shut out of his hunting grounds by some Marshall Lea land purchase.

"In that case," I said, "you'd probably remember him if he'd started hanging around here a year or so ago. Dignified. Dresses well."

"Unlike you and most of my regulars," said Jake. "Yeah, I'd probably remember anybody who was dignified and well dressed and hung around the place. But I don't. The dignified, well-dressed types who wander in here usually don't come back. Maybe you should ask Helen or Clancy. Maybe one of them will remember more than I do."

I thanked him for his help and advice and went back to the truck. As I drove away, a few degrees too cold for comfort, I decided that I would definitely get Clay to fix my heater. If I was going to keep the Land Cruiser, I needed a way to make it warmer in the winter.

Of course I didn't have to keep the truck. It was forty years old, after all. Maybe I'd been too cheap for too long. Maybe I should bite the bullet and spend some money on a newer vehicle. The prospect was both pleasant and unpleasant; pleasant because a new truck was bound to be more comfortable, unpleasant because there actually wasn't anything really wrong with the old Toyota. It was cold in the winter but I'd never caught pneumonia or been frostbitten while driving. Besides, Clay was going to fix the heater.

I circled around the Flying Horses then took Circuit Avenue out to Wing Road and went on to Barnes Road. I parked near the narrow lane that led up to the old Olmstead place, took note of the car and truck tracks that had recently used it, ignored the No Trespassing signs, and walked up to the fallen house. There was yellow police tape around the site, and a lot of the rubble that had been in the cellar hole when last I'd been there was now piled outside of the foundation walls, where it had been deposited by a backhoe. The area where Nadine's body had been found was now fairly clear of debris.

I wondered if the police had found anything useful to their investigation. A signed confession by the killer would have been a nice discovery but I didn't think they'd found one. How about the murder weapon, covered with bloody fingerprints? How about the murder weapon without the fingerprints?

I studied the site. Whoever had deposited the body could have driven right to the cellar hole, then dumped the body, covered it with rubble, and left. I remembered the bartender, Clancy O'Brien, telling me that it had been a bright, moonlit night, so the killer probably could have turned off his headlights down at the road and not turned them on again until the burial job was done and he was headed home. No one would have seen him come or go.

I wondered if I should start questioning the people who lived nearby on Barnes Road, in case one of them had seen something, but I was pretty sure that the police had already done that and that I wouldn't learn anything they didn't know. So, instead of talking with the neighbors, I went to Clancy O'Brien's house. It was about time for him to be up and about.

And he *was* up and about, albeit still a bit blurry-eyed. However, when I described Justin and Genevieve he couldn't remember ever seeing such folk in the Fireside, and he thought he'd remember them if they'd been there more than once.

I declined his offer to join him in a midday beer and breakfast and asked instead to look at his phone book. In the book I found and noted the telephone number and address of Justin and Genevieve. They lived in Chilmark, off North Road. I had nowhere else to go, so I went there.

Justin and Genevieve's mailbox was one of several mounted in a row on a long timber beside a narrow sandy lane. Their house wasn't one of the new mansions that were going up all over the island. Rather, it was a fair-sized old farmhouse at the end of the winding drive, from which smaller drives took off on either side, each marked with a tiny sign naming the family or families who lived in that direction. The Geller-Wyner farm buildings—barn, sheds of various kinds, and what looked like a couple of rabbit hutches—were worn but well maintained. The house had a nice view of Vineyard Sound, the Elizabeth Islands on its far side, and, in the blue distance, the mainland beyond Buzzards Bay. A Range Rover was parked in the yard. I parked my truck beside it and studied the two. There was no doubt that the Range Rover would win if they had a beauty contest.

When I knocked on the door, Genevieve Geller answered and, before she could stop herself, looked at me disapprovingly. But her training in gentility quickly asserted itself and she said, "Why, Mr. Jackson. What brings you this way? Please come in."

I followed her into an entrance hall that held a rather ornate wooden coat-and-hat rack that was actually holding some winter coats and hats. There was a worn Oriental rug on the wide boards of the floor, and two large old pewter plates were mounted on a wall beside a door through which she led me into a living room made warm by both the fire in its fireplace and by its decor. There were paintings from the Hudson River School on its walls, more Oriental rugs on its floor, and an ancient blunderbuss and a pair of muzzle-loading pistols mounted above the fireplace mantel. The chairs and sofa were large and old and comfortable-looking, and bookshelves held Victorian knickknacks along with old books bound in leather.

Not bad.

"Would you like some tea?"

"Please don't bother. I just came to ask your husband a question."

"I'll call him. He's in his study writing his memoirs for our grandchildren. Our son is constantly at Justin to write them because if he doesn't, no one will know what sort of life he lived. I think it's a good thing to have a written family history, don't you?"

"I do," I said. "But I've never tried writing one. Perhaps I can talk with him in his study. I'll only interrupt him for a minute."

"Come right this way."

I followed her down a hall to a small room. The door was open and Justin Wyner was sitting in front of a computer, pecking away with two fingers like the newspaper reporters always did in old movies. He looked up when his wife rapped on the open door.

"You remember Mr. Jackson, Justin. From the other day when we were at the Olmstead place looking for that unfortunate young woman."

"Of course." He stood up and shook my hand. He had the firm grip of someone who used his hands for more than hitting a keyboard with his trigger fingers.

"Mr. Jackson has come to ask you a question," said Genevieve.

"Ask away," said Justin.

"Did you ever drink beer at the Fireside?"

He squinted at me through what looked like thin-rimmed reading glasses. "That's the question?"

"That's it."

"Well, the answer is yes. A long time ago I drank beer in a lot of places, including the Fireside. You remember me taking you there, don't you, Gen? Back when we were up at Harvard and Radcliffe in the winter and down here in the summer."

"You took me to a lot of dives in those days, dear. The Fireside was one of them. I believe the idea was that if you plied me with cheap drink you might have your way with me later."

"And it worked like a charm. We've been married longer than you've been alive, Mr. Jackson. Is that the answer you were after?"

"I take it that once you got her in your clutches you no longer had a need to buy her beer in Oak Bluffs bars."

He smiled. "That's the truth. I don't think I've been in the Fireside for fifty years. Maybe we should go back, Gen, just to see if it's as wonderfully decadent as I thought it was in those days."

"It's decadent in its own way," I said, "but I'm not sure you'd call it wonderful."

"You came just to ask that question?"

"Yes. Thanks for answering it."

"May I ask why?"

I realized that I didn't want to tell them my reason because it now embarrassed me. "Yes, you may," I said. "I wondered if you knew Nadine Gibson. If you might have met her when she was working in the Fireside."

Justin and Genevieve looked at each other, raised their eyebrows, then looked at me.

"Ah," said Genevieve. "You thought one of us might be a murderer. Is that it?"

"Somebody is," I said, "but I'm taking you off my list of suspects. You weren't on it for long, if that makes any difference to you."

"I don't think we've ever been murder suspects before, have we, dear?" asked Justin Wyner.

"Not that I know of. Mr. Jackson has a low opinion of the Marshall Lea Foundation and thinks my conservation ideas are idiotic, but I don't believe even he ever thought of us previously as mad-dog killers. Am I right, Mr. Jackson?"

"You're right, but I haven't changed my mind about the Marshall Lea Foundation."

"Or about my views of conservation?"

"Or those."

"Have you changed your mind about having tea? I'm going to be making some because it's time for Justin to take a break from his literary chore so he doesn't wear out those two fingers he uses."

"I'd love to," I said, surprising myself by meaning it.

As she headed for the kitchen, she paused and turned. There was a thin smile on her thin lips. "Would you like yours with or without poison?"

I was not Mithridates, so I returned her smile and said, "Without, please."

— 26 —

Genevieve Geller served her tea in fine china cups. While we drank it, she and her husband asked me why I was so interested in the death of Nadine Gibson. I told them it was because of my fondness for Bonzo, and my concern that his already difficult life might be made worse by suspicions that he was somehow involved in the killing.

"Gracious," said Genevieve. "You sound quite sentimental. I never noticed that aspect of your character when you called me a fanatic at conservation meetings."

"I don't have much tenderness in me, so I save it for special occasions."

"Probably a wise policy. Tell us about your investigation so far. Not about your arrival here, because we already know about that, but about what came before that."

"It's a pretty dull story," I said. "I've talked with people and they've told me next to nothing. You'd be bored."

"I don't see why we should be," said Justin. "Murder stories are always interesting. Besides, it may be good for you to tell your tale to a new audience. Maybe you'll hear yourself say something you never paid any attention to before."

"Anyway," said Genevieve, "you owe us for having put us on your suspect list."

"You weren't on for long."

"Long enough for you to tell us about your sleuthing. We deserve payment."

I was unexpectedly comfortable with them and could think of no good reason not to describe my efforts on Bonzo's behalf, so I said, "When the tedium gets too much for you, let me know," and launched into my tale, beginning with the phone call I'd gotten from Bonzo's mother and ending at Justin and Genevieve's doorstep. It took longer to tell than I'd guessed it would, but they both listened with what seemed to be interest.

When I finished, Genevieve went into the kitchen and came back with more tea and some cookies.

"And there you have it," I said, when she returned. "What do you think?"

"What comes to mind," said Justin, "is a list of questions: Who knew Nadine? Who knew where she worked and lived? Who knew the place where she was buried? Who knew all of those things? Who knew some of them? Who hated her? I think her killer did because of all the blows he struck. Why was she hated?"

"I think she was probably hated because of fear," said Genevieve. "Most hatred, to my thinking, is based on fear of one thing or another: fear of being hurt or having a loved one hurt; fear of being robbed of something treasured; fear of being betrayed; fear of having the very foundations of your world shattered. If you aren't afraid, you don't hate."

Justin sipped his tea and nibbled a cookie, then said, "The killer knew her, hated her, knew where to find her, knew how to kill her, and knew where to bury her. Find the man who knew all those things and who was deathly afraid of her and you'll have your murderer."

"Goodness me," said Genevieve. "You sound like one of those detectives who sits in his study and solves mysteries without leaving the house."

"To take your requirements one by one," I said. "First, a lot of people knew Nadine and she didn't lack for male admirers. Second, everybody who drank beer at the Fireside knew she worked there. Third, her landlord and neighbors and God knows how many of the men who were after her body knew where she lived. Fourth, probably half the bird-watchers on the Vineyard and half the members of the Marshall Lea Foundation, including you two, have been to the old Olmstead place."

I paused and Genevieve said, "Which, all in all, doesn't cut the suspect list down much."

"Leaving us only hate as a differentiating factor," said her husband. "Out of all of the people who knew her, who hated her? And why? Lovers are the first people to consider, I'd venture. Jealousy and all that."

"But none of the boyfriends and would-be boyfriends I talked to seemed to resent the others," I said, running these ideas through my mind and feeling perplexed for the umpteenth time. "Nadine seemed to be a spell thrower. When she left an old lover for a new, she cast an enchantment that forbade both parties to be jealous. I didn't talk to a single male who was resentful of her other beaus."

"Too bad she didn't live long enough to write a book about how to accomplish that," said Genevieve. "She could have made a fortune."

"Well, somebody certainly wasn't charmed," said Justin, helping himself to another cookie, which he waved at his wife. "These are very good, dear."

"Fattening, too," said his wife, giving him the disapproving glance she'd often given to me at conservation meetings.

"Wives are like that," said Justin to me. "They bake delicious goodies, then criticize you for eating them."

"You both look pretty trim to me," I said.

"My only thought about this murder business," said Genevieve, "is that you should go back and talk some more with that neighbor woman. What's her name? Loretta Aldrich? She may have seen more than she told you. She just might not have wanted you to know how snoopy she really is."

Justin Wyner arched a brow. "That's a cynical remark, my dear. Are you saying that all women are nosier than they want others to believe?"

"I don't know about all women," said Genevieve, lifting her cup to her lips. "But I certainly am."

When I left the house I considered the possibility of minding my tongue more carefully in the future when Genevieve and I crossed ideological swords at public meetings. Had I really called her a fanatic? It was more than just possible. Perhaps I should be more politic in the future.

Or maybe not, since the truth of the matter was that I still considered the Marshall Lea Foundation to be a sort of fundamentalist religion of conservatism insofar as it was totally dogmatic, had sacred texts and a hierarchy of saints, and was composed of true believers intent upon converting the world.

So, on third thought, since such institutions and such proselytizers had irked me all my life, it seemed likely that I wouldn't change my ways after all. Which suggested that I was just as stubborn and inflexible as Genevieve Geller, and that this was something I should think about, but not right then.

Right then I was taking Genevieve's advice and going to revisit Loretta Aldrich.

As I drove slowly through the narrow streets of the Camp Meeting Grounds I looked at the houses. Many of them were empty, without insulation or furnaces. When summer came, they'd be full of folk: families enjoying holidays, lovers escaping the prying eyes at home, kids running where there were few cars to endanger them. Now, as spring slowly approached, the working men and women who'd rented the few winterized houses would be leaving so the home owners could use the places themselves or rent them out at summer prices their winter clients couldn't afford. Nadine Gibson had been one of the lucky ones. She'd managed to find a year-round rental she could afford. Or at least could afford with her boyfriend's financial help.

How had they managed that on a barmaid's salary and that of an architecture student? Probably, I thought, Adam Andrews had a parental pension of some sort. He was, after all, going to Harvard, no doubt with financial help from his parents, and after his breakup with Nadine he had been taken by his mother out to Arizona to heal his broken heart.

But when Adam had departed, Nadine had stayed on and given no indication that she needed to move on herself. Did she have some private income or store of cash that allowed her to stay in her house? Or was she depending on the next boyfriend to help pay the rent? Or was there some other explanation?

I parked in front of Loretta Aldrich's house and as I got out of the truck saw a window curtain move in Gordon Brown's house just up the street. As I walked to Loretta Aldrich's door I saw another curtain flutter in her front window. There were a lot of window watchers in this neck of the woods. Loretta Aldrich smiled at me when she waved me inside. "You've returned. Something you forgot to ask me when you were here before? I think I've told you all I know."

"I've been wondering how Nadine Gibson could afford to live in her house. Do you have any thoughts on the subject?"

Her old eyes glittered. "Perhaps I do, but they're only guesswork."

"Will you share them anyway?"

"When I was younger and could get out more, I was too busy to wonder much about my neighbors. Nowadays, as I told you before, I like to keep track of things."

"In the summer I imagine there are too many people around for that, even if you wanted to," I said.

She nodded. "In the summer I put a rocker on my porch and sit out there. I love to watch the children and the young families. I'm sure they think of me as the old lady who's lived across the street as long as anyone can remember." She smiled. "Of course, I've been here since I was a young woman myself. I doubt if they even think of that possibility."

"In the winter there's a lot less activity. Anyone with an interest in the community could probably keep track of what's happening."

"If you're talking about me, you're absolutely right." She crossed her thin hands on her chest in an almost theatrical gesture.

"You," I said. "And Gertrude Brown up the street. And probably other people in the neighborhood that I don't know. I expect a lot of people look out of a lot of curtains whenever a car passes or a person walks by. It's what I'd do and what most people would do. On Martha's Vineyard in the wintertime we all notice things we wouldn't necessarily notice in the summer."

"Gert," she said, nodding. "You're certainly right about her. She's locked herself away in her house but she doesn't miss a thing. I'll bet you she keeps binoculars right there by her bedroom window. She probably sees more than she did when she was still walking around."

"Tell me your thoughts about Nadine," I said. "You say you're only guessing, but I'd like to know what those guesses are."

She hesitated, then made up her mind. "Well, the girl's dead, so I guess it doesn't make any difference, and I can't prove it anyway, but if you ask me, I think Gordy was giving her a real break on her rent. I know what he used to get for the place in the summer because I've been living here a long time and I hear things, and I don't think she could afford to stay there year-round on her salary. You ask me, I think he rented it to her cheap because he liked to have her around, and then he lied to Gert about doing it. You wanted to know what I guess. That's it."

"You don't think Nadine might have had some other income? Or that the boyfriend might have shared the rent?"

"She didn't act like a rich girl, and she worked hard, so I don't think she had much money. I know she never hinted at anything like that when we talked. As far as Adam is concerned, he wasn't making any money from that firm where he was working, but maybe his parents helped out. Still, after he left and the last time we talked, she wasn't planning to move."

"Maybe she figured her next boyfriend would kick in for the rent."

"Maybe."

"What do you think Gordon Brown got out of his deal with the girl? Sex? Romance of some sort?"

She gave a small, ladylike *humph*. "If there was any romance, it was all in Gordy's mind. She was sweet to him, but the same way she was sweet to everybody. She wasn't interested in being lovey-dovey with a man old enough to be her grandfather. She liked young men. I think Gordy just liked having her live nearby. He and Gert are twenty years past being man and wife, if you take my meaning, and Gordy is a man who likes to be with women, especially pretty ones."

"You told me before that he's a Caspar Milquetoast. Do you think there might be another side to him?"

"You mean a violent side? Violent enough for him to kill Nadine Gibson in a fit of pique?" She shook her old, white-haired head. "Not in a million years. Gert's had him wrapped around her thumb since they were newlyweds almost fifty years ago. They both seemed to like it that way then and I think it's still that way whether or not he likes it now."

I went to the front windows and looked out. I could see Gordon Brown's house and the house Nadine Gibson had lived in. How many secrets could there be in such a small neighborhood? Someone must have noticed something on that fatal night a year ago. I tried to imagine the scene bathed in white moonlight. Nadine came walking up Clinton Avenue at midnight, wearing her loden coat and her winter cap. She passed through alternating patches of shadow and light, going home as she always did, not knowing that it would be her last such walk. Was someone following her? Or was someone waiting for her, blunt instrument in hand?

Had she gotten home before her killer approached? Had he knocked on her door and struck his first blow when she opened it? Probably not, because her body had been found still wearing that loden coat. It had happened, therefore, either before she'd gotten home or after she'd gotten there and left again, outside in the silver moonlight. The weapon had smashed down again and again, and if she'd tried to cry out, no one had heard her.

And then the killer had driven her corpse to Olmstead's farm and covered her body with rubble in the farmhouse basement. But if that had happened, surely there would have been blood at the scene of the crime, but the police had found none. Why?

Maybe her killer met her on the street before she got home and had taken her to the farm in his car and killed her there. But why would she have gone with him? Was he a lover who prevailed on her to go on a moonlit drive? If so, how had he known about the farm?

I turned back to Loretta Aldrich and asked, "Were you up late the night Nadine disappeared?"

She shook her head. "No. I've since wished that I had been. I might have seen something. I might even have been able to save her. But I was in bed, asleep, when she came home."

"Did you notice anything unusual the next day? A strange car on the street? Some person who normally isn't around? Anything at all?"

"No. I do remember that it looked like it was going to snow and that Gordy went to the landfill that next morning, but the only reason I remember is because he'd gone just a couple of days before and had asked me, like he always does, if I had anything I wanted him to take. That morning he didn't ask."

"Did you attach any significance to that?"

"No, but Gert seemed to. She watched him from her window while he loaded a rubbish bag into the van and kept watching until he drove out of sight."

"Just one rubbish bag?"

"That's all I saw. Gert's usually not interested in trips to the dump. She's a strange one."

I thought that Gertrude Brown was probably even stranger than Loretta Aldrich imagined.

27

When I left Loretta Aldrich's porch I once again saw a window curtain move in Gordon Brown's house. I felt eyes watching me and wondered if someday my private life would interest me so little that I'd be one of those people who constantly watch their neighbors.

Were their internal lives worse—less rewarding or pleasurable—than their external ones? Was the outside world more real and important than the inside one, the private one that no one else could share?

My own persuasion was that both were ultimately meaningless, but that didn't prevent me from thinking about values and acting as though they mattered. It just prevented me from believing my life had any purpose other than the one I invented as I went along. I thought of people who had religion. Gordon Brown had described his wife as one such. Their biggest problems were trying to figure out what their gods wanted them to do (the worst believers were sure they knew), and explaining the existence of evil. Although I lacked the solace of faith, my agnosticism at least freed me from dealing with those two classic problems.

I did, however, have similar ones having to do with how to live morally in an amoral world. Usually love was a good guide, but I had too little of that in me to be a saint, and I distrusted the concept of justice as an alternative.

Thus, feeling neither loving nor just, motivated only by the idea that the island would be fractionally safer if Nadine's killer was prevented from killing again, I walked to Gordon Brown's house and, as I neared it, saw the window curtain fall.

Gordon Brown opened his front door to my knock, frowned, then brightened a bit as he recognized me, and said, "Mr. Jackson, isn't it? You were here last week."

He glanced behind him, then stepped out and pulled the door almost shut, although it was too cold for him to be outside wearing only a sweater over his winter shirt. He gestured over his shoulder with his thumb. "Don't want the chilly air to get into the house. My wife's not well."

"So I've been told. Sorry. Is she bedridden?"

He looked startled. "Bedridden? No, no, not really." He tapped a forefinger alongside his head. "She's just . . . she just doesn't like to leave the house anymore."

"She was a large, lively woman when she was young, I'm told. Does she ever get outside anymore?"

He rubbed his jaw. "I can't remember the last time. It's been a while."

"You must do all of the outside work, then. Shopping, going to the dump, mowing the lawn."

"I don't mind, really. What can I do for you, Mr. Jackson?" He glanced at his wristwatch and seemed to be listening to the inside of his house as much as to me.

"It must be particularly hard for you to live with the woman you love when there's nothing wrong with her physically, when she's strong and looks perfectly normal but isn't."

"I'm used to it. I really have to go back inside." He crossed his arms and hugged his chest. "It's cold out here."

"The morning after Nadine Gibson disappeared, you made a trip to the dump. Do you remember that?"

His eyes grew worried and wary. "No, I don't. Did I? I go every couple of weeks, whenever stuff begins to pile up. Maybe I went that day. I don't remember."

"You went just a couple of days earlier, so you wouldn't have had much rubbish that morning." He stepped back toward the door, but I put a hand on his arm. "You put a rubbish bag into your van. What was in the bag?"

He brushed weakly at my hand. "Rubbish, I guess. How can you expect me to remember? It was a year ago. Let go of me."

I let go, but before he could duck into the house I said, "If you go inside now, I'm going right to the police, so talk to me."

His face was touched with fear. "What do you want?"

"You don't have much of a social life anymore, do you? You and your wife used to go bird-watching and do other things that young couples do. But that's all ended, hasn't it?"

"I guess so. But that's because Gert is sick. She's sick and she doesn't want me to be away from her."

"That's right. You get out of the house to do chores like mowing the grass where she can keep an eye on you, but the only times you get away from her is when you go to the store or the dump. And she doesn't like that, does she?"

"No. But that's understandable. She's sick."

"You're a sociable guy, Gordy. The neighbors like you and you like being their friend, don't you?"

"Sure. Of course I do." He was shivering.

"You chat with them when you see them. You like it in the summertime when there are people around for you to talk to."

"Yes. It's cold out here. Aren't you cold?"

"We can go inside if you prefer."

"No, no. This is fine."

"Gert doesn't like it when you're outside talking, does she?"

"I guess not, but you can't blame her. She's—"

"I know. She's sick. She especially doesn't like it when you talk with women. Isn't that so?"

"What are you trying to get me to say?"

"She didn't like Nadine Gibson, did she? You told me Gert thought the girl was a sinner, the way she lived with her boyfriend, and that she was glad when the boy left."

"That's right."

"But a couple of nights later another man spent the night at Nadine's house. How did Gert feel about that?"

He looked past me and said in a small voice, "She called her a whore."

"How did she feel when she found out you weren't charging Nadine full rent?"

He turned visibly pale. "What!"

"You heard me."

He pressed his fists hard against the sides of his face. I saw that his teeth were gritted. He made not a sound.

"What I think happened," I said, "is this: Your wife had never liked the attention you paid to the girl, and when she found out about the rent deal you'd been giving her and then saw another man spend the night with her, the combination of betrayals was too much for her. She left the house that night when she knew Nadine would be coming home from work and she met her out somewhere along the way, probably in the shadow of a house or a tree a block or more from here, out of the moonlight, and she beat her to death with a piece of pipe or a tool of some kind she probably got out of your truck. I don't think you knew anything about it until she came back home. It that pretty close to what happened?"

He said nothing, but only stood there with a silent howl of pain on his face. I went on.

"I think she was wearing clothes covered with blood, because beatings spatter more blood than you'd think possible. I think you got her out of her clothes and into the shower, and that you made her go to bed while you put her bloody things into a rubbish bag. You didn't take the bag with you because you were afraid the clothes might be found and identified so you left them there while you got a sheet and drove to where the body was. You wrapped the body so you wouldn't get blood all over the inside of your truck. Then, because it was too cold to dig a grave and because you remembered the old Olmstead ruin, you took the body up there and buried it under the rubble in the cellar, where there was a good chance it wouldn't be found for years. How am I doing so far?"

He was staring into nothingness. "How do these things happen?" he asked the gods who live out there.

I said, "The next morning you took the bag of bloody clothes to the landfill, where the chances were they'd never be found. And they never were found. Then you got even luckier: a snowstorm covered the place where the murder occurred, and the snow didn't melt for a long time. For a year, the body wasn't found and maybe you were beginning to think everything was going to work out after all. But then one day my friend Bonzo found a bird's nest made in part from long red hair and that was the beginning of the end for you and Gertrude."

"She's sick," he said. "She has been for a long time."

"You need a lawyer," I said. "I imagine there's a good chance that your wife will get off with an insanity plea, but even if she doesn't, there's no death penalty in Massachusetts."

His eyes were watery and he was shivering. "Oh, poor Gertrude. Poor Nadine."

Poor you, I thought. Poor all of us.

"I'm going to the police with this," I said. "You go back inside and don't upset your wife if you can help it. She saw me coming here and she'll want to know what we talked about."

"What'll I tell her?"

I couldn't think of an answer to that, so I just said, "Wait for the police. Don't do anything unusual. Make some tea. That might help."

As he opened the door I heard her voice. It reminded me of a crow's cawing. "Gordon! What are you doing out there? Is that man trying to sell you something? I saw him come from Loretta Aldrich's house. Get rid of him!"

He shut the door and I walked back to my truck and drove to the state police station.

Dom Agganis was at his desk sifting through the pile of

papers that was always on his desk. Between the papers and the computer he didn't have a lot of spare space.

"I think you need a bigger file cabinet," I said. "I suggest the trash barrel out behind the barracks. If anything there is really important they'll send it to you again."

"I know you're right," he said, "but I never know when the governor might walk in and I wouldn't want him to think I'm not working on something."

"Has he ever walked in?"

"Not yet, but it could happen anytime. What brings you here? Nosing around in police business again?" He leaned back in his chair, stretched, and put his thick hands behind his neck.

"'Tis better to give than to receive," I said, sitting down. I'd felt tired before I'd even finished talking with Gordon Brown. I was more tired now, wearied the way we are by angry argument or depravity.

"You look to be in a giving mood," said Dom, eyeing me keenly. "If so, I'm in a mood to receive."

So I sat and told him of my day. My voice droned in my ears like the buzzing of a distant swarm of bees. There was no inflection in it, no tone, only words following other words until, after what seemed a long time, the words stopped abruptly and I was looking almost sleepily at Dom.

I saw a tape recorder on his desk and wondered how long it had been there. From the beginning, I guessed. Now he leaned forward and turned it off.

"We'll need more than you got," he said.

I nodded. "I know, but it's a start. Maybe you can still find the clothes he threw away."

"I doubt it. It's been a year. We can look."

"I imagine he's cleaned his truck, but there might be bloodstains that he missed."

"There's a chance of that. Luminol should find it if it's there."

"He probably put the weapon in with the clothes if she

brought it home, but maybe not. I forgot to ask. He has a van probably loaded with pipes and plumbing tools. Gertrude might have used his favorite pipe wrench, and maybe he loved it too much to part with it."

"Not likely, but possible."

"There must have been a lot of blood where the killing took place. Brown couldn't have cleaned it all up in the middle of the night, even with all that moonlight to help him find it, and he wouldn't have wanted to stay on the scene very long for fear someone would come by."

"If you're right, that spot is somewhere between the girl's house and the Fireside, which is quite a stretch of territory. And a year's gone by and God knows how many people, dogs, and kids have messed up the crime scene. Too bad about that snowstorm. If it hadn't been for that, we might have figured this all out a year ago."

"Maybe you can use luminol in the likeliest spots. I figure it happened in the shadows. Maybe that'll narrow the possibilities."

"Maybe we can get Gertrude to lead us to the spot."

"Maybe."

"There are a lot of maybes in this conversation. You got anything else for me to think about? No. Then thanks and good-bye."

I went out into the cool, clear March air. A wind was coming off the water and I could see a ferry coming around West Chop bringing cars and travelers to the Blessed Isle.

I climbed into the Land Cruiser and drove home. It was the middle of the afternoon and I felt the way a writer friend had once described his feelings when he was "between books": slightly ill at ease, existential, wondering if I had wasted my life and if I would ever do anything worthwhile. What I needed was company and a beer. Or maybe two or three beers.

I stopped on Circuit Avenue and went down the stairs into the Vineyard Wine and Cheese Shop, the island's only basement liquor store. I bought a six-pack of Sam Adams lager and, because neither my wife nor my children were yet at home, drove to Ted Overhill's barn. There I found Clay Stockton whistling as he worked.

The barn was warm and comfortable. I climbed up and sat in the schooner's cockpit and invited Clay to join me in a Sam. He was glad to do it.

"What's up?" he asked as I handed him a bottle.

"Oh, nothing much," I said. "Cheers."

We touched bottles and drank. The clean, fresh, cold beer slid down my throat and I felt myself relax. God was a brewer. There was no doubt about it.

28

They launched the *Horizon* on the last day of May, just after Clay had finally gotten around to fixing the heater in the Land Cruiser. As he observed as he wiped his hands afterward, now that it worked, I didn't need it. It was still fine with me, because I'd love having it next winter. The schooner had gotten her name because Ted Overhill had always hoped to do blue-water sailing and still did. Boat names fall into three general categories: great, awful, and commonplace. *Horizon* wasn't the worst I'd ever seen.

When you don't have a regular job, which was my situation, you can make up your own mind about which work you'll do today and which you'll do later, if at all, so once the boat was in the water I took some time to help with her rigging and ballast. As in the old days Clay and I worked well together, and it was still June when the *Horizon* was ready for a sea trial.

She was sweet but a bit tender, so we added and relocated ballast until she was up to having her lee rail in the water and flying as fast as you wanted to go. Clay and I took her out into the sound several times in a variety of weathers until we were persuaded that she was as strong and stable as she was swift, and that she could be handled by a two-man crew if necessary. Then we put her on her mooring outside the Vineyard Haven seawall and invited Zee, Joshua, Diana, and Eleanor to join us and Ted for an official First Sail.

There was food and drink for all, and a nice fifteen-knot wind blowing from the southwest, making small whitecaps on gentle waves. Perfect. We put up the main and mizzen, dropped our mooring line, and eased out of the harbor, raising the foresails as we went. The *Horizon* cut smoothly through the water like one of the swans that we could see from our house, on Sengekontacket Pond.

We first sailed around East Chop and reached over to Cape Pogue before coming about and returning. Past West Chop we hauled in the sheets and beat up Vineyard Sound to Tarpaulin Cove, where we dropped anchor and had lunch and took turns jumping off the bow into the still-chilly water, swimming back to the ladder and climbing aboard and then jumping off again before coming aboard for a last time and lying in the warm sun to dry.

Then we raised the sails again, hauled anchor, and slid in front of wind and tide back down the sound before rounding West Chop and tacking up to fetch our mooring as the long summer day slowly darkened.

"Splendid," said Ted, beaming. He was in love and his paramour was the *Horizon*. Looking at his happy face I thought that many a woman had lost her man to a ship.

That evening, as we sat on the couch drinking a last glass of cognac in front of a June fire in the stove, I mentioned that thought to Zee.

"A lot of women went to sea with their husbands during whaling days," she said. "Maybe because they didn't want that to happen. They didn't want the seductress ships to have their husbands alone for three or four years. How about us, hunk? Do I need to be jealous of the *Shirley J.*?"

"I'd much rather sleep with you," I said. "I'm very fond of our catboat, but I prefer a live woman in my arms."

"Good, as long as I'm the woman."

She was and knew it, but just in case, I said, "You and only you, sweets," and meant it.

After a while, she said, "Love can surprise you. Gordon Brown loved his wife even after she murdered poor Nadine. Do you think she loved him back?"

"She was jealous, but I don't know if that's really love. I

think of love as wanting good things to happen to your lover. She was a very sick woman."

"I think there's a dark side to it," said Zee, "like there is to a lot of things. Look at all the killings that involve husbands and wives and girlfriends and boyfriends. Passions can get very twisted."

"The poets and shrinks of the world would probably agree."

"What's going to happen to the Browns?"

I didn't know, of course. "My guess is that she'll end up in a hospital and he'll do some jail time as an accessory. Something like that." Whatever happened to the Browns was too late to save Nadine.

"At least Bonzo isn't worried about anything now."

"No. He has little memory of the dark side of things."

"I know you don't believe in an afterlife," said Zee, "but if there is one, do you think that killers and their victims ever meet there?"

"If there is such a thing, I think they probably do."

"Really? You don't think there'd be a heaven and hell, one for the innocents and one for the brutalizers?"

"It's an old question," I said, feeling lazy and comfortable sitting there beside her inside our house, shut away from the troubles of the world. "Somebody wrote that there are deer in the heaven of tigers but no tigers in the heaven of deer."

"But you think the killers and victims will meet. Why?"

"Because I don't think that good and evil exist. I think they're both just products of our imagination. Things are or they aren't. They don't have any moral character. Events happen, but they aren't moral either. They're just events, like falling rain or the way sunshine feels on your skin."

"I think that last's a sensation, not an event."

"I think we've both had just enough cognac."

"Do you think that Jack Blume and Mickey Monroe will come back?"

"No. Why should they? There's nothing here for them."

"There's the money."

"They think Clay gave it to the Feds."

"But he didn't. He still has it."

"He's keeping it for Mark Briggs."

"But Mark Briggs is in Rio de Janeiro or somewhere down that way. Unless he comes back to the United States and gets in touch with Clay, Clay has the money. And since Clay doesn't know how to get in touch with Mark Briggs and Mark Briggs doesn't know how to get in touch with Clay, Clay will have the money forever."

"What do you think he should do with it?" I asked.

"Well, it's out there in California, so he should probably go get it and put it somewhere safer than it is."

"Then what?"

"Then he should use part of it to buy Elly an engagement ring!"

I looked at her. "Really? With his record with women? He's never had a relationship last yet."

She had an expression on her face that was hard for me to decipher. "He's just had bad luck. Now he's ready to settle down and Elly is just the right woman to settle down with him. They love each other; she's got a house for them to live in, and he's got several million dollars. It's perfect for both of them!"

"But they're not his millions."

"They are until Mark Briggs comes to get them, and he won't be coming."

"If Jack Blume and Mickey Monroe could find Clay, Mark Briggs certainly can."

"So?"

"So he might just want his money."

"But he won't get it."

"Why not?"

"Because Clay gave it to the Feds! You said so yourself!"

"But I was lying."

"But Mark Briggs won't know that."

I put my arms around her shoulders. "I'm not often glad that I'm poor, but this is one of those times."

"You're not poor," she said, snugging closer. "You have everything you need."

True.

More people are married on Martha's Vineyard than anywhere else in America, outside of Las Vegas. In the spring, summer, and fall, and even in early winter, the churches are booked, wedding houses are full, and tents are up in fields, on beaches, and on lawns, including, conspicuously, that of the Captain Fisher House in Edgartown. Every day, almost, you can see people decked out in gowns and tuxes, and limos unloading brides and bridesmaids. You can spend a fortune on a Vineyard wedding, and a lot of people do.

Clay and Elly didn't. They got married in August, in our oceanside yard, with us and a few other friends and kin in attendance. I was best man, Zee was matron of honor, Diana was a flower girl, and Joshua was ring bearer. We had champagne, several kinds of shellfish appetizers, and lobster rolls. The sun was shining just like it was supposed to do, and we had Mary Coffin and Hazel Fine playing early music for anyone who wanted to listen.

In September, on a gorgeous fall day, but with their eyes and ears open to all reports of low-pressure systems moving across the Atlantic from Africa, Clay, Elly, and Ted Overhill sailed out of Vineyard Haven harbor and pointed the *Horizon* south. Zee and the kids and I drove over to East Beach on Chappy and saw them moving down through Muskeget Channel, heading for the open sea.

"Where do you suppose they'll end up?" asked Zee.

"I know they have a copy of *Ocean Passages for the World* aboard, so they can go anywhere they want to go. Maybe they'll go to Rio de Janeiro."

"You don't suppose . . ."

"Why not? Clay still has the key to that storage locker in San Diego. Maybe he wants to give it to Mark Briggs in person."

"If he can find him."

"If he can find him. Or maybe he wants to see that girl from Ipanema."

"He doesn't need a girl from Ipanema. He's got Elly."

"Hey!" said Diana. "Look there!"

We brought our eyes closer to shore and there, sure enough, was funny water. Bluefish! We trotted to the Land Cruiser and I got the others' rods off the roof rack and handed them out. Before I could join them, Zee was already at the water making her beautiful long cast, and Joshua and Diana were right beside her making their short but straight ones. It was a miniblitz, with blues both far out and close in, and they were taking whatever you threw at them. I stood by the truck and watched as fish hit all three lures and the rods bent and the lines began to sing.

I stuck my rod in the spike on the front of the truck and went back and opened the rear door so we could get at the hook removers and more lures in case anybody's got bitten off. On both sides of our parked truck, men were running from their pickups and SUVs down to the surf, rods in hand, some casting as they ran.

Zee had a good fish and was playing it carefully. As I watched, it leaped and twisted, trying to throw the hook, but she gave it no slack and reeled it in steadily. Diana was almost in the water, pulled there by a fish that didn't want to be caught. Beside her, Joshua was leaning back, then reeling down, then hauling back again, steadily bringing his fish to shore. I started to go help Diana but forced myself to stop. It was a battle she'd not yet lost, though she'd not yet won it, either.

Zee's fish and Joshua's came flopping ashore almost at the same time, and the two fisherpeople hooked their hands in the gills, carefully avoiding the razor teeth and spiny fins, and stood watching Diana's titanic battle. It ebbed and flowed, with Diana first losing a step, then gaining one as she reeled in line and then lost it and then reeled it in again. Then, almost imperceptibly, she was gaining, taking two steps back for every one forward. Twenty feet out in the water the fish suddenly broke the surface and we could see that it was a good one. Diana reeled in and backed up the beach, staggered but recovered, and reeled some more. And then, twisting and turning, the fish came through the last wave and slithered up the wet sand. Zee walked over and put a foot on it to hold it down while Diana got her hand in its gills. Then my wife and children came up to the truck, rod in one hand, a fish in the other. They looked happy, the way fishermen look when they're on East Beach and the blues are in. I got my rod and walked down to the surf to join the fun.

When the blitz was past, I looked to the south. The *Horizon* was only a dot. I watched it grow smaller and smaller as it moved toward a future none of us could guess. I remembered Clay saying that he'd never liked being in a place as much as he liked being on the Vineyard, where he had good work and good friends; but with the launching of the *Horizon* the wanderthirst had come upon him as it had so often in his life, and now he was off on another adventure. I wished him well and knew that many would envy him, but when I looked at my wife and children, close by me on the golden sand, I felt content.

RECIPES

SPINACH LASAGNA

My wife, Shirley, and our daughter Kim have an ongoing contest concerning whose lasagna weighs the most. That may not seem like a meaningful criterion for quality to you, but it supports the theory that you can't have too much of a good thing.

1-lb. package of wide egg noodles
½ lb. sliced mushrooms
1 large onion, diced
2 cloves garlic, minced
½ sweet green pepper, diced
2 (10-oz.) packages frozen chopped spinach (cooked and well
    drained)
1 lb. ricotta cheese
½ cup grated Parmesan cheese
1 tsp. salt
½ tsp. pepper
½ tsp. dried oregano
¼ tsp. nutmeg
3 cups spaghetti sauce
12 oz. mozzarella cheese, shredded

Cook noodles al dente and drain. Sauté mushrooms, onion, garlic, and green pepper in a little olive oil and add with cooked spinach to noodles. Add ricotta and Parmesan cheese, salt, pepper, oregano, nutmeg, and 2 cups spaghetti sauce. Pour mixture into buttered 9-by-13-inch baking dish (or two 9-by-9-inch pans). Top with remaining sauce and mozzarella cheese. Bake at 350 degrees for 30 minutes or until heated through.

May be frozen, well covered. (Cover lasagna with plastic wrap before wrapping again in aluminum foil. Defrost and don't forget to remove the plastic wrap before reheating.) *Serves 8–12.*

LINGUINI WITH SHELLFISH
AND GARLIC SAUCE

J.W. sometimes brings home more quahogs than the Jacksons and their guests can eat on the half shell, as casinos, as stuffers, or than he can use as chowder makings. (There are lots of quahogs in Edgartown ponds!) This is a good way to use the extra ones. Serve with a fresh green salad and some crusty bread to dip in flavored olive oil.

2–3 dozen quahogs (or equivalent amount of shrimp, scallops, or mussels*)
6 tbsp. butter
2 cloves garlic, finely chopped
1 shallot, finely chopped
¼ cup dry white wine
Generous pinch dried thyme
Freshly ground pepper
Salt, if desired
1 lb. linguini, cooked according to package directions

Steam quahogs in ½ cup water over high heat, just until shellfish open. Cool, remove quahogs from shells, and chop coarsely. Reserve ¼–½ cup broth.

*If using mussels, steam them in the same manner. Shrimp or scallops should be lightly sautéed.

Melt butter in heavy saucepan. Add garlic and shallot and sauté until soft. Add chopped quahogs and broth to taste, along with wine, thyme, and pepper. Heat through over low heat. Serve over cooked linguini with freshly grated Parmesan cheese.

Serves 4.

PASTA WITH SALMON

The Jacksons and the Craigs eat a lot of pasta. This is a good way to do it.

3 tbsp. unsalted butter
4 oz. sliced mushrooms
8 oz. salmon, cooked and flaked (a good use of leftovers)
1–1½ cups asparagus, cooked to crisp-tender and sliced
    diagonally*
½ cup freshly grated Parmesan cheese
½ tsp. ground nutmeg
8–12 oz. spinach noodles, cooked according to package
    directions and drained
1 cup dairy sour cream
Paprika

Melt butter in Dutch oven (or large saucepan). Sauté mushrooms until they've released their juices. Add salmon, asparagus, cheese, and nutmeg to pot and heat gently over low heat. Add noodles, stirring gently until hot. Fold in sour cream and heat until just hot (add a bit of milk if sauce needs thinning). Spoon into a heated serving dish and sprinkle with paprika.

Serves 4–6.

*You may substitute edible pod peas (or tiny frozen peas) for the asparagus in this recipe.

ACKNOWLEDGMENTS

Philip R. Craig passed away on May 8, 2007, after a brief battle with cancer. At the time of his death, Phil had completed and submitted this novel, but had yet to acknowledge the contributions of those who had provided him assistance during the writing of the book. The success of the J.W. Jackson series was due in no small part to the support of Phil's friends, family, and colleagues, who would often help Phil and J.W. navigate some particularly sticky part of the mystery with which they were currently embroiled. Some would provide answers about poisons or weaponry, others about police procedure or methods of tracking down people online. Phil would certainly have wanted to thank all of those who contributed ideas and suggestions for this book; and though we don't know your names, you undoubtedly know who you are!

Phil's family would like to express our gratitude to all of the many people, named and un-named, who've contributed in any way to the success of the Martha's Vineyard Mystery series over the years. You were all part of the experience that fed the writer's soul.

Shirley Craig
Martha's Vineyard
January 2008